Heist

Also by Kiki Swinson

Wifey
I'm Still Wifey
Life After Wifey
The Candy Shop
A Sticky Situation
Still Wifey Material
Sleeping with the Enemy (with Wahida Clark)
Playing Dirty
Notorious

Also by De'nesha Diamond

Hustlin' Divas
Heartbreaker (with Erick S. Gray and Nichelle Walker)

Published by Kensington Publishing Corp.

Heist

KIKI SWINSON

DE'NESHA DIAMOND

KENSINGTON PUBLISHING CORP.

www.kensingtonbooks.com

DAFINA BOOKS are published by

Kensington Publishing Corp.
119 West 40th Street
New York, NY 10018

All Kensington titles, imprints, and distributed lines are available at special quantity discounts for bulk purchases for sales promotion, premiums, fund-raising, educational, or institutional use.

Special book excerpts or customized printings can also be created to fit specific needs. For details, write or phone the office of the Kensington Special Sales Manager: Kensington Publishing Corp., 119 West 40th Street, New York, NY 10018, Attn. Special Sales Department. Phone: 1-800-221-2647.

Dafina and the Dafina logo Reg. U.S. Pat. & TM Off.

ISBN-13: 978-0-7582-5178-7
ISBN-10: 0-7582-5178-5

First Printing: December 2010
10 9 8 7 6 5 4 3 2 1

Printed in the United States of America

CONTENTS

The Ultimate Heist

KIKI SWINSON

Todd

CRASH! *BANG!* "What the fuck?!" I was out of bed and on my feet with one big jump when I heard the sounds of crashing glass and wood smashing. I immediately started searching the side of my bed for my ratchet. I felt down around on the floor in the place I usually kept it.

Nothing.

"Fuck," I cursed as the sounds grew louder and louder. Shannon had moved my shit. I told her not to ever move my shit without telling me. She was always so worried about guns being around Lil Todd.

"What the fuck!" I exclaimed as I heard feet thundering in my direction. My heart pounded through my wife-beater like the shit was going to jump loose of my chest bones. My mind was not foggy with sleep anymore; I was wide awake and on alert.

I didn't know if it was jealous motherfuckers from the hood or those hating-ass five-o bastards who had a vendetta against me, banging up my fucking minimansion doors. The shit sounded like a fucking earthquake was happening right there in my crib. At first

I didn't hear them say "POLICE!" but as soon as I was facing down the end of an MP5, I knew what the fuck was up.

"Get on the floor! Get the fuck on the floor!"

Those commands were very familiar. I put my hands up, folded them behind my head, and assumed the position. I was pushed down to the floor roughly, and about five of those bastards dropped knees in my back and legs. My arms were yanked behind my back, and I was cuffed and made to lie facedown on my own fucking floor. Those fucking pigs were swarming my crib like flies around a pile of freshly dropped shit. It seemed like there were a million of them. All of them against just me.

"Punk bitches," I grumbled under my breath. I recognized one of them—a big-headed white boy who thought he was the shit. A snake motherfucker named Labeckie. He was the sergeant of the Norfolk Police Department's narcotics and gun unit, and he hated my ass.

"Take out that wall! Tear this fucking place up until we find some shit!" I heard that bastard yell as he looked down at me and smiled.

I closed my eyes when I heard them axing down walls and cabinets. Didn't they fucking know they could've just opened that shit up? My mind was racing, and I immediately hoped that Shannon didn't walk in on this shit with Lil Todd.

I lay there, facedown, knowing right away that somebody in my camp had snitched. I knew my gun-running shit and five-o radar were airtight. There was no fucking way they could have known about my operation unless somebody told them. It had been three years since I had done my last bid on a drug charge, and when I got home, I had gone into a different line of work. Before I got knocked on the trumped-up drug charges, I was one of the biggest kingpins in the Norfolk area. I had all of Tidewater on lock, and I was bringing in at least fifty thousand a week. Almost all of the trap boys in the area were employed by me. I ran a tight ship, and the narcos found it hard to get my ass. The cops who arrested me the last time weren't gonna rest until they got my ass. I had beat so many charges because of my high-paid attorney, and those fucking pigs were mad as hell, so when they finally got me on some ol' caught slipping shit, they was happy as hell.

When I came home, I promised my wife I was leaving the drug game behind me—the money, the bitches, and the fucking five-o too. I knew she was tired of riding with me through all this bullshit, so I told her I was going legit, and that is exactly what I did . . . at first. I opened my own short-distance trucking company. That shit was all good, but it wasn't enough money for me. Shannon was used to living a certain lifestyle, and I was going to provide it. I got into the gun-running shit by coincidence, and it was all up from there. I was bringing in cake, and my wife and kid were fucking happy. I was sure I was careful, and I surrounded myself with only a few cats who I thought were real. It seems one of those motherfuckers wasn't a real cat but a fucking snake-ass rat.

These bastard-ass cops had me facedown on the floor for mad long. The circulation in my hands felt like it was completely cut off. All I could hear was them destroying my beautiful home and rummaging through my shit. I bit into my cheek until I drew blood when I heard one of them whistle and say, "Hmm, the missus must be a pretty bitch—look at these pretty-ass panties." Then the bastard took a long sniff and said, "Ahhhh, pretty pussy smell. Think I could fuck his wife while he does his life sentence?" and then he started laughing. I squirmed around with the handcuffs biting into my skin. He was so lucky I was shackled like an animal or else I would've fucked his ass up. Shannon was my world, and I didn't want a nigga, especially a bitch-ass pig, even looking in her direction.

"Yo, these cuffs is tight!" I called out while they continued going through my shit.

"I don't give a fuck! You lucky we don't hog-tie you like the animal you are," the pig guarding me barked in my ear. His punk ass knew if I could get out of the fucking handcuffs, his wig would be twisted back.

It seemed like they were searching for days when one of them yelled, "Jackpot! I knew we would find something!" I just shut my eyes and thought about Shannon and our little man. I was a three striker, and my ass was going down. I had always made it a practice not to bring my shit where I live, but Jock—one of my boys—had met up with me the night before with a military-grade AK47 left over from his sales meeting. Apparently the cats he met up with had gotten cold feet on that shit and didn't buy it, leaving Jock to drive around with the shit on his way back to Norfolk. Jock was shook and didn't know where to take the shit, so being the man I am, I met up with Jock and took that load off of him. My intention had been to get that shit sold today. Either I was a few hours short or I was set the fuck up.

"Yo, I get a phone call, right?" I asked as two cops hauled me up off the floor.

"Don't ask for shit!" one of them barked.

Shannon

"How do these look?" I asked Satanya as I sashayed around the Saks shoe salon.

"Mmmm, girl, those shits are hot on your little-ass feet," she said, smiling.

"I'm about to get them, then," I said, sitting down to let the salesgirl take the hot-ass Christian Louboutin booties off my feet. "I will take those and the other two pumps too," I told the girl as she scrambled to get the shoes together. We both knew her commission depended on me.

Satanya wasn't buying nothing, and I thought about slipping in a pair for her but changed my mind. *Not today,* I thought. I dropped $2,885 on my shoes like it was nothing. Then I went upstairs to find something for my hubby and baby boy. I always picked up something for my two men. As long as Todd was providing, I was buying. He always said he wanted to repay me for riding with him through his bid. Damn, how I loved that man.

"Girl, you the shit," Satanya said, paying me a compliment as I peeled off enough bills to pay for my merchandise. I already knew I was the shit, but I played modest.

"Oh, girl, please, I don't do this too often," I lied. Shit, I still had like five g's in my bag to spend. As we eased off the escalator in the men's section, my cell phone started going crazy. "Who is calling me?" I asked, looking down at my phone, annoyed as hell. I knew Todd was at home sleeping after a long night's work. It seemed like a bunch of old texts were coming through on my phone.

"I hate being in that shoe section in Saks. I never get my messages," I said to Satanya. It turned out to be a bunch of voice mails coming through. I decided to check them later. Chances were it was my begging-ass family, who called me almost every day begging for shit. My cousins still couldn't believe I was with Todd and living like a star. They had all shitted on me when I was younger because their mothers worked, and my mother was cracked the fuck out and never bought me shit. Well, the tables were turned now. All those bitches were scrambling for rent money even though they were on Section 8, and I was living in a minimansion in the exclusive Ghent section of Norfolk. I had a good man while they had those fake-ass hand-to-hand corner boys. Those chicks were glad to take my designer hand-me-downs now.

I wasn't trying to hear their begging-ass messages today, talking about can they borrow a hundred dollars to pay their rent or get food—that shit was always their story.

Satanya and I continued to blow Saks out, and I dropped another $2,500 before we left. Feeling bad, I took her back downstairs and picked her up the cheapest pair of Gucci slides they had. The shits were only $395; it was the least I could do for her keeping me company. Don't get me wrong; Satanya wasn't no slouch, but her man was on lock right now, so shit had gotten tight for her. I had been in her shoes once, too, when Todd was locked up, so I couldn't judge her. I knew she'd be back on her shit sooner or later, and besides that, she was my girl.

"I'm going to my house to drop this stuff off, and then we going to pick up the baby from day care," I told her.

We laughed and joked all the way to my exclusive gated community. As I pulled through the black gates, something seemed a little different today. A bunch of my neighbors were standing outside on their lawns looking up and down the street. Now, I knew most of these rich folks didn't work, but usually they stayed inside, and I would only see them coming in and going out, or if they hosted dinner parties, I'd see them greeting their guests. As I drove, some of them pointed at my car and looked like they were whispering to each other and talking about me.

"What the hell is going on? I ain't never seen this many people out in your neighborhood, Shannon," Satanya said, looking out at the neighbors.

"Damn right. I have no idea," I replied, confused as hell. As I rounded the corner toward my house, which was the biggest one at the end of the cul-de-sac, I noticed a bunch of tire marks on my circular driveway. My heart immediately started thumping. Todd's Mercedes CLS was in the driveway but looked like it had been sideswiped.

I didn't want to alarm Satanya, so I decided to play it cool; meanwhile, my bowels felt like they were going to release. I threw my car in park and took the front steps in one leap. As soon as I reached the door, I knew.

The front door was splintered like it had been hit a million times with an ax. There were no locks left on it. I gently pushed the door open, and it practically came apart with pieces of wood falling. I threw my arms up, and Satanya was right on my heels. When I looked through the doorway, my eyes widened so big they felt like they were going to just pop out of the sockets. My chest started heaving, and my entire body became numb. I couldn't breathe, and I grabbed on to Satanya to keep myself up.

"Girl, what the fuck!" she screamed.

"Oh my God! Todd!" I screamed out before my knees buckled. Satanya held on to me as we both moved forward.

"Todd!" I screamed out again, breaking free of her grip and running through the mess toward the stairs. It looked like a tornado had hit the inside of my house. All of my furniture was either chopped up or thrown over. I could hardly get up the steps—the entire banister on the winding staircase had been broken into pieces, and wood splinters littered the carpeted stairs. I slid on wood as I scrambled up the stairs to try to find Todd. I finally got up the stairs and ran through all of the Sheetrock and plaster in the long hallway straight to the master bedroom.

"Todd! Todd!" I screamed out with tears flowing down my face like a river and my pulse racing so hard it felt like it was beating in the back of my throat. Todd was nowhere to be found.

Our bedroom was in even worse condition. The artwork that usually adorned my walls was sliced up and the expensive frames shattered. The wall right before you enter the suite had a huge hole in the center like someone had taken a sledgehammer to it.

"Oh my God!" I yelled as I raced around what was left of our once-beautiful bedroom. All of my clothes were on the floor of my walk-in closets. My dresser drawers had been emptied onto the floor, and the dresser had been hit down the middle, completely split in two. The dresser mirror lay shattered on the carpet in a million pieces. The mattress and box springs were on the floor, and cotton spilled from the middle like a gutted pig. I knew from the looks of things it was definitely the police that had come up in my house and destroyed it. If it had been one of Todd's rivals from the streets, there may have been bullet holes, but all of this destruction couldn't have come from anyone else but those hating-ass police.

As I tried to compose myself, my mind immediately went to Todd's safe. It contained our life savings and all of the money I needed to live off of if something happened to him. It was a plan that Todd had put together after the last raid and prison bid. He promised me that he would always make provisions for me and the baby so that I would not have to struggle if he had ever gotten into anything again. The safe also contained his "attorney stash"—an allotment of money Todd set aside for his defense attorney should some shit like this ever happen. I immediately scrambled toward the closet for the safe. My body immediately became hot and drenched with sweat as the possibility of the safe being gone made me see my life flash before my eyes.

I swallowed hard and climbed through the piles of clothes and shoes boxes that littered the floor of my closet, falling and pushing shit aside until I was at the back of the closet. Before I could reach the spot in the floor that had the loose piece of carpet, I dropped to my knees.

I could clearly see that the carpet was peeled back, and the big hole in the floor that usually contained the safe was empty. The electronic hoist that lifted the safe out of the floor was smashed to pieces, and the large Picasso that usually covered the switch for the hoist was also destroyed.

"Noooo!" I screamed, holding on to the side of my head as my ears began ringing. I screamed so loud I scared the shit out of Satanya.

"Shannon! Oh my God, girl!" Satanya screamed, too, rushing into the closet. She grabbed me and we both fell to the floor screaming together.

It seemed like a lifetime had passed. My eyes were swollen, and my throat was sore. I just spun around and around in circles trying to figure out how this had happened. Satanya helped me compose myself. I had a banging headache, and I had to think. I dumped out my purse and saw I had a total of $2,500 left after my shopping spree. Todd never really kept money in the bank because of the fucking questions and those fucking stupid-ass suspicious-activity reports those bank people filled out if a person brought in certain amounts of money. He had explained to me that even if he kept his deposits right under ten thousand, the bank would start filling out those reports after he did that a couple of times. In his case, it would send off red flags to the police, especially since those bastards hated the fact that Todd had gone legit. Todd also always wanted to have his money at his fingertips in case we had to get the fuck out of dodge. I had a bank account that I opened for Lil Todd, but it had only about another two g's in it. Todd just always encouraged me to put money away in the safe stash. When I calculated what I had in total right now, I began to cry again. Five thousand dollars couldn't do shit for me.

I was used to spending that in one day. My house mortgage was $6,500 a month alone. Not to mention me and the baby had to eat, plus the light, gas, and other expenses we had. This little-ass bit of money wouldn't last no time. I took a deep breath and realized that I would have to wait on Todd to tell me what to do next. I was hoping he had some money stashed somewhere outside of the house. After calming down, I found a copy of the fucking search-and-seizure warrant and the arrest warrant lying on what was left of my granite countertops. Those motherfucking cops had finally gotten their wish and got something on Todd. In my assessment, since Todd told me he had gone legit, those pigs had to have made something up on my husband.

Satanya was good enough to go pick up Lil Todd for me while I stayed and tried to make sense of all this shit. I paced the floor up and down trying to think of all the places Todd would have money. First I looked in the exercise room under his weights; they had gotten the little stash he kept there. Then I looked outside in the fertilizer bin; they had gotten that one too. The more I searched, the more I realized that $5,000 was what I had to my name right now. They had taken all of my jewelry, both Rolexes, Todd's diamond Jesus piece, and basically anything worth a lot of money. Those crooked-ass cops probably pocketed all that shit. I didn't even have enough fucking money to call that expensive-ass attorney who got Todd off the last time. That bastard had a $5,000 retainer up front, not to mention what he would want after he went to just one court appearance. If I gave him that, how the fuck would me and Lil Todd eat?

My cell phone rang and I raced over to it. "Hello?!" I breathed hard into the phone. My shoulders slumped when I heard Satanya's voice.

I thought for sure it would be Todd. Satanya had gotten the baby and was taking him to her house. She said he didn't need to see the house in that condition, and she was right. I found it strange that the word hadn't gotten out on the streets yet and that none of Todd's boys had contacted me yet. I knew sooner or later, Todd would get his one phone call, and he would definitely be calling me. I was sure he would be able to tell me where he had hidden some more money. So I waited. And waited.

Todd

"Yo, straight up. Y'all niggas got the wrong dude if y'all think I'm speaking to y'all asses without my lawyer," I barked. These fucking cops didn't know who they were fucking with. They had me in this interrogation room talking that let's-make-a-deal shit. These motherfuckers were crazy! First of all, who the fuck would I snitch on?

I am my own boss. They wanted to know who I got the weapons from. "What fucking weapons?" was my question back to them. As far as I knew, I didn't have no weapons; that was my story and I was sticking to it. They weren't fucking with no little corner dude who would be running his mouth before his lawyer showed up.

That big white boy sergeant, Labeckie, hated my ass. He got so mad at me that he banged his hands on the little metal table until his shit was swollen. It was obvious that somebody in a high place had told that motherfucker that he'd better get me to roll or else his ass would be back on the beat.

I kept asking for my phone call every time they came in and out of the room. They knew they couldn't hold me longer than sixteen hours without a call, and it was coming close to that time. I was hoping that Shannon remembered the codes I had taught her for the phone conversation in case something like this ever happened again. We hadn't practiced those codes in a long time. I couldn't trust talking on no fucking precinct phone, so we had developed some codes for an emergency just like this.

I had my head in my hands when Labeckie and his little ass-kissing cronies came back into the room. I knew they had been watching me through the blacked-out glass that looked like a mirror. I guess they thought a nigga was stressed, so they came back to make their move.

"So, Todd Marshall, here's the fucking deal—if you don't play, you stay. In other words, talk and you might walk. This is your final offer," Labeckie said as he flexed his jaw. The sergeant was angry. I watched his chest swell and his jaw flex a million times a minute.

He was on the edge, and I knew it. I wasn't bending over so these crooked-ass cops could fuck me with no lube—hell no!

"Yo, I need my phone call. Y'all got ten minutes," I said calmly, looking over and leaning my head toward the institution-style clock above the steel door. The sergeant knew all too well that I was fully aware of my rights, and it just pissed him off even more.

"Andrews, take this pantywaist for his phone call. Then you can go fuck his wife right after—" Labeckie spat, smiling wickedly.

Before he could fully get the words out of his mouth, I jumped up and pushed away from the table, sending it sliding right into Labeckie's chest.

He jumped up ready to flex.

"Don't mention my wife!" I barked.

"Sit the fuck down!" Labeckie screamed as the two other cops slammed me into the table, knocking the wind out of me.

When I was finally given my phone call, I dialed Shannon's cell and hoped to God she answered. I knew that by now she would be a nervous wreck, probably crying and all fucked up over this shit. I would've given anything to see her beautiful caramel face with those long-ass eyelashes she loved to bat at me. Those eyes always made me melt like a stick of butter in the sun. Thinking about my beautiful wife, with her slim waist and thick hips, being out in the world alone while I did another bid was enough to send cramps into my stomach. Shannon had told me that during my first bid, so many dudes who were supposed to be my boys had tried to fuck her it wasn't even funny. I knew that most of the street dudes in Norfolk were envious of me, especially when they peeped my wife with her long hair; clear skin; and those round, perfect D-cup tits. Damn! I was fucked up just picturing her beautiful ass right now.

"What up, baby?" I whispered into the phone, secretly thanking God she had answered. I closed my eyes and moved the receiver away from my ear as my wife screamed out my name at the top of her lungs. It was breaking my heart to hear her in so much pain. "Calm down, baby. I don't have that much time," I comforted as Shannon wilded out on the other end. When she told me these fucking pigs had taken my safe, my stomach clenched and I felt like shitting on myself. Everything I owned was up in that safe, including my get-outta-jail-free lawyer stash. Shannon was crying so hard I knew I couldn't fall apart now, too, even though I felt like it. "Listen, listen," I said, making sure I had her full attention.

"Remember what we practiced?" I asked, trying to get her to calm down so I could tell her what to do next. Through her tears, she said she remembered. I told her, in code, to go to Jock, Zack, and Billy to collect on some loot all three of them owed me for recent sales and to collect on debts that they all owed me as well. Then I told her to go to the garage where I parked the trucks for the business; there was a small stash in a lockbox in the office. Shannon sounded like she finally started to breathe easy. I knew that between what my dudes owed me and what I had up in the garage, she could at least pay the bills on the house for two months and get a retainer up for my attorney. It was a solid plan. The only other person who knew about the garage stash was my dude Jock.

"I love you, Shannon, and I'm gonna get outta this shit," I said to her before getting ready to hang up.

She told me over and over again how much she loved me too. She held on to the phone as long as she could; then these fucking assholes were breathing down my neck, telling me my time was up. I told her that I had to go, and it was probably the most painful thing I have felt in a while. It just sounded so final. I knew my wife wasn't made for the streets, so I prayed real hard that she was able to handle the tasks at hand before my first court appearance.

Shannon

As soon as Todd told me what to do, I set out on a mission to get the money so I could try to get a good lawyer and be prepared for Todd's arraignment. My first stop was to see Zack, since he lived closer and since, through code, Todd had made it seem like Zack owed him the most money. Zack was much younger than Todd, and I remember Todd taking him under his wing and showing him the ropes on the street.

So I was sure collecting from him wouldn't be a problem.

I pulled up to the corner of Church Street and Johnson Street, where I knew Zack had his trap house. There were a bunch of niggas out there, gambling and standing around waiting for their customers. I hadn't been to this side of town in so long I immediately got disgusted. All the run-down buildings and crack fiends running up and down the streets. Even though I grew up around here, it was a place I wanted to forget.

At the corner I spotted Zack.

"Zack!" I called out the window. All of those niggas turned around like they were ready to flex. They were all staring at me like

I was crazy. Zack put his hand up to his eyes and moved his head in and out like he was having a hard time recognizing me. This nigga looked confused and shit. I called out to him again, this time bending my head down a little so I was sure he could see my face through the window. I knew damn well he knew just who the fuck I was, but I played it cool. Finally, he bopped over to the car.

"What's up?" I asked.

"Oh, damn, Todd's wife—Shannon, right?" he asked, putting a little phony-ass smile on his face. I could've slapped the shit out of his skinny ass. How dare he act like he didn't fucking remember me!

"Yeah. You don't remember staying at my crib when you first got home?" I asked, reminding that nigga just who took care of his ass and got him back on his feet when he was hungry.

"Nah, I'm saying I remember and shit, but you look different and shit," he said.

"A'ight, well, I'm sure you heard about my husband, right?" I asked, not even giving him time to answer, because the way the streets of Norfolk was, I knew he already knew about Todd getting locked up. "Well, Todd sent me here," I started again.

"Oh, yeah, I heard he got locked up on some ol' life-sentence shit," Zack said. His words hit me right in the gut, and I felt like doubling over as if he had actually punched me.

"Nah, that's what niggas might think. He gonna get out as soon as I collect from all the dudes who owe him so I can pay his attorney," I said with an attitude. "That is the reason I'm here. You owe Todd twenty thousand, right?" I said with more of an attitude. How dare this motherfucker put my damn baby behind bars for life before he was even arraigned! I wasn't getting a good vibe from this nigga at all.

"Ummm . . . I thought me and that nigga had settled that," Zack said dismissively.

"Settled it? Well, that ain't what he told me. I really need to collect that as soon as possible," I replied, not trying to hear this nigga right now.

"I'ma see what I can do," Zack said, starting to back away from the car like he was dismissing me.

"When should I check back?" I yelled out the window. This nigga had moved fast as hell.

"I'll get back to you. You don't have to look for me. I'll get at you," he said, turning his back and returning to his little group of corner boys. I could see them huddling around him to find out what I wanted.

I was well aware that there were several of them who wished they could have me. I was fucking pissed. Todd was always like the Robin of the hood, helping all these little niggas out, putting them to work and shit, and now this motherfucker was acting like he didn't owe my husband shit. I was driving with tears in my eyes. That meeting didn't seem too damn promising. I was on the next dude.

I pulled up to Billy's house and blocked his driveway. He had graduated from the corners, so he lived in a pretty decent neighborhood. It wasn't as high class as where we lived, but it was nice enough. I rang his bell, and within minutes he was at the door. He pulled back the door and was standing there in his wife-beater and boxers.

"Wassup, Billy? I'm sorry if I woke you up, but this is an emergency," I said.

"Nah, I'm good. I heard about T. But you a'ight?" he asked.

I felt like breaking down, but I held my head up and got to the point. "I'm good. Todd asked me to come by and check for some loot that you got for him," I explained. Billy's eyebrows went down and his face changed. He asked me in and told me I could sit down on the couch. I didn't want to be rude, but I wasn't there for all that sit-down bullshit. I wanted to get to the point—did he have the money or not?

"Yeah, yeah. I owe him a few dollars. Whatchu need?" he asked.

"I need what you owe Todd. For real, shit is crazy right about now, and I just need to get up some money for his lawyer," I explained, feeling like I was doing too much explaining. I felt like I had to cop a plea to these niggas who owed my fucking husband money!

"Hold up," Billy said, disappearing toward the back of his house.

I looked around and could tell by the flat screens, the expensive furniture, and the artwork that Billy wasn't doing too bad financially.

He came back with two plastic bags in his hands with some money in them. "Here is a little something," he said, tossing the bags at me, then he plopped down on the couch beside me. My eyes immediately lit up. I was happy to see that he was coming up off the money.

"How much is this?" I asked.

"That's like two g's. I'ma have to work on the rest," he explained.

I wasn't trying to be ungrateful, but I was thinking what the fuck is two g's gonna do? I still wouldn't be able to pay for that lawyer. Unlike that little punk-ass Zack, at least Billy came up off of something. I put the money in my bag.

The next thing I knew, this nigga had moved real close to me on the couch. He shocked me when he put his arm around me and got close to the side of my face.

"Yo, if you need a nigga to take care of your pretty ass, all you gotta do is holla," he said, breathing on my cheek.

"What the fuck is you doing?!" I screamed, pushing him away and trying to stand up. My heart was racing fast, and I was in such shock I didn't even know what to say.

"Don't be acting like you too fucking good for a nigga," he growled, holding on to my arm so tight I felt a sharp pain.

"Get the fuck off me!" I screamed again, yanking my arm away.

"I could take your pussy right now and nobody would know. Ya man ain't fucking getting out no time soon. You better get with a nigga who can take care of you without getting his ass locked up every other year," he said cruelly.

"Fuck you, Billy!" I spat, twisting my arm out of his grasp. I ain't gonna front; I was scared as hell, but I was mad as hell at the same time. I rushed toward the front door to get the fuck out of there. Billy looked like he was liable to rape me right there. I guess I wouldn't be getting no more money from him. I was feeling so conflicted inside. I really couldn't believe these niggas was shitting on Todd for real.

When I got back in my car, my mind was racing in a million directions. This shit wasn't going to be as easy as Todd made it seem. I slammed my hands on the steering wheel. I started to feel angry because my husband had told me he had gone fully legit. *How the fuck did this happen?* I asked myself as I pulled away from Billy's driveway wondering what the fuck would happen next.

"Think positive, Shannon, think positive," I pep talked myself as I drove. Shit couldn't get any worse . . . or could it?

As a last-ditch effort, I was sure praying that Jock was going to hook me up with some cash. Jock and Todd had been friends since they were little kids, and my husband shared everything with him. Todd trusted him with everything, including his secrets and his business dealings. Jock was Lil Todd's godfather, and he had been the best man in our wedding—that was how close he was with my husband. I was still wondering why the hell Jock hadn't come to check on me yet.

I drove to Jock's house and he wasn't home. I went to every place I knew he hung out and couldn't find him. I left him three voice mails, and he had not returned my calls. I had no choice but to wait for him to get in touch with me now, because I didn't know where he was.

I couldn't even go to Todd's garage, because Jock had the spare keys and with my house tossed up like it was, I had no idea where Todd's keys were.

With only an extra $2,000 to add to what I had, I went home, mentally and physically exhausted. Todd would be in court tomorrow, and I had no way to help him. As soon as I pulled into my driveway, I broke down. The tears just came flooding and didn't stop until my tear ducts were completely dry and my mind completely numb.

Todd

My arraignment was quick and fucked up. They were trying to stick me with all kinds of gun charges—fucking possession and intent to distribute illegally. Since I was already a predicate felon, that fucking judge denied bail. Shannon was in the courtroom, but she hadn't been able to get up enough money for a lawyer, so they gave my ass a court-appointed attorney. Right then and there, I prepared myself for a trip to prison. That little skinny-ass lawyer looked all sloppy and shit, papers and folders spilling out of his hand. Not the well-dressed, sharp-ass attorneys I had hired in the past to beat charges. This scrawny little bastard was acting all scared of me and shit. I knew right then and there he thought I was guilty as a motherfucker too—not a good sign. Something was gonna have to give.

Three meetings with that little bitch-ass lawyer and he was trying to convince me to take a plea deal.

"Ten to fifteen years! Motherfucker, is you crazy? I ain't pleading to that shit!" I hollered at him.

"That's what they are offering you since you are a three striker," he'd said, his voice cracking like a little bitch.

"Nah, I'm taking this shit to trial," I argued, shaking my head, but I knew deep down inside if I took the shit to trial, I would be facing life. I wouldn't stand a chance with the evidence they found in my crib. If I took it to trial with this little fucked-up lawyer, I would definitely lose. Taking a ten-year bid would be better than getting fucking life. Leaving one of the many meetings I had with the lawyer, I knew right away I would be going down for another bid if something didn't give.

I had my next court date fast as hell. That little bitch-ass lawyer had made a motion to dismiss, which was denied and I was set for another court date in six weeks. Six fucking weeks of sitting in the fucking Virginia Beach County Jail would be fucked up. Seeing my wife screaming and crying in the courtroom fucked me up inside and had me ready to kill a nigga for real. I looked back at her one last time before they took my ass back to the courtroom cells, and all I could do was hang my fucking head.

Right after that, they carted my ass off on that dirty-ass prison bus. As soon as I stepped up on that shit, I could feel the eyes of some of my enemies staring at me and grilling me. No matter when a street nigga like me went to jail, I was always gonna have enemies.

I wasn't no fucking punk, and I was going to let these niggas know right now that I wasn't to be fucked with. I kept my head up as I took small steps with my feet and hands shackled. I kept a confident air about me and screwed up my face, staring those bitch niggas right back in the eye. Without a word, I knew I was letting them know "don't fuck with me."

When I arrived back at the jail, I got into a different state of mind.

I wasn't trying to hear the COs or none of these fucking inmates up in here. Of course, I was strip searched, body-cavity searched, and sprayed with cold-ass water from a hose—in other words, I was fucking dehumanized. I was given a fucked-up jumpsuit and those little piece-of-shit slippers. The CO handed me my fucking sheets, a blanket, and pillow. When I arrived on the tier, a bunch of niggas playing spades stopped to check me out. I kept eye contact with them, letting them know what was up. I wasn't to be played with. It was important that I sent a message early. Shit, for all I knew, I might be doing a fucking life sentence.

I walked into my cell, and there was a dude on the floor doing push-ups. Looking down at him, I noticed his fucking arms were huge and he wore long dreads. When he heard the COs bringing me in, he got up to check me out. He looked me up and down, and I did the same shit to him. As long as he looked me in the eye, I did the same back. He had real dark skin and a scowl on his face like he wanted me to know he was a tough guy. I ignored him and placed my shit on the empty top bunk. The COs left, and shortly after, they called gate lock for the count. That's the shit I didn't miss. The constant fucking counting heads in jail—after every meal, at yard time, for new inmates, anything they had to do a fucking count.

I looked around the cell and noticed that the dude had mad legal books stacked on the floor. *Oh, boy. Another prison lawyer trying to come up with his own defense,* I thought to myself. I got up on my bunk, put my arm over my eyes, and remained quiet until it was time for lights-out.

*   *   *

Waking up in jail was the worst feeling in the world. I opened my eyes to gray cinder-block walls and a pissy-ass cell. Damn, I covered my nose and mouth because this nigga had taken a piss and didn't flush the toilet. It was breakfast time, and I really wasn't feeling like dealing with the niggas in general population.

I knew from experience these motherfuckers always thought they had shit to prove. I walked out of my cell toward the chow hall and wished a nigga would try me. I could hear some of them whispering and trying to figure out who the fuck I was. I looked around the chow hall tryna see if I recognized any of my boys, but I didn't see nobody I knew yet. I got in the line for food. Looking at the slop was depressing. As I stood in line, sure enough niggas tried to start some shit with me.

"I smell new pussy," I heard one of them say. The next thing I knew, one of the dudes was right up on me, while two more of them moved in position to try to surround me.

I crinkled up my face like the Incredible Hulk and turned around quickly, getting ready to bang those motherfuckers in the face with my tray. I wasn't going to talk to these niggas; it was all action from Todd Marshall. I wasn't no punk-ass nigga. Before I could do anything, my cellmate stepped between me and the dude.

"Yo, bitch ass, step the fuck off my celly and go find some other asshole to run up in, faggot nigga," my cellmate barked, cracking his knuckles and flexing those big, black-ass arms.

Those niggas nodded and backed off, like they knew the deal with my cellmate. Obviously he had a reputation up in the joint.

"Dray," he said to me, reaching his hand out for a pound.

"Todd," I said back, giving him dap. "These motherfucking punk-ass niggas always trying to find new ass to catch," Dray said, grabbing a juice.

"I don't need no protection," I assured him, letting him know that I could hold my own. I wasn't trying to let nobody fight my battles.

"Nah, I saw you about to handle yours with that tray, but it ain't worth getting sent to the hole for," Dray explained.

He was right. I was about to get an extra assault charge added to the fucking book of charges they had already put on me.

At yard time, me and Dray held a good conversation. He pointed out all of the new gangs and cliques that had arrived up in the prison since I had been out.

"Yo, those Spanish cats are a motherfucker. They all about cutting niggas down the middle to leave their mark," Dray explained, pointing out the tatted-up Spanish dudes who were huddled around the pull-up bars. "Those Muslim dudes are solid. They keep to themselves, but if you cross them, you're dead," he continued, nodding toward a group of black dudes with little things on their heads. I knew about them when I was up in prison, but from what Dray was telling me, they had become more ruthless. In fact, he told me the jail-gang tracking unit now considered the Muslims inside the walls a gang and not a religion.

Two weeks up in the joint and me and Dray had gotten mad cool. He was always spitting legal terms and shit, telling me all the things I should be telling my court-appointed lawyer until I could get my new attorney. I was usually leery about cats I didn't know, but Dray was cool, and I was kind of digging his style.

One day, we had worked out and afterward, I went to use the phone to call Shannon. I needed to find out what the fuck was going on with her and my son and with the money for the lawyer. I got more and more heated by the minute as I spoke to her. She was all crying and shit, telling me how none of those dudes I sent her to was trying to come up off the money they owed me. I was on fire inside when she told me that she still couldn't find that nigga Jock and that the garage where I kept my trucks had been cleaned the fuck out—stash and all. The more I spoke to her and found out what was going on on the outside, the more this whole shit sounded like a fucking setup.

When I got back to my cell, I was fuming mad. I paced up and down the floor. I didn't sit out on the tier and watch TV, nor did I feel like working out. My mind was racing, and my anger level was over the top. It seemed like shit was dim for me, and as I looked around, I started realizing this little fucking dank-ass cell might be my fucking reality.

Dray came into the cell and sat down on his bunk. He watched me for a minute, then asked what was up.

"Yo, I just met you, man. I ain't into telling cats I don't know my business," I said.

"Nah, man, I fully understand," Dray said.

But as I paced and paced and thought longer and longer, I just grew angrier by the minute. I wasn't into telling dudes my business, but I was so heated I just let it out. I told him how my fucking wife was down to almost nothing. She was barely able to pay the mortgage on the house and was going to have to move to a small-ass apartment. I told him how niggas in the streets who owed me money thought I was gone for good, so they wasn't trying to come up off paper that they owed me. Dray was looking at me like he was thinking as I was talking.

"And, yo, the thing that gets me the fucking most is my main partner, Jock, ain't nowhere to be found, and the whole reason I'm in this shit is because I took a fucking ratchet off his hands. I ain't even got money for a fucking defense attorney right now!" I barked, with regret and anger behind my words as I continued pacing up and down my little cell. I regretted the words as soon as they left my mouth. You just never knew who was who up in prison. I knew I had run my fucking mouth enough already.

"Yo, man, it ain't all bad," Dray said, rubbing his temple like he was feeling my pain.

"Nigga, this shit ain't bad—it's fucking tragic!" I screamed. Right now I ain't have shit—no fucking lawyer and no chance to try to fix the chopped-up fucking job that court-appointed bitch-ass attorney had done.

"Yo, man. I think I can help you. I know a way you can make a lot of money in a little bit of time," Dray blurted out.

"What? Whatchu talking about, nigga? You in the same boat as me," I fumed, not trying to hear no bullshit fake-ass outside hook-up.

"Yeah, nigga, I am. But me and you are two different people. You ready to hear how you can get money to feed ya family and get a fucking lawyer for appeal before you sit in here and rot while ya boys fuck ya wife?" Dray said, not holding back his words.

Even though I wanted to punch him in the fucking mouth for what he had just said, I couldn't front. I was interested in what the fuck he was talking about.

I was all ears. What did I have to lose? At this point, nothing!

Shannon

It had been almost a month since Todd got locked up and still no sign of Jock. Todd was fucking heated off the situation, because if he didn't get a good lawyer soon, they were definitely going to be pressuring him to take a plea at his next court appearance.

These so-called street cats weren't trying to come up off the money they owed Todd, and I was down to absolutely nothing. I was having one more fucking garage sale today to sell off some more of my bags, shoes, and coats so I could scrounge up enough money to get a little apartment up in Dolphine Cove on Military Highway. I wasn't about to wait around for the marshals to come put my ass out once the fucking foreclosure proceedings started on the house. So far, I had had two sales and made a little cash to get me and Lil Todd through the month and enough to put some on the books for Todd. For real, though, I never knew how good I had it with my husband around until now, when I was left to survive on my own.

I was busy packing when I got a call on my cell from Todd.

"Wassup, baby?" I said, trying to sound upbeat so he wouldn't be all stressed out in there worrying about me.

"I got something to tell you. It's real important," he said, sounding all excited.

His excitement confused the hell out of me. Shit, I couldn't feel the same. There was nothing he could tell me right now—except that he was getting out—that would make me excited.

"What is so important?" I asked him, twisting my lips and rolling my eyes, glad he couldn't see the look on my face.

"I gotta tell you about a foolproof plan to get this one big lick. Shannon, I'm telling you, with what we can make, you will be able to get me an attorney for my appeal and get the fuck up outta dodge until I get out," Todd said, still sounding all excited.

By this time I was annoyed. *How can this nigga even sound the least bit excited at a time like this?* I thought while I listened to him talk.

"What is it?" I finally asked, sitting down on the couch, leaning my head on my fist. To me, it already sounded like a fucking pipe dream. I didn't want to sound all negative, but what the fuck did he expect me to do now? It was easy for him to sit up in that fucking jail and say "Shannon do this" and "Shannon do that." He was locked up, three square meals a day and not facing all the embarrassment I was facing from my friends and family, not to mention the streets was talking like a motherfucker. The street chronicles already had me on welfare; sucking dick for money; and, the best one yet, I was a paid informant for the same pig-ass cops who arrested my husband. I'm telling you the streets could spread some bullshit.

And to top it all off, when my hating-ass cousins had heard about my situation and heard I had to sell my most prized possessions, they all came over to rummage through my shit. Those bitches was spending they last dollar on my shit. They was buying up all my exclusive shit with their little welfare checks just so they could turn around and say they had Shannon's shit on their backs. Pride aside, I took their money too. I had no fucking choice.

During the conversation, Todd was rambling on in fucking code again, talking some shit about how his so-called master plan was gonna involve me and how I needed to be a "soldier." At first, I was saying hell fucking no when I figured out that I would have to be involved. But the more my husband spoke and the more I looked around at all of the boxes containing what was left of my belongings and thought about having to move and feeding my son, I got right into a ride-or-die bitch mind-set.

"What's the plan?" I asked again. He had my attention now; he had kind of got me interested in the money part. Todd instructed me not to speak over the phone. I would be visiting him tomorrow, and I guess I'd be finding out what I was about to do.

Todd

"A'ight, tell me again about this nigga Bobby Knight," I asked Dray as I paced again. My mind was racing with a million fucking thoughts about the money Dray had said this cat Bobby Knight had up in his crib.

"Yo, I'm telling you, nigga. He is fucking crazy paid. He owns all the strip clubs in the Chesapeake, Virginia, area. He is not just a two-bit hustler—that motherfucker is basically the head of his own fucking cartel. On my word, he got paper. Yo, what I'm talking about would be the ultimate heist. But I'm telling you, your people would have to mirk this nigga, because if not, he will kill you, your crew, and ya whole fucking family—puppy dogs, grandmas, and all," Dray informed me. Once again, the sound of a money machine was ringing in my ears. I could just see the fucking paper this nigga had, and I could also picture my fucking hands right on it.

"So if the nigga is so thorough, how you think this shit gonna go down?" I asked, rubbing my chin deep in thought. It was obvious this ultimate-heist shit was gonna take some planning.

"Listen, T-man, the one thing that is Bobby Knight's weakness is pretty women," Dray said, giving me a telling glance.

"Whatchu saying?" I asked, crinkling my eyebrows, knowing what he meant.

"I'm saying that I've seen your wife on visits. No disrespect, but she is gorgeous and she is one hundred percent Bobby's type. All she would have to do is get in and set that shit up," Dray said, his words tumbling so fast I couldn't think.

"Nah, nigga, that sounds like some indecent-proposal-type shit," I replied, not willing to give no nigga at no cost a taste of my fucking wife.

"She don't have to fuck him. All she gotta do really is get that nigga to sweat her. Listen, man, I used to work around that dude, and I know his weaknesses. The cat got low self-esteem, and if you saw him, you'd know why. But see, he keeps the most pretty bitches in his stable and on his arm so he can make other niggas believe these gorgeous-ass woman are really attracted to his hideous ass," Dray explained, chuckling. "I'm saying I know Knight very well, and he would definitely latch on to your wife from day one," Dray continued.

"So, why you trying to get that cat set up?" I asked. Not trying to look a gift horse in the mouth, but I needed to know why Dray wanted to do this nigga Bobby Knight dirty.

"It's simple. Bobby Knight is a backstabbing prick bastard," Dray gritted, spit flying out of his mouth as he spoke. "He turned his back on me, and he had my brother killed. We had been loyal street soldiers in Bobby's army. See, that nigga Bobby Knight got a God complex, and he thinks he is untouchable. Basically he is, unless you know his inner workings and how he operates," Dray explained, his eyes getting small and squinty like he was either gonna cry and shit or kill a nigga. I could feel his pain of being betrayed too. I was now convinced that that nigga Jock had turned his back on me in the worst way.

"So how much money you think this dude is sitting on?" I asked, trying to change the subject since Dray seemed to be having a hard time talking about why he hated Bobby Knight. His explanation was good enough for me. Shit, I lived by the death-before-dishonor code, so I was feeling Dray all the way.

"Nigga you couldn't understand the magnitude of this dude's bank. He is a millionaire a thousand times over. We talking Pablo Escobar–type money . . . rooms full of money. See, he can't put that shit up in no bank with all these money-laundering and money-tracking laws, so the nigga got rooms in his house just filled with boxes and boxes of money!" Dray said, spreading his arms wide to illustrate how much and sounding like he was getting lifted just thinking about it. "I'm talking about boxes of money. You ever seen that movie *Blow*? How them dudes had money in a room from floor to ceiling? That's the type of money I'm talking about," Dray explained.

I knew just what the fuck he was saying. I had watched that movie at least ten times; aside from *Scarface*, it was probably my favorite movie of all time.

"When I went down, this motherfucker Bobby ain't so much as put a dime on the fucking books for me, and he took away my brother, leaving me with nobody," Dray continued, his chest heaving a little bit.

I could tell Dray was trying hard to keep his composure. I noticed that it was a sensitive topic when he spoke about Bobby Knight.

"Boxes of money sound good to me. Where this nigga stay at?"

I asked, putting a halt to my pacing. Dray started drawing on the inside of a small cereal box. He drew zigs and zags like a fucking maze.

"We talking about a complex. It ain't no regular house—that's what I'm trying to tell you. This nigga live behind big iron gates with a massive security system. He got his own closed-circuit TV security system that he can see anywhere in the house," Dray explained, passing the little drawing to me. I examined it closely.

"Dayum, it's like that?" I said, opening my eyes wide.

"For real, for real. This nigga Bobby Knight is a thorough dude. That's why this shit is gonna have to be done from a trust standpoint, and Bobby don't trust many niggas. But bitches, especially grade A beauties, now that's his weakness. I have seen him bring bitches to his home after a first date when he knew absolutely nothing about them. He got a bad weakness for pretty women. I'm telling you, your wife got what it takes to get that nigga's eye," Dray said with extra emphasis on Shannon having what it took. "After she gets inside, she can map out the house and assemble a team to get it done. But it gotta be thorough, with cats you can trust," he continued.

I was all ears, but I still didn't know if I wanted to send Shannon out there as fucking bait. Dray was right about one thing—this shit was gonna have to be planned out like some *Ocean's Eleven* shit. It wasn't gonna be no regular fucking stickup-type robbery; it was going to be a heist!

Shannon

I simply hated visiting Todd in jail. I hated seeing him locked up like that. This ride-or-die shit was played the fuck out too. I had done it for so long. Nonetheless, I prepared for our weekly visit. I put on a hot little Dolce & Gabbana jean skirt that I hadn't sold off and a pair of Gucci stilettos that I had left. I knew no matter what, Todd was gonna need to get a quickie between the vending machines, so the skirt was a must.

After the whole jail search bullshit—you know, open your mouth, let me feel under your bra straps, take off your shoes, open your bag—I was finally allowed behind the heavy iron gates to the visiting room.

It was packed as usual. The smell of chicken, shitty diapers, and old plastic made me want to throw up. I looked around at all of the loyal women who had come to do the same thing as me—visit the nigga who was taking care of them but had left them high and dry. I could feel niggas and bitches alike staring at me. I knew my outfit had caught more than a couple of eyes. I sat down at one of those fucking *Romper Room* tables—I mean, really, did they think inmates and their visitors really wanted to be at those little-ass tables and sit on those little-ass colorful chairs? Anyway, I saw when they brought Todd in.

I immediately smiled at him as he bopped over to me. He hadn't lost his swagger one bit, and he was looking very fucking ripped, which immediately made my pussy wet. Todd stood six feet two inches, and he had always had a washboard stomach and muscular arms. But since he had been locked up, his arm muscles seemed to have grown by a couple of inches, and his washboard was now a fucking twelve-pack. He licked his thick lips, and I noticed my baby still had his low-cut waves spinning on his head. People always told Todd that he looked like LL Cool J, shit I thought he looked way better than that—same complexion and eye shape maybe, but Todd's face was much finer than LL's.

Before he could even make it all the way to the table, I jumped up and grabbed him around the neck tightly. I hugged him so hard and kissed him ferociously. I held on to my husband so hard the CO had to come between us and break it up. You know they didn't allow all that contact just in case I was trying to pass him contraband.

We finally let go of each other and sat down across from each other at the table. I immediately slipped my foot out of my sandal and secretly placed my foot between Todd's legs. I could feel his dick flexing on my foot, and that shit was driving me wild. I held on to his hand and smiled at him. Damn, I wanted him so bad. I missed his twelve-inch dick so much. Todd looked over at a tall black CO who was in charge of guarding the area where the vending machines were. There was a small bench over there, and the machines kind of blocked the view of the bench from the rest of the visiting room. I could tell another couple was over there getting their fuck on right now. The CO gave Todd the eye.

"We got next, baby," Todd said, turning his attention back to me.

"So how are you?" I asked, rubbing the top of his hand, really concerned about him. I knew Todd was worried about the lawyer thing, and he was always asking about that fucking traitor Jock.

"Nah, fuck asking about me. How are you and my little dude?" Todd asked, always thinking of me and the baby before himself.

"We hanging in there. Satanya got the baby because I knew we had to talk today. It's hard, Todd. I'm telling you. Without that safe, we are fucked up," I said, tears starting to rim my eyes. I had promised myself I wasn't going to cry during this visit. That crying shit was getting old.

"Well, that's all about to be a done deal," he said, leaning in closer to me so he could whisper.

I knew eventually he would be getting to his "plan" that he had mentioned over the phone.

"Shannon, I found out about this major playa named Bobby Knight from Chesapeake," Todd whispered.

I listened and was just looking at him, confused.

"I hear this nigga is paid like a motherfucker. I hear he got boxes of loot in his crib just sitting up in there because he got so much that he can't even put that shit in the bank," Todd continued, his eyes seeming to light up.

I just listened. I was still trying to figure out what this all had to do with me.

"Remember the nigga Dray I told you I met up in here who was mad cool and had my back?" Todd asked.

I nodded.

"Well, this nigga used to work for Knight and—" Todd started, but I cut him off.

"Todd, tell me what I'm going to be doing, because all this shit you talking still ain't getting to the point of how this is gonna help us or how it involves me," I said seriously.

The next fifteen minutes of our visit was taken up with Todd telling me what I needed to do in order to set up this Bobby Knight guy. He made it seem so simple.

"Just catch that nigga's eye, get real friendly with him, and set him up," Todd said.

I stared at him as he spoke but didn't really believe what I was hearing. I had been down for whatever for a long time, but Todd was making this shit seem way too easy.

"All you gotta do is get inside his house and get a layout," Todd continued.

And how the fuck did he suppose I do that? Basically what Todd ended up telling me was, "Shannon, all you gotta do is seduce this nigga and set him up to be robbed and murdered!"

Todd had finished giving me my instructions, and I wasn't fucking happy at all. I played it off, though, because I didn't want to ruffle his feathers. Finally, the CO gave us the signal for the bench, and we went over acting like we were buying shit out of the machines. Truthfully, I wasn't in the mood for fucking at that point, but I sure didn't come all the way up here to hear bad news and not get no dick. Todd sat down and took his dick out of a little opening in his jumpsuit.

I hoisted my skirt up, pulled my thong aside, and sat on his throbbing dick. "Ahh," I gasped as I ground my pussy down on his dick so hard. I could feel his shit throbbing like a heart, and I kept grinding it hard.

I knew we had a only few minutes, so I reached under my skirt and touched my clit, trying to seed up my nut before Todd beat me to it.

"Mmmm," he groaned, which drove me crazy.

I was about to cum all over his dick and soak it with my juices. I pulled my body up so just the tip of his dick was in my tight pussy, and then without warning I plopped back down, putting my entire deep pussy on it. That was all I needed to do.

"Argh!" Todd groaned into the back of my neck, breathing hard.

"Yes!" I cried out as I came too. We hurried and got up before anyone detected us and so the next visit couple could get their quick fuck on. At least I could say I got one good thing out of that fucking visit—some much-needed dick. I was still thinking about what he wanted me to do when the COs called time's up.

Todd hugged me and said, "Remember what I said."

"I will," I said softly, my mind heavy. I walked out of the jail with the name of a big-time hustler, a hangout spot, some instructions on how to plot what my husband had called the "ultimate heist," and a cold and broken heart. I was about to become a ruthless bitch, because I realized that now it was all up to me.

Todd

Me and Dray spent all our days talking about this Bobby Knight cat. Dray supplied me with information about where Shannon should focus once she was inside the house. He described how some of the faucets and doorknobs were solid-gold plated. Dray also said that it wouldn't be easy for Shannon to get out of Bobby's eyesight to map the way to the rooms where the money was kept, but if she was really focused, she would be able to do it. Dray explained that it was going to take a team to make the shit go down, and that the team had to be comprised of niggas who were smart and fast. I decided that my only two loyal boys were Bam and Black; they would be the ones to help Shannon, and she told me that she had Satanya down on her team too. I was a little skeptical about having Satanya involved, because that bitch ran her mouth like a leaky faucet. I had been telling Shannon to stop telling that bitch our business.

But this dude Dray was a real down nigga. He wasn't even demanding a certain cut outta the heist loot. He told me to use what I needed up front and give him what I wanted in the end. Dray said bodying that motherfucker Bobby Knight would be enough pay-ment for him. I could dig that shit too. This was more about an eye for an eye for Dray.

I was trying to put the fire under Shannon's ass, because my next court date was in four weeks and I needed a lawyer. She had already moved outta the house and told me that she was going down to one of Knight's main hangouts tomorrow night.

I tossed and turned the whole fucking night thinking about my wife. Would she be able to get at this nigga without letting him touch her? Would she be able to get in, find out the setup, and get the fuck outta there so my boys could do their thing? I was going crazy with thoughts.

When we got up the next morning, Dray started talking about the shit right away and I wasn't really in the mood. As we were get-ting ready for chow, Dray got into more detail.

"Bobby Knight had my brother killed because he fucking thought my brother was working for the cops," Dray blurted out. "He tortured my brother. He made him get on all fours like a fuck-ing dog. Then he had one of his henchmen make small cuts all over my brother's body—even on his dick. That nigga went and got table salt, boxes of that shit, and poured it all over my brother. Then he used rubbing alcohol," Dray told me, biting down on his lip. "The whole time he was calling my brother a cop. Then he held me down and made me watch as he blew my brother's head off right there," Dray continued, closing his eyes like he was about to spaz out just thinking about it.

I was silent. There was nothing I could say that could comfort this nigga right now.

"You see, Bobby was under investigation by the Feds, and he

thought it was my brother who was the rat in the camp," Dray started up again.

I listened but I didn't wanna hear no shit about who Bobby Knight had killed. Not when I was sending my fucking wife into the fire with this nigga.

All I wanted to do was hear from Shannon first, and then I would be all right. I wanted to know what was going on so far.

After yard, I jumped on the phone to holla at Shannon and find out what was up. The phone just rang and rang. I called like five times in a row. The last time I left a message. "Yo, what's up with you not answering your phone and shit? I'm fucking worried about you!" I barked into the receiver before I slammed it down.

I stormed back to the tier.

"Yo, T. You wanna hit this game of spades?" one of the inmates yelled at me. I just kept walking fast to my cell. If something had happened to my wife, Dray was a dead man, and then I was gonna put my own lights out for putting her up in the mix. On the other hand, if this shit all worked out, I could be walking out of this shit hole a rich man.

Shannon

I saw Todd calling my phone, and I ignored his call. Right now I didn't want to speak to him. Lately, all he wanted to speak about was the fucking Bobby Knight shit. In the past couple of days, I don't think he has even asked about Lil Todd. I had thought about this shit long and hard. I had talked it over with Satanya, and she had said, *Shit, girl, if I could just set a nigga up to be robbed and get my fucking husband outta prison, I would do that shit in a minute.* I thought about her words, and I felt like if I didn't do this shit, I would be shitting on Todd after he had taken my ass up out of the hood and given me the good life. That's not to say I haven't been down for him when he had done bids the other times. I had always sacrificed and stayed loyal to the nigga.

After our conversation, me and Satanya had it all planned out that we were going to Bobby Knight's known hangout spot that Dray had given Todd. We would go check out this Bobby Knight cat and then get started with the plan. I didn't need to tell Todd shit. What I needed was a fucking drink to get my mind right.

"Satanya, let's go get a bottle of Goose before we get dressed," I said somberly.

"Girl, you know I keeps a bottle of that shit handy. Drink all the

Goose you need, then get the fuck dressed so we can get this shit on and popping," Satanya said, walking away and coming back. She handed me some Grey Goose and cranberry juice in a martini glass. I grabbed that shit and gulped it down real quick. It wasn't gonna be no sexy sipping tonight. My fucking nerves needed calming down. Satanya and I sorted through what was left of my high-end outfits—there had been some shit I just wasn't parting with. Satanya picked me out a dark purple Diane von Furstenberg minidress and a pair of thigh-high Lanvin boots.

"Girl, ya ass is phat as hell in that dress," Satanya complimented.

"I heard this cat is attracted to a nice big ass," I said, laughing out loud in an attempt to relieve my fear.

When me and Satanya pulled up to Blakelys, it looked packed. All kinds of high-class cars were up in front of the spot. The one that caught my immediate attention was the Mercedes Maybach with the presidential tint on the windows. This spot was strictly valet only, so we hopped out and let them park my shit. The one fucking thing I was glad to see was that my BMW 745i was able to hang with the cars at this spot. That was the one fucking thing I wasn't trying to sell or give up. Todd had bought it for me outright as an anniversary gift a year ago when life was good. I had been so happy that day. He was always doing shit like that for me. Now shit had drastically changed.

I walked into the dimly lit club, and it was immediately apparent that this place was a league above what me and Satanya were used to. There were men in there dressed in fucking tailor-made suits and shirts that required cuff links. I peeped more than one pair of diamond-encrusted cuff links. There were absolutely no big chains, jeans, or baseball cap–wearing niggas up in this spot. The music was that slow-jam, mellow type of shit.

"Mmmm, girl, what the fuck?" Satanya asked, noticing the same things that I had noticed. All I could do was shrug my shoulders. We certainly recognized that we were two reformed hood chicks in a place that was out of our league. We found a table and sat down. There were eyes on us for sure, but it wasn't the usual all-eyes-on-me attention I got in the regular clubs. There were a lot of beautiful women up in there, and their gear was tight. Todd had described Bobby Knight to me, but I didn't see anyone fitting his description—tall, really dark-skinned, big-lipped, and always wearing dark glasses and hanging with a group of niggas.

A girl in an all-black leotard came over to me and Satanya. "What can I get you ladies?" she asked, smiling.

"Um, can I get like an amaretto sour?" Satanya ordered.

"Oh, miss, I'm sorry. We only serve top-shelf liquors. Mostly things that cost over three hundred dollars a bottle," she said smugly.

"She's new here. Give us a minute," I said, fronting like a motherfucker. When the girl left, I looked at Satanya and she looked at me.

"What the fuck? I'm new here all fucking right. Girl, I don't know about this shit here," she whispered.

I was thinking the same thing. We sat there for a while before I heard a rowdy crowd coming into the place. When I looked over, I saw an entourage of people flanking someone like the person was a celebrity, and everybody up in the spot started turning toward the door. Girls started fixing their makeup and moving closer to the noise. My heart started thumping wildly, and something inside me told me that it was Bobby Knight coming up in here. Sure enough, I heard one of the waitresses tell the other one, "Get ya shit together. Bobby just stepped up in here, and if you want to get paid, you better be looking good."

I strained my neck to get a glimpse of him, but he was surrounded on every side. Every now and then, I caught a quick glimpse of his face, which was covered by dark-ass glasses as he shook hands and exchanged pounds with a few dudes.

There was definitely a lot of fanfare surrounding Bobby Knight. They changed the music in the club, waitresses neglected everyone else to pay special attention to him, and even grown-ass men seemed to stop in their tracks for him. Bobby kept his dark shades on, and from where I sat after he took his seat, I could peep his getup. He wore a purple-label Polo button-down with French cuffs and some hot-ass cuff links. On his feet were a pair of Salvatore Ferragamos that I'd seen in Neiman Marcus two weeks ago for $1,600. And that ring. A huge diamond pinky ring, not diamond chips like those wannabe niggas in the hood. That was a solitaire as big as a gumball on his pinky. I couldn't tell where he was looking because of his shades, and I was hoping he couldn't tell how hard I was scoping him out.

I turned to Satanya and said, "Let the games begin."

She just smiled, and we both got up and moved toward the bar. We had to be seen or this night would be a complete waste of time. I switched my ass as hard as I could, and Satanya kept an eye out to see if Bobby was taking notice.

"Girl, it's so many bitches around him he ain't even got time to look over here," she said disappointedly. I didn't let that stop me. Once at the bar, I wedged myself between two guys I had seen in Bobby's crowd, and I ordered the most expensive shit I could.

"Whew, damn, baby girl, you got expensive taste," one of the men whistled and said. I looked up at him, winked, and licked my lips seductively. For real, it was like somebody else all of a sudden was living inside of me. I understood what Beyoncé was talking about when she said that her alter ego was Sasha Fierce and comes out when she was onstage performing. It was kind of like that for me. The usually laid-back Shannon was gone; I was now a bitch with a mission.

I knew I had gotten up in their heads, because when Satanya and I returned to our table, I noticed one of them pointing us out to Bobby. Of course, he was going to play it cool at first, but that didn't last long.

It was about thirty minutes later when Satanya's eyes grew wide, and she bent over to me. "Girl, one of his dudes is coming toward the table," she whispered.

"Bitch, play it cool. Don't let them see you whispering like we desperate and shit," I whispered back, making sure to keep a smile plastered on my face. Sure enough, a tall Tyrese-looking dude came to the table.

"Excuse me. Sorry for interrupting. On behalf of Bobby Knight, I wanted to ask if you ladies would like to join us," he said, all polite.

"Who?" I asked, acting like I didn't know who the fuck Bobby Knight was. The dude looked a little thrown off.

"Bobby Knight," he said, clearing his throat as if to say, *Bitch, don't act like you don't know.* "The owner of damn near every club in the Tidewater area," he continued.

"We can join you. But for the record, I had no clue who Bobby Knight was," I explained indignantly. Satanya was looking at me like *Bitch, you crazy as hell.*

Walking over to Bobby Knight's section of the club seemed to take forever. I could feel every step, hear every syllable of the music, and all of a sudden I started thinking about Todd and the plan, and sweat just broke out all over my body.

"Ladies, this is Mr. Knight," the guy introduced us.

Bobby Knight stopped talking, stood up, grabbed my hand, and kissed the top of it. I was shocked and had a fake smile plastered across my face. He then extended his hand to Satanya for a handshake. I guess he was telling us which one he preferred.

"Please, have a seat," he said, putting out his arm like an usher. Satanya and I sat down. The fact that this dude had money was evident. Champagne flowed like a river, and I was blinded by all of the bling around the table. I sat there thinking I could get used to some shit like this. Todd was caking a lil something, but we never did it up like this. Bobby turned out to be very polite and well spoken. Although I could tell he was from the South, he didn't use that broken-ass slang like these niggas around here. He asked a lot of questions, which I expected. I guess you could say talking was his strong point, because we did plenty of that. Satanya took particular interest in the Tyrese-looking dude, whose name was Captain. I had to ask if his momma really named him that, and Bobby interjected, "I named him that. When you're down with me, what your momma named you don't matter. Got it, sweet pea?" He had given me a pet name already.

After that first night, it seemed like we were in like Flynn. I gave Bobby Knight my phone number. He told me he didn't own a cell phone. He said he was more of a face-to-face person and that he'd be in touch. When he asked me if I was married or in a relationship, I almost choked on my champagne. I couldn't tell a complete lie, because the tan line on my left ring finger told the story. "I'm recently divorced," I said deceitfully, the lie burning on my tongue like the sting of a poisonous insect.

Todd

When I finally spoke to Shannon, she told me all about Bobby Knight. She had definitely caught his eye, and she was in. Shannon told me that she was set to go out with him and one of his dudes on a kind of double date with Satanya. I can't front—I was so heated that if Shannon had been in front of me, I probably would have slapped the shit out of her. I know it was all my idea, but now I was having fucking jealousy issues. Another man wining and dining my fucking wife was hard to hear. I told her to hurry the fuck up and get in that house so all of this shit could be over with.

When I returned to my bunk, Dray was being led out by two COs. "Where you goin'?" I asked, confused. I knew Dray hadn't been in any fights and hadn't done anything to get himself sent to the hole.

"Mind your business, Marshall," one of the COs barked.

"Fuck you. That's my boy and I'm talking to him," I replied.

Dray kept his head down and his eyes to the floor. They carted him off the tier, and none of the other inmates even made any noise like they usually did when a nigga got banged and put in the hole. It was almost like they were used to seeing Dray get carted off. I was real fucked up in the head behind my conversation with Shannon right now, so I hopped up on my bunk, turned my face to the wall, and tried not to think about my wife and Bobby Knight.

Shannon

It was two weeks and a day since I had met Bobby the first time. Yes, I was now on a first-name basis with him. We'd gone out almost every day. While I was getting to know Bobby, the neighbor was looking after Lil Todd. He told me he hung out on every day of the week, except Sundays. I found that quite amusing—a well-known hustler observing the holy day. We'd gone to more than one high-class restaurant, and he had laid gifts on me like a comfort blanket. I can't front—I was getting a little addicted to the lifestyle again. Although Bobby was nowhere near as attractive as my husband in the face, with his rough dark skin and huge gorilla lips, he made up for it with swagger. Bobby Knight's swagger could not be fucked with. He had the whole Rick Ross shit going on, and it kind of drove me wild. Then every time he pulled out the fucking knot of paper from his pocket, I got even more enthralled with his ugly ass.

Satanya was hanging hard with Captain. She confided in me that she had already fucked him and that she was even thinking about leaving her husband for Captain. I told her she was fucking crazy and that she better get focused and remember the mission at hand. I could only pray that this silly bitch didn't lose her god-damn mind over no dick. Todd had warned me about her, but I still considered her my fucking girl.

I had just gotten off the phone with Todd. He acted like he wanted to know *everything* that was going on, but when I told him, he just got angry and started acting stupid. I had to remind him that it was his idea and that I was doing this all for us. All of the shit I had put up with from Todd over the years was nothing com-pared to this. I was fucking risking my life every time I got with Bobby. Shit, if he were a mind reader, I would be fucking dead.

But it was hard to dismiss Todd's bullshit attitude. He wanted updates, updates, and more updates. He was getting antsy. But I tried to explain to his ass that shit like this took time. If all he wanted was a regular fucking robbery, then he could've told Bam and Black to just run up on Bobby and gank him. This was some whole-other-level type of shit. I had told Todd that I loved him, and he refused to say it back. Jealousy was getting the best of him. Did he not remember he was the one who put me in the mix of this shit in the first place?

As soon as I hung up the phone with Todd, it rang again.

"Hello?" I answered with little anger in my voice.

"What happened, sweet pea—you not happy to hear my voice?" Bobby asked, his fucking smooth-ass voice giving me goose bumps.

I immediately tried to change my tone. "Nothing, I'm good," I lied.

"Well, I'm outside," he said, and I went to my window to find the black Maybach parked out front.

"I'm not dressed," I whined. How dare he just show the fuck up at my house! This motherfucker really had power issues. But I was loving it. I started to wonder what kind of little bauble he would be bringing me today. I smiled to myself.

"I like the natural beauty anyway. Now come downstairs," Bobby said demandingly.

This motherfucker was power hungry but a charmer too. I wasn't mad for that long. I couldn't front. I started rushing through the house trying to find something to put on. He said he liked the natural look, I kept telling myself. It took me less than fifteen minutes, and I was rushing out the door. Once I got downstairs, I tried to take a slow, sexy stride to the car. Can't make a nigga think I was too eager.

"See, you are too beautiful to worry," Bobby said as I slid into the buttery-soft backseat next to him. He had Musiq Soulchild's "So Beautiful" playing. I moved a little closer to him. I was starting to think that I really liked Bobby. Which could be a dangerous thought for me.

The driver drove for what seemed like two minutes, but it had actually been almost an hour.

"What are your dreams?" Bobby asked. It was a question I had never thought about. Todd had never really wondered what I dreamed of. "To be a world-renowned fashion designer," I said, almost whispering. I wanted to cry. The wrong man had asked me the right questions.

The conversation with Bobby was so refreshing I didn't even notice how long it had taken. He was very well versed in world news and the stock market, and I found out he had been to college. A far cry from Todd. Conversations with my husband were always about the streets and how this nigga is a snitch and that nigga is running this. Bobby was different. I started to feel slightly guilty about what I was planning, because Todd had given specific instructions that Bobby was not only to be robbed, but he also had to die.

When we pulled up to the huge golden gates of Bobby's estate, my heart almost stopped. It was almost as if everything Todd had told me was happening like clockwork. The gates opened to a long winding road leading up to the house. The road had beautiful trees and well-manicured lawns on each side. At the end was a tan brick circular driveway. The driver pulled up to the front doors of the house to let us out. There were about six steps and large columns to the left and right of the door.

"Your house is beautiful," I said, trying to keep my mouth closed. His shit looked better than the homes on *MTV Cribs*; it was more like one of the houses I'd seen on VH1's *Fabulous Life of* . . .

Once inside, I was even more overwhelmed. The foyer was a huge, beautiful marble expanse decorated immaculately. The winding staircase looked like it was solid gold, and there were fresh-cut flowers everywhere. The ceilings were painted with beautiful portraits of black angels. I stared up at them in awe.

"It's the black version of the Sistine Chapel," Bobby said, looking up with me.

I was even more impressed. What hood nigga would know about Michelangelo and the damn Sistine Chapel ceiling?!

"Come this way," Bobby said, breaking up my gawking.

"Bobby, I'm really not dressed to be here," I said, feeling slightly ashamed and inadequate. Even though it was just his house, I felt like I needed to be dressed up to be in here. Here it was I thought me and Todd lived well. Shit, this house made ours look like the projects.

"You don't need to be dressed. I brought you here because I wanted to let you know that I am ready to take things to the next level. I like you, Shannon," Bobby said, grabbing my hand. The words fell on me like a boulder off a cliff. Here was a big-time dude telling me he wanted *me* to be in his world and that he trusted me enough to bring me to his crib. Meanwhile, I had larceny in my heart. I was speechless for a minute. I had to regroup and think about the mission at hand. I closed my eyes and tried to picture Todd's face. It wouldn't come to me for shit. I just stared into space, dazed, confused, and having second thoughts.

"You okay, sweet pea?" Bobby asked.

Why the fuck did he start calling me sweet pea? How had he gotten into my head like this so goddamn fast? I started getting angry for liking him so much and letting him get in my head. I shook my head slightly so I could get my ride-or-die mentality back on track. I could finally picture my husband's face, his sexy lips, his pleading eyes sitting in that fucking courtroom.

"Let's go out back for some lunch," Bobby said, tightening his grip on my hand and breaking my trance.

When we walked through the huge glass doors, I noticed the beautiful S-shaped swimming pool and a man-made waterfall. I also noticed the security guards walking the perimeter of the gates around it. There were two of them out back, and I had noticed two by the front gates and two positioned near the front doors.

Out on the back patio, there were tables with umbrellas, and one of the glass tables was all set with stemware, champagne on chill, and fruit. I squinted when I saw two people sitting out there already. When I got closer, I noticed it was Satanya and Captain. My heart jerked in my chest. Why hadn't she called to let me know she would be here? This bitch was really tripping. She looked different. Her complexion was golden, and she wore an expensive Diane von Furstenberg bathing suit. When she noticed me, she waved and gave a stupid little grin.

"Shannon! What's up, girl?!" Satanya screamed out all loud, smiling from ear to ear. I had known her for years, and I could tell she was definitely different. The silly-ass giggling and laughing at nothing in particular just wasn't like her.

Just as Bobby and I approached them, Captain grabbed Satanya in a bear hug, pulled down her bikini top, and started sucking her titties right there in front of us. His ass must've been fucking high too. I just didn't get down like that. I turned my face away, but I could hear Satanya giggling like a little schoolgirl, and it made me uneasy. Bobby didn't seem to have a problem watching them until he noticed my face.

"Hey, hey. Get a room," Bobby said, chuckling like he found the shit amusing. I squinted and looked back over toward them and just shot Satanya a dirty look.

"Shannon, what's wrong, homey? Lighten up!" she screamed out, sticking out her tongue all silly and shit.

What the fuck is going on? I thought to myself. When she took off her shades, I could see in her eyes she was high. Growing up around addicts all my life, I knew when a person was high with those dilated pupils and shit. Satanya getting high could be fucking dangerous for us.

I grabbed her arm and said, "Hey, girl, let me talk to you in private," trying to keep my voice as soft as I could when I really wanted to scream on her ass.

"Anything you gotta say, you can say in front of my boo," Satanya slurred.

I smiled again and pulled her out of Captain's and Bobby's earshot. I was damn near dragging her like a mother dragging a little kid through a mall. Finally I stopped when I thought we were far enough away from the guys and spun her around to face me.

"Satanya, what the fuck are you doing coming here without me?" I asked, gritting my teeth. She started laughing again. *Here the fuck we go,* I thought.

"Shannon, this is not about you. You got your thing going on, and I got mine. You here to set a nigga up. I'm here to fall in love," she said, her words catching on her tongue, making her sound like a stupid-ass retard.

"Shhhhh," I said in a low whisper, placing my finger up against her lips. "You're just fucked up right now. Keep your fucking mouth shut or we both could get killed," I continued, gritting out the words with emphasis.

Satanya pulled away from me, pouting her dumb fucking lips. "My lips are sealed, but my pussy is wide open," she said, laughing again, sounding like a fucking wild hyena. She was so loud Bobby and Captain looked over at us. My heart was racing as if Thoroughbred horses were trampling through my chest. Right then, I decided not to speak about her behavior again or else she might blow the whole shit up. I started having regrets about getting her ass involved.

After Satanya's bullshit episode, we walked back over to the guys. I plastered a fake smile on my face, and Bobby and I sat down for our planned lunch while Captain and Satanya went back into Bobby's house. I kept watching the door. I was really worried about her and was having an anxiety attack about what she might be telling Captain.

Bobby was talking and I wasn't even listening. I did hear when he asked me back into the house. I gave a halfhearted smile and got up slowly with my legs quivering like crazy. I was so scared Bobby was gonna try to get me to fuck him. I wasn't in it for that, and I made sure I kept telling myself that. Although he had some redeeming qualities, he was still what I considered the vic, and I was gonna make sure of it.

Once we were back in the house, I followed Bobby down a long hallway, through the indoor basketball court to the swimming pool area. I made a mental note of the path that we took. Looking out the window inside of the indoor swimming pool, I could tell the house basically went in one big circle. I noticed more armed security guards out there and a couple on the roof. What the fuck did he need so much security for? Was he that fucking paranoid?

Finally, he opened a door for me and said, "This is my private wing."

I tried not to act too shocked, but I wanted to fall down on the floor all over again. I stared out at the huge area, thinking I could get used to living here. There were custom drapes, Italian marble floors, art pieces that I recognized as authentic, and the bed . . . The shit was a custom-made circular bed bigger than the one Shaquille O'Neal had showed off on his *MTV Cribs* episode. Bobby's "wing," as he had called it, was bigger than the apartment I was living in right now. Bobby placed his arm out in front of him.

"Right this way," he said softly. It seemed like my feet were stuck in quicksand and I couldn't move.

"Bobby, I . . . don't think I'm ready for all of this," I stammered, feeling the heat of embarrassment on my face.

"Ready for what? I don't expect anything from you. I know you are a good girl, sweet pea," he said, and with that I walked into his private wing.

Bobby and I talked into the wee hours of the night. We lay side by side on the bed but never touched. He was a perfect gentleman. I did not even remember drifting off to sleep.

When I woke up the next day, I was nervous as hell. I jumped up with thoughts swirling in my head. What if Todd had been calling my phone and Bobby noticed? What would Todd say if he knew I had not only gotten into the house but also spent the night? I couldn't believe I'd slept that hard in a strange place. I looked around to get my bearings and try to clear my head so I could scope out some more of the house.

Bobby was not in the room, and there was a tray of breakfast at the end of the bed. I looked down at myself and saw I still had on all of my clothes. That was a good fucking sign. I knew I hadn't slept with him. I stood up and crept over to the door, and that's when I noticed the security system screens that were embedded in the wall. There were about seventeen different panels on the screens showing different parts of the house. I recognized the front foyer, the pool area, and Bobby's wing. The rest of the screens looked foreign to me, but one caught my attention real quick. It was a shot of a long hallway of doors, and as the cameras panned up and down the hallway, I could see that the doors had Onity locks on them.

"Shit," I cursed. This must be the area of the house with the rooms of money, but I knew that Onity locks required a code.

Then I noticed that one of the doors on the screen looked familiar. I peeked around the room; then I remembered. There was a door in Bobby's huge-ass bathroom that stayed closed. I rushed into the bathroom to check. Sure enough, the door that led to the hallway with all of the doors was located inside his bathroom. There was a huge lock on it as well. I raced back over to the security screens to see if there were any other shots of the house that looked familiar. I made a note that there were armed security guards at almost every entrance, exit, and door. "Fuck!" I cursed under my breath.

"What's the matter . . . never seen a security system before?" Bobby's voice boomed from behind me.

I jumped so hard a little bit of piss escaped my bladder. "Heyyy," I sang out, nervous as hell. I was hoping he couldn't see my lip quivering like a motherfucker. "I was just admiring the other parts of your house," I lied.

"You didn't eat your breakfast," he said dryly.

"I'm not a breakfast person. I really have to go. I . . . need to take care of some things," I stammered.

"I will arrange to have you taken home," he said like he had something else he had to do. I was trying real hard not to look back over at those security screens. I started mapping shit out in my head. I needed to call the guys and get this shit popping before Bobby was on to me. I knew from all of our conversations he wasn't no dumb-ass street dude. In fact, Bobby was so sophisticated I started to doubt our ability to carry out this heist.

"Can you call down to Satanya and Captain for me?" I asked as Bobby walked me toward the front doors.

"They are not here," he said.

My heart sank. *What the fuck is Satanya thinking?!* I screamed in my head. She was steadily making fucking moves without letting me know. Satanya was trying to come up at a bad time in her life, and I understood that, but so was I, and I wasn't about to let her fuck everything up. I was gonna see her ass. Me and this bitch needed to have a serious talk. I just hoped I could get to her before she did some dumb shit.

As soon as I was in my apartment, I peeled off my clothes, took a hot shower, and called Bam and Black over. It was time to get this under way. I was afraid that if I stayed around Bobby any longer, I might get caught up. He was easy to like, and his dough was especially easy to fall in love with. I had seen enough of the house; by looking at the security setup, I figured out just where the cameras were. I had counted the security guys at the front and around the perimeter. All it had taken was one visit. I had to get the ball rolling. There was money to be made, and I wasn't fucking sitting around playing games. Bobby and his charm were no match for the fucking mission at hand. I knew for sure now that this motherfucker definitely had a shitload of paper up in that house. I was going to get Todd out, but I was also going to set aside something for a rainy fucking day for myself. Granted, Todd was the one who had picked me up out of the gutter, but a bitch had been through the wringer with his ass too. Bitches, bids, being broke—it was time for Shannon Marshall to come up. I had a new fervor back to my attitude. I was gonna get that paper.

"Fuck Bobby Knight!" I said to myself after thinking about what I had been through. That bastard had tried to charm my pants off, and if I had been weak, he would've fucked me and then he would've thrown me away.

I had everything sketched out on paper by the time Bam and Black arrived at my house. I had taken that little drawing Dray had given Todd, and I put the two together until I had a complete drawing of the house and all the areas we needed to be concerned about.

"Damn, ma, you are focused," Bam commented, walking in wearing all black. He picked up the drawings I had made to examine them. He stared at them, rubbing his chin like he was thinking hard.

"I'm telling you the house is huge," I said. "There is a hallway off of this wing that I think has the rooms full of money Dray was talking about. Those got Onity locks, so either y'all shooting off the locks or blowing those doors off," I continued.

"Looks like we gonna need a lot more people for this shit," Black said.

He was also dressed in all black. That nigga looked like he had been through a war with scars all over his face and neck. I recognized a nigga who had been shanked, and somebody had definitely taken a razor and fucked Black up. Todd told me that Bam and Black were professional heist niggas. They were responsible for one of the largest jewelry heists that ever happened in Virginia. I remembered seeing it on the news. Those niggas grabbed two million dollars in jewelry and cash. They had drilled fucking holes right into the jewelry store's walls, burrowed themselves underground, and blew the fucking doors off the safes. Some real TV type of shit. The police couldn't understand how they had avoided the surveillance cameras. Bam told me that they had these suits that the military uses that mask the body heat so in the dark the night vision on the cameras could not detect them. Shit, you could buy anything on the black market in the hood. After he said that, I was pretty confident that these dudes were the truth. There was no way they would leave Bobby's house without most, if not all, of that fucking money.

We sat and devised a plan. They told me they did not want to tell me too much about what would go down once they got inside; my job was to get them in and get to the money and get the fuck outta Dodge while the mayhem was going on.

"You know that he gotta die, right?" I asked.

"That's not a problem. We have Usef the Nigerian on our team to carry out the hit. There will be no witnesses, so whoever is there who is not on the team gotta die," Black said, sounding ruthless as hell. That shit brought a cold chill over my body. I had to hurry up and get in touch with this bitch Satanya.

Todd

Word on the tier was that Dray was gone because he was a snitch. Those fucking rumors kept me up at night. I paced the cell thinking that this bastard Dray had fucking used me and my wife, and he was working with the police. I had ransacked all his shit in the days he was gone. When he finally got escorted back to the cell, I was on his ass like a tick on a fucking dog. I grabbed his bitch ass by the collar.

"What the fuck is going on with you, nigga?" I growled in his face. My eyes were bugged out of the sockets, and I could see my spit landing on his nose. "I heard you a fucking snitch! My wife's life is on the motherfucking line out there!" I continued, feeling the veins in my arms bulging.

"Yo, nigga! Get the fuck up off me!" Dray yelled, grabbing on to my hands and pushing me off him.

We started tussling. I grabbed his bitch ass in a headlock and started choking the goddamn life out of his punk snitch ass.

"Yo, Todd, man . . . I am not no snitch! These motherfuckers tried to get me on some ol' trumped-up shit saying I had hidden weapons in the wall near the shower area. Said they had me on camera," Dray started explaining, barely able to squeeze the words out as hard as I was holding his fucking neck between my arms. "Man, I wouldn't be working with no fuckin' cops!" Dray screamed, letting his body go limp like he was about to pass the fuck out.

I knew how to put a nigga's lights out, but I also didn't wanna catch a fucking assault charge and get sent to the hole. I released his ass with a push. I was huffing and puffing. I didn't know what to think—my head was spinning. I felt like I was going crazy. It was only two more weeks before my court date, and I needed a fucking good attorney. The stress of being locked up, my wife seeing another man, and the whole heist shit had me bugging. Shannon was hardly answering my calls. I hadn't gotten a visit that week. I didn't know what the fuck to think.

"Yo, nigga, I told you already. We good. You can trust me," Dray said.

Shannon

When my phone rang at two in the morning, I knew it wasn't good.

I reached over and picked it up. "Hello?" I answered, all groggy.

"I need to see you right now. I am downstairs," Bobby's voice boomed through the receiver.

"I'm asleep. What time is it?" I said, sitting up in the bed, trying to wipe sleep out of my eyes.

"Come downstairs," he barked, and hung up. I hadn't seen this nigga in two days after he got all bent out of shape at me looking at his fucking security system. How he gonna just keep showing up at my fucking crib demanding me to come outside? This nigga really thought he was the biggest boss and shit. I got out of bed and peeked out the window. Sure enough, he was outside with his dark-tinted windows. At first I thought about ignoring him, but knowing him, he would just keep calling me and sit out there until I came out. Maybe he was just thinking about me in the middle of the night. That better be the fucking reason. I picked up my cell and called Bam.

"Change of plans. This nigga is at my house right now. I may already be at his crib. I will send the text when I'm ready," I said on Bam's voice mail.

I slipped on some jeans and a T-shirt, threw my hair in a slick ponytail, and went outside. Before I could get to Bobby's car, the door swung open.

"What's going on?" I asked, acting like I was still rubbing sleep from my eyes. "You can't keep popping up on me like this," I complained.

"I need to show you something," Bobby said dryly. Without saying another word, I climbed into the backseat. After I closed the door, the driver pulled off.

"It's two in the morning. It couldn't wait?" I asked. It's a damn good thing Lil Todd had gone to my neighbor's house for a slumber party.

Bobby didn't speak much on the ride like he usually did. I had the call in to Bam because I had had enough of the games. Bobby's behavior was a bit strange. No calling me sweet pea, no long conversations, just silence. My hands were wet with sweat, and I could not control the urge to rock my legs back and forth. The silence was fucking unnerving.

We arrived at the marina near Virginia Beach, and the car stopped abruptly. Bobby turned to me, grabbed my arm with a little force, and said with a strange tone to his voice, "Sweet pea, I want to know if I can trust you."

"Ahem . . . sure you can," I said, trying to stay calm, placing my hand on top of his because he was hurting my goddamn arm.

"Good, then I want to show you something," he said, summoning me out of the car.

"What is it, Bobby, that it couldn't wait until the morning?" I asked, trying to act very annoyed to mask my fucking nerves. All kinds of thoughts were running through my head. What if he had had me followed? What if he had my phone tapped? I was paranoid as a bitch. We walked halfway down the pier, and that's when I noticed her, and she obviously noticed me too.

"Shannon! Help me! Help me!" Satanya was screaming at the top of her lungs. Captain had his huge hands wound all up in her hair; her neck looked like it would break. My eyes almost popped out of my head.

"Shannon, tell them! Tell them so they will let me go!" Satanya screamed, her face filling with blood, taking on a maroon color, almost like the inside of a beet. I swallowed hard and took a deep breath. My legs felt like they would give out, and I crossed my arms in front of my chest like I was mad, but it was really to keep me from throwing up.

"Bitch, what are you fucking talking about?" I screamed, squinting my eyes into little slits. "What the fuck is going on, Bobby? Make him let her go," I screamed, playing it off big-time.

"Shannon! You know the plan! Tell them! They don't believe me! Ahhh, pa-lease!" Satanya screamed.

I couldn't believe this bitch.

"Satanya, what the fuck are you talking about? This bitch is crazy!" I yelled, turning away from her to look at Bobby.

"Well, she says you planned to have me robbed or something crazy like that," Bobby said calmly, looking over his dark glasses so his eyes could meet mine.

"What?!" I shouted, crinkling my eyebrows. "Bobby, look, this bitch is obviously on some serious drugs. I don't even know you like that to have you robbed. You know how I feel about you and this thing we are building," I said, pleading my case. I knew Bobby had a soft spot for me and wanted to believe me. I could see it, even though he played hard that he was conflicted. I was in fucking utter shock at this bitch Satanya. We had been friends for years, and I thought for sure I could trust her with the biggest fucking secret I'd ever had.

"Shannon! Tell the truth or they will kill me!" Satanya continued as Captain dragged her down to the ground and took his other hand to punch her in the face. Blood spurted out as if her face were a popped cherry.

"Bitch, shut the fuck up! I don't know what the fuck you are talking about!" I hollered. I had to save my own fucking life. This bitch had ruined her own. I wanted to just kick the shit out of her, but I felt bad about the way Captain was beating on her. Our lives were on the fucking line right now for no fucking reason. Why? Why couldn't this fucking hoodrat bitch just have kept her fucking legs closed and her mouth shut? But this was my fault. I should have set this whole thing up alone. I had just been so nervous to do it all by myself. Now shit may be ruined for real.

"If I can trust you and you say she is a liar, then she has to die," Bobby said, nodding at Captain, who opened up another assault on Satanya.

I closed my eyes; I couldn't watch. I felt like a coward for not saving her. My ears started ringing.

"She has to die."

It felt like his words were a loud bell up against my eardrums.

Captain kept his grip in Satanya's hair, and she continued to scream. I could tell he was hurt and angry at the same time. He really looked like he was kind of fucked up over what was going on. But I also knew he was a killer. There were like six other niggas there; there was nowhere to run. Satanya's screams kept echoing, and she kept pleading for me to tell them the plan. It was a good thing I had never given her any details or else the whole shit would've been over. They were not trying to hear shit.

"Well?" Bobby said.

"Look, Bobby, why are you talking crazy? When she dries out, she won't be talking this crazy shit. Just let her go and I will make sure she never takes another drug," I said, shaking up and down on my legs to emphasize my desperate plea. I could feel my ass cheeks shaking—that was how scared I was.

"I don't fucking think you understand! If she's lying, she dies. And if she's telling the truth, then I'm gonna torture you until you bleed to death," he growled, grabbing my cheeks forcefully.

Bobby gave me a hard look, then told Captain, "Take the girl home and clean her up." But I knew that's not what he meant. I was seeing my girl alive for the last time.

"You're going home with me," Bobby said forcefully, placing his arm around my neck. I looked back at Satanya and our eyes met.

Bobby waited for me to get myself together. I couldn't help but look back at Satanya a few times.

"You all right?" Bobby asked.

"No! No, I'm not all right. You just threatened to kill me!" I screamed.

"Yeah, I threatened to kill you because Satanya came to me with all that shit," he said calmly.

"Yeah, because your fuckin' boy keeps her so skied up on shit that she is fucking hallucinating. She is harmless. If your fucking boy harms a hair on her head—" I started.

"What? Will you beat my ass?" Bobby asked sarcastically, chuckling.

"I want to go home," I demanded.

"You will, but when I say you go," Bobby said, grabbing my hand like I was a little kid and leading me back to his car.

We drove straight to his house. When we arrived, I was scared as hell all over again. But I guess if he wanted to kill me, he would've done it already.

Once inside, we went to his wing. Bobby loosened his tie and took off his shades. I couldn't even bear to look at his ugly-ass face. I just sat all shook up on the end of the bed.

"Listen, I want you to understand—" he started, touching my shoulders gently.

"I can't. This shit ain't for me," I sobbed. I cried for so many reasons. Because my fucking husband had put me in this predicament; because I knew the task at hand; and most of all, because my heart had grown so cold over the last few weeks that I didn't give a flying fuck about anybody but myself. Bobby grabbed me and hugged me tightly. He began kissing my neck with his big soup cooler lips and then moved to my breasts. A feeling of disgust came over me, and suddenly I wanted him dead. I could feel Bobby's hard dick up against me.

Bobby pushed me back gently on the bed. My mind was swirling with all kinds of mixed feelings. He started pulling off my jeans. I cried even harder. I knew that if I didn't fuck him, he might think I was down with what Satanya had said. I let him undress me. Then I watched him undress himself. He walked back over to the bed, climbed over me, and stuck his dick straight up in me.

"Ahh." I let out a loud sigh.

"You like that?" he asked.

Oh, he was so lucky I didn't have a knife or a gun. It was like I had left my body. Bobby was like an animal. He grunted and groaned and sweat dripped off of him. He pounded on me like a maniac. I faked it and let out moans to make him think I was into it, but the entire time I thought about Satanya and Todd. I thought about how fucking much I hated Todd for putting me in this predicament because he had gotten himself locked up again after all of his empty promises that he would never put me through some shit like this again. I thought about how I was going to watch Bobby die because he was a ruthless piece of shit who thought he could do what he wanted just because he had money. I could feel his dick deep in my gut now. It was like he was trying to pull my pussy inside out. No fucking condom at all, and I just lay there and let him fuck me over and over again. I was basically no better than a prostitute right now, fucking for money, except Bobby didn't know he was about to fucking pay. I was fucking for a means to an end.

True to form, Bobby was knocked the fuck out after he nutted twice.

I eased out from under his heavy dead-weight arm and sneaked into the bathroom. I sent the text that Bam and Black would have been waiting for. *It's on now.* Then I hit SEND, returned to the room, and waited. I would have to keep Bobby occupied and away from the cameras. It would be dawn in another two hours, so these niggas needed to hurry up.

When I got a text right back, I started kissing this ugly motherfucker on his neck and face to wake him up.

"Mmm," he grunted.

"Can you come shower with me?" I asked seductively.

"Hell yeah," he said, pulling me down on top of him. I watched
him look over at his security screens. This motherfucker was always looking at those things; that's why I knew I had to get him
into the bathroom.

"C'mon," I said like a little whiny kid.

Bobby let me lead him by the hand into the bathroom. He had a
big smile on his face. With the lights on and his shades off, I finally
realized just how ugly he was. He was a cross between Biggie
Smalls and King Kong. One of his eyes was doing its own thing,
just roaming. I turned on his rainfall shower and climbed behind
the glass door. I pulled down the detachable showerhead and put it
up against my clit; then I pointed at him and used my pointer finger to summon him. I was fucking Shannon Fierce right now; I was
somebody altogether different. Bobby smiled, grabbed his hard
dick, and came behind the glass door with me. The steam was fog-
ging up the entire bathroom, just what I wanted. I didn't want him
able to see mirrors, doors, screens, nothing. He came up from behind me and grabbed both of my breasts. I closed my eyes because
I felt like screaming. He started kissing me roughly and breathing
all hard. I was praying that these niggas were gonna make it there
and get shit under way. I had told them what time Bobby's security
people changed shifts; I hoped they had the shit timed to a tee. Just
as Bobby grabbed his dick to drive it up in me, all of the lights
went out.

"What the fuck?!" he shouted, snatching back the doors.

Thank God, I thought.

"Bobby, baby, I'm scared. Don't leave me," I whined, knowing damn well what the fuck was up.

Bobby grabbed a towel and scrambled out of the shower. He couldn't care less about my ass. I was close on his heels. He ran over to the wall with the screens—it was black. He then rushed over to his huge closet and pulled back a door. I started scrambling to get my clothes on. I was going to need to get the fuck out of there. I watched him rush into the closet and start doing shit in the dark. I was shocked. He started punching buttons and shit, and another door opened up. It was a huge gun safe.

Damn, I thought, *how the fuck did he find those codes in the dark?! Shit!* I was trapped with this motherfucker. He grabbed a huge rifle. I was crying and doing my best acting job.

"Oh my God. Bobby, what is going on? First Satanya, now this!" I cried.

"Shut the fuck up and take this," he said, shoving what seemed like a long gun in my hand. I wish there were light for me to see. Then I saw a ray of light from a flashlight Bobby had picked up from somewhere. He shined it out the door. I couldn't tell if it was light outside, because the way Bobby had his bedroom was like fucking Fort Knox—no sunlight in or out. My hands shook as I looked down at the gun. The shit said DESERT EAGLE on the side. I had heard Todd talk a lot about this gun. My hands were not the only thing shaking. I didn't know if I should just shoot his ass since he wasn't expecting it.

"Stay here!" he demanded. He raced over to his nightstand, picked up his cell phone, and called someone. Then he threw it across the room. Before Bobby could make it to the door, the shit came crashing down like a bomb had gone off.

"Ahhhh!" I screamed, genuinely scared. We had not gone over this. There were five niggas in all black with their faces covered. I wasn't expecting this, and I was hoping that Bam and Black weren't going to kill me and make off with the fucking money.

Bobby immediately started shooting. *Tat, tat, tat,* his gun went. One of the guys went down instantly. I raced for cover. More shots rang out.

Tat, tat, tat.

I was cowering in the corner. Next thing I knew, *BANG!* Bobby dropped like a fucking sack of potatoes. I could still hear feet coming toward us. It was more of Bobby's team trying to get to him to save his life.

BANG! Tat, Tat!

There were so many gunshots going off I couldn't even hear. Niggas were dropping like flies right in front of my eyes. What the fuck had I done? I had masterminded a bloodbath. I heard an explosion, and the door to the hallway with the rooms flew off the hinges. This shit was turning into a mess. I made a mad dash for the hallway. Finally, I saw Bam.

He lifted his mask and grabbed my arm. "Get to the first room and just grab boxes. There is a truck outside behind the last room on the left. There is an exit. We need to be out of here in five minutes."

"Okay, okay," I said, putting the gun into the back of my jeans. My chest was heaving. I raced for the hallway as Bam went along door by door, shooting off the Onity locks and taking out the cameras. Although all of the power had been shut down, he didn't want to take a chance that Bobby had a backup generator on those cameras. I really felt like a renegade bitch. I wasn't leaving the fucking house without enough money to set me straight. The first room was filled with boxes. I tried to grab more than one, but they were fucking heavy as hell. I started dragging one toward the door so I could get outside. Bam and the two dudes who were still alive grabbed boxes too. I couldn't even think to ask where Black was. When I didn't see him, I just figured he was a casualty of war.

"Wait!" I heard Bam call out. He stopped and used a knife to strip off the tape on one of the boxes. Sure enough, the shit was filled with neatly rubber-banded stacks of cash. He wanted to make sure we weren't wasting our fuckin' time.

"Go!" Bam screamed, and we raced outside toward the truck. I kept dragging my one box. As soon as we made it toward the front, more gunshots rang out. Two more of Bam's dudes dropped. Now it was just me and him. I was too fucking scared to cry or scream. I just kept ducking and running for the truck. I had a warrior mindset, and I was gonna get the fuck out of here alive. I had a baby boy to pick up and start a new life with.

There was a dude in the driver's seat of a black van. He got out and hoisted my box into the van. Bam was still struggling to get out with his boxes. The driver helped him, and Bam turned around like he was going back in.

"Where are you going?!" I screamed at the top of my lungs.

"Yo, that ain't enough," Bam said, but as soon as he turned around, one last security guard was there. Bam and the guard shot at each other at the same time, and they both dropped.

"Ahhhhh!" I screamed, jumping into the van.

The driver sped away, the van swerving all over the road leading out of the estate.

"Oh God!" I screamed, and started crying.

"Shut up!" the driver barked. He looked to be no older than eighteen. He was shaking and could barely drive. He finally got the van to go straight and slowed up a bit so that we wouldn't bring attention to ourselves. My nose was running, my heart was thumping, and the tears just flowed and flowed. I had done it. I had carried out the ultimate heist, and I was the only one left standing. Todd would've been proud of me. The little boy drove and drove until we were on the highway. The plan was that me, Bam, and Black were all supposed to meet at the Hilton across from Pembroke Mall on Virginia Beach Boulevard to split up the money. We also planned to lay low for a few days before leaving the hotel. Now it was just me and this little boy I didn't even know.

"What's your name?" I whispered, my voice hoarse from yelling.

"Little," he said.

"Can I trust you, Little?" I asked, flashing the Desert Eagle at him.

"Yeah, I'm not telling shit. I ain't going down over this shit," he said, his voice shaky as hell.

Once we got in the parking lot of the hotel, I told him that we needed to go in separately and that he would go to the front desk to get the key under the name Bam had told me. I wasn't trying to be up on no surveillance camera from the hotel. When Little returned to the van, we used a luggage cart to off-load the boxes.

"Can I help, miss?" a bellboy asked.

"No!" I barked, not meaning to scream at him but so fucking

nervous I couldn't see straight. We pushed the cart through a side exit so that we wouldn't be seen in the front lobby of the hotel carting these boxes looking spooked as fuck. Once I was safe in the room, I asked the boy what he was promised.

"Yo, they said they were going to give me ten thousand," he said.

How fucking stupid was he? He let them fucking promise him that tiny bit of money off of a big-ass heist like this. I opened one of the boxes and pulled out a stack of bills. The boy's eyes lit up. I took the Desert Eagle out of my pants and pointed it to his head and said, "If you even breathe a word of this to anyone, I will not only put this entire shit on you, but I will also kill you."

"You ain't gotta worry about me. I . . . I . . . don't even know your name," Little gulped out as he swallowed hard, grabbed the money, and got the fuck up out of there. After he left, I opened the boxes and started spreading the money out. It was unbelievable how much money this motherfucker Bobby really had just sitting up in his crib. Just there, in boxes, while motherfuckers all over were hungry and homeless. I lifted stacks of it, sniffed it, and let it fall all over my head. Then I dropped to my knees and just cried and cried. Everything had gone wrong, and there were at least twenty people dead.

I stayed in the hotel for three days. I had called my neighbor and arranged for her to meet me on the border of Norfolk and Virginia Beach with my son. I'd paid one of the housekeepers to buy me two large suitcases so I could put the money in and leave the hotel like I was just a tourist. I stacked the money tightly in the suitcases. I was finally ready to face the world. I dragged my two suitcases down to the front lobby and let the bellboy call me a taxi. I hadn't watched the news at all while I was in the hotel, and the first glimpse of the massacre I saw was a headline on the *USA Today* newspaper in the lobby: BLOODY MASSACRE IN PALATIAL ESTATE REVEALS HIDDEN MILLIONS OF COP-KILLING GANGSTER. *Bobby was a cop-killing gangster?* I thought to myself as I climbed into the taxi and told the driver where I was going. As we drove through the city, I knew I would be leaving the place I'd grown up. As we passed the Virginia Beach 2nd Precinct, I stared at the front doors, thinking about how dirty most of the cops were.

When I arrived at Shoney's restaurant near the Norfolk and Virginia Beach line, I was so damn happy to see my little boy. He made all of the worries I had hanging over my head just melt away. He jumped into my arms, and I knew that I had something to live for. I thanked my neighbor and asked her to take me to the Avis rental car place. I hoisted my suitcases into her trunk.

"Girl, did you hear about your friend?" she asked as I sat in the back kissing my son profusely.

"Who?" I asked, stopping to hear what she had to say.

"It was in the newspaper. The girl I always saw you with. Satanya, I think the paper said she was identified as," she continued.

"What about her?" I asked, but I already knew it was bad.

"She was found shot to death in her house," my neighbor said, the words coming out of her mouth like bullets hitting me.

I put my hand over my mouth and immediately started to cry. I knew that motherfucker Bobby was still going to kill her. He probably was planning on killing me, too, but he wanted to fuck me first.

"I'm sorry—I thought you knew. I thought that is where you

disappeared to," my neighbor said. After a moment of letting me cry, she continued: "Jock came by looking for you. I told him I would tell you to call."

I was surprised to hear that Jock was looking for me. I thought that nigga was gone for good. If I'd been able to get Todd's stash from him, I wouldn't have had to seduce Bobby to take care of myself and pay for Todd's lawyer. For a moment I thought about not calling Jock, then decided to call him once I was on the road with Lil Todd.

When we finally pulled up to the rental car place, I dug down into the front of the smaller suitcase where I had put some of the money. I peeled off a few hundred-dollar bills, folded them, and placed them in the palm of her hand.

She looked at me, surprised. "You don't have to. My son just loves to play with Todd—it was no trouble at all," she said.

"No, you take it. Thank you for taking care of the only person I have left in the world and keeping him safe," I said with feeling. "I need you to do me another favor. Take this down to the jail and put it on the books of Todd Marshall. Then mail this letter afterward," I told her, and she agreed to do it.

I took a deep breath, looked around, and said my final good-byes to life as I had always known it.

"Mommy," Lil Todd called out.

"Yes, baby?" I answered.

"Cars," he said in the cutest little voice.

His voice was music to my ears. Then I took my suitcases and my son and got me a car. I was going to drive and drive until I found a place that looked like it was where I wanted to be. I knew better than to try going through an airport with all of this fucking money. I convinced the clerk in the rental place to give me a car with cash, of course. I had to give her a little something because they wanted only credit cards. Those shits could be traced, and I wasn't trying to be found. I pulled out of the rental place on my way to nowhere in particular with a trunk full of unmarked cash and with a new lease on life.

Todd

I had been sent to the hole for fighting. I had grown tired of niggas saying I was hanging with a snitch and fucking with Dray. I had not spoken to Shannon in days. I had started flipping, just thinking about the Bobby Knight shit. I saw on the news that a big-time massacre had happened at the nigga's crib and that more than twenty people were dead. I didn't fucking know if my wife was dead or alive, so I just started bucking on niggas up in that jail. The day I saw the story on the news, I busted a CO's whole snot box. That was it. I was beat the fuck up and put in the hole. I had stopped fucking counting the days in there; that shit would make a nigga go crazy for sure.

I don't know what time it was when they came to my solitary holding cell to get me.

"Marshall, let's go," the CO shouted, prompting me to put my hands through the slot. I turned around and assumed the position so they could cuff me. I wasn't in the mood to fight them, and besides, I was looking forward to getting out an hour to at least take a shower. Then they slid back the metal doors. It felt strange being out. They had me on twenty-four-hour lockdown since my assault was on an officer. That was just another charge added to my shit. If Shannon hadn't come through by now, I knew some shit was wrong.

As I was being led out of the solitary-confinement area, I noticed we weren't going toward the search area and pods that they take you to before you return to general population, nor were we headed toward the yard or showers.

"Where the fuck y'all taking me?" I asked.

None of the COs answered me. All suited up in riot gear like I was crazy, they just held on to the cuffs and pulled me along. The only sound down that long-ass hallway was the foot shackles around my ankles clanging against the concrete floor as I walked along. I felt like somebody should be calling out "DEAD MAN WALKING" like they do to those niggas on death row. This shit was eerie as hell. I was led into a room with a steel table and four little steel chairs. Up in the corner I could see the eye in the sky— the security camera. The walls were all fucked up and scratched. The room kind of looked like the attorney/client visit area, except it was slightly bigger and had more chairs. I hadn't been in the attorney/client visit area since I told that fucking court-appointed piece-of-shit attorney to get fucking lost because I thought for sure by now I'd have a good one on retainer.

As soon as I was placed in one of the little steel chairs, the COs left, leaving me alone. All kinds of shit was running through my mind. I thought they might be putting me in here to tell me my wife was one of the people found dead in the Bobby Knight estate massacre, as they had called it on all the news channels. I shook my legs back and forth, picturing something happening to Shannon. She was the one person who stuck by my ass no matter what I put her through. After a few minutes of sitting there letting my mind wander, fucking Dray walks in with a white dude. When the door opened, I lifted my head, my eyes widening in surprise. For real, I had to do a double take and shit. I crinkled my eyebrows in confusion. This motherfucker walking in right now looked like the Dray I had bunked with, except this bastard in front of me was not in his prison jumper. I had to squint my eyes to make sure I was seeing right. I folded my bottom lip into my teeth, trying to make sense of what the fuck I was seeing. Dray wasn't handcuffed, he wasn't being followed by COs, and he was in regular street clothes. Dray was real friendly looking with the white dude he came in with. I could immediately tell the white dude was a cop or some sort of law enforcement; he just had that look. Dray and the white pig sat down in front of me.

"What's up, Todd?" Dray asked, trying to gauge my reaction.

"Yo, nigga, what the fuck is up?" I growled, flexing my jaw so hard it became painful.

"Maybe you were right about me," he said, sliding an open black leather case with his badge and credentials across the table in my direction. ANDRE BURKETT it read. When I looked down and read those infamous fucking letters DEA, I bit down so hard into my cheek that blood started forming at my lips. Dray, who I had trusted with my fucking life and with my wife's life, was an undercover fucking DEA agent! Word life, I'm telling you, if I wasn't a man, I would've fucking cried right there on the spot. How could I have been so fucking stupid? I could've kicked my own ass because I've been a street nigga all my life, and yet I easily trusted someone like that. I was caught fucking slipping for real. When those niggas on the tier called this motherfucker Dray a snitch, I had taken up for him. I had gotten into many a fight trying to defend that motherfucker's reputation, and all along he was a fucking Fed! I refused to look at this traitorous, pig-ass bitch in the eye. I just hung my head thinking about what I would've done to him if I wasn't in these handcuffs and leg irons.

"I know it's fucked up because you trusted me. But I got to tell you what's really going on. I could've let my bosses come up in here and talk to you, Todd, but I wanted it to come from me," Dray said, folding his hands in front of him like he was remorseful. Like by him telling me this shit he was doing me a favor or somehow showing loyalty after he had already stabbed me in the back and turned the knife round and round. Even the way Dray spoke had changed. He no longer had a Southern accent; instead, he now sounded like he was from New York or New Jersey.

Dray was steady talking, his words just falling around me. I couldn't even hear that nigga right now. I was just rocking back and forth like a mental patient. I couldn't even see straight. Suddenly the door to the room swung open again. Startled, I shot my eyes toward the door. As if shit couldn't get any worse for me, fucking Norfolk Police Sergeant Labeckie walked in the room with a big-ass white-toothed smile on his face. Sweat broke out all over my body, and my stomach just tightened up. Not this motherfucker too! What the fuck was going on?! I'm thinking to myself that this has to be a fucking bad dream. By now I'm balling my fists so tight I could feel my skin cracking around my knuckles.

"Well, well, well, if it isn't bad-ass gangster Todd Marshall. I knew I'd get you one of these days. You can't always beat the case," Labeckie said snidely.

I turned my head and took a deep breath. It was all I could do to keep myself from flipping the fuck out. This had to be the worst day of my life. Obviously they weren't there to give me any news about Shannon . . . or were they? I would've flipped if I wasn't cuffed and shackled.

Labeckie handed Dray an envelope. Dray opened it and took out a few pictures.

"You recognize him?" Dray said, sliding a picture toward me.

I looked down and my heart sank. It was a picture of Jock. I fucking knew it! I knew that motherfucker had set me up! The vein on the side of my head and in my neck started throbbing, and I started feeling like I could bust out of these fucking cuffs and murder all these bastards.

"Well, you have him to thank for all of this," Dray said with his cocky attitude.

I looked at him confused.

"Your boy here got busted with guns on him, and it took nothing for him to agree to give you—his so-called boy—to us on a silver platter to get himself off," Labeckie said, tapping his fingers on the table to make the point. "No honor among street thugs," Labeckie said, laughing like he had heard a funny joke.

Then this fucking traitor Dray started talking again. "Bobby Knight was a cop killer. He killed my partner, DEA agent Greg Mathison, three years ago, so when I told you he killed my brother, that wasn't a lie," Dray said seriously. "When Jock agreed to tell us where he got the guns, we knew you'd try to beat the case, so we worked our plan. We had you set up Bobby Knight because we knew you'd be so desperate to get out that you'd do anything. Jock told us where to find your safe and all of your stashes so you would be dead broke and without money for an attorney. Jock knew you so well that he told us you would be down with any plan to get money. See, we wanted Bobby dead, and you were the perfect one to carry it out. You were facing life anyway, so what did it matter?" Dray finished, sliding his chair back. "Besides, I heard that your wife did get away with some of Knight's money. I guess you haven't heard from her either, huh?" Dray said with finality.

When Dray said the words *Jock told us where to find your safe,* something inside of my head clicked. I knew Jock didn't know where the safe in the house was. The only people who knew were me and Shannon. When I first got locked up, she made it seem like the cops had found the trip switch for the safe when they wrecked the house. But now that I thought about it, I had never heard those fucking cops say anything about the safe when I was lying facedown in the house.

Although I was relieved to hear that Shannon had gotten out of Bobby Knight's house alive, I still hated that motherfucker Dray, and I hawked up all the spit I could muster and sent it flying in Dray's direction.

He jumped back. "Yo, Todd. I really did enjoy passing the time with you, homeboy. You weren't half as bad as some of these other losers I tried to get to do this," Dray said, then turned his back.

Labeckie was still standing there. "So, we just added conspiracy to commit murder to your charges. Thanks to your boy, we finally got you, Todd Marshall," Labeckie said, smiling.

"Fuck you, pig!" I screamed.

Dray and Labeckie shook hands. "Good job. This was truly the ultimate heist," Labeckie said, cackling like a witch.

That was the final straw for me. All sanity went out the window. There was nothing left for me.

I started flipping, thrashing my body up and down. The COs couldn't even control me. I had nothing else to live for. I had got got. The government had finally taken me down. My life was over. I was kicking and spitting at those fucking COs. They carted my ass back to the hole.

Shannon

I drove and drove until I found a place I thought was far enough from Virginia and where people didn't know me from a hole in the wall. I had stopped only to feed my son and get gas. I knew shit was hot, and I also knew that the police would've been on to the Bobby Knight heist by now.

When I passed by the sign on the highway that said WELCOME TO DALLAS, TEXAS, HOME OF THE COWBOYS I was satisfied that I was far enough away from the bullshit. I drove around and scouted areas that I thought would suit me and Lil Todd. We stayed in a hotel for a few days, and I just relaxed and appreciated every hair on my son's head. Finally, I rented a three-bedroom apartment where the lady allowed me to pay in cash. The apartment was not too far away from the new Cowboys stadium. From what I could see, Dallas was a nice city. It was a far cry from Virginia, and a damn far cry from where I had grown up.

After getting settled into the apartment, I went shopping, cut and dyed my hair, got a new cell phone, and mentally prepared for what was in store for my new life. Once I was sure I was comfortable, I made the telephone call that I had put off until now.

"Hello," I said as seductively as I could when the line picked up. The voice on the other end was sexy as hell. Mmm, I just wanted to touch myself already.

"Yes, I'm in Dallas," I said. Then I gave my new address. It seemed like that was all I had to say. Seven hours later, there was a knock at my door. I started smiling right away.

I peeked in on Lil Todd to make sure he was sound asleep.

I checked myself in the mirror one more time and rushed over to the door. Standing on my tiptoes, I looked through the peephole and there he was, as sexy as I remembered him to be. I felt like a giddy little girl. I let a smile spread across my face, and I loosened the belt on my silk robe. I pulled back the door and let him see what I was working with.

"Dayum, baby!" Jock called out when he saw me looking fucking sexy as hell.

I giggled and threw my arms around his neck. His caramel skin and thick chest and arm muscles glistened. His gear was tight as usual. He was rocking a hot pair of Prada sneakers that I had never seen in the store before; a nice, neat pair of True Religion jeans, and sexy black motorcycle jacket. The long diamond-encrusted Jesus piece and chain Jock rocked around his neck definitely looked better on him than it had ever looked on Todd.

"Damn, I can't believe you let me go through all that shit," I said as Jock lifted me off my feet and carried me into the apartment.

"Yo, you was a true ride-or-die bitch, baby," Jock said, laughing as he started kissing my neck and breasts.

"I'm just lucky it turned out all good," I said. I just wanted him to fuck me; I didn't want him to remind me of the drama I'd just gone through behind Todd.

Jock threw his tongue down my throat, and I closed my eyes in ecstasy. I had missed him. I had been fucking Jock for almost two years. It had started when Todd got locked up the last time. Once Todd got home, I tried to stop my thing with Jock, but he was just so goddamn good in bed. It started off with Jock being there as a shoulder to lean on every time Todd cheated on me or got locked up. Or when bitches came to my front door holding babies, talking about Todd being the father. Jock was always so attentive and caring. That's why I was so disappointed when Jock didn't check on me after Todd's arrest. But when I called Jock from the road, he confessed to setting up Todd to get caught with the guns. He didn't like the way Todd treated me and wanted him out of the way so that he could have me himself. I just wish I'd known Jock's plan before I'd seduced Bobby to get at his money. But now that I had Bobby's money, life for me, Lil Todd, and Jock was going to be easy from here on out.

Jock laid me down on the bed and immediately licked down my stomach until he got to my dripping wet, waiting pussy. Jock took his long tongue and went to work on my clit; then he went down to my hole and back up to my clit.

"Ahhh," I yelled out. I had missed him the entire time he was lying low. He must've licked me for about twenty minutes, and I came over and over again. His tongue-play was not to be fucked with.

"I want you so bad," I called out right before Jock crawled up and took all nine inches of his beautiful, rock-hard dick and drove it up in my pussy.

"Damn, girl, this pussy is so fucking good. Too bad for your fucking husband he didn't appreciate it," Jock said as he rocked his hips against mine, grinding my pussy until I started coming again.

"Whose pussy is this?" he asked. I held on to him so tight. I never wanted to let go of him. "I said whose pussy is this?" he asked me again.

"Yours, Jock!" I screamed out with not one bit of guilt. I had completely put Todd out of my mind, just like he had done to me so many times.

Jock and I had been in Dallas for about a week, and I was still thinking about the possibilities of our new life. We'd decided to lie low for a while before moving into a new neighborhood and enrolling Lil Todd into school. I wondered if I was going to be foul enough to let Lil Todd call Jock *Daddy*. As I lay in bed lost in thought, I heard it. *Knock, knock!* Somebody was knocking on my door?

I leaned up on one arm and looked at Jock with my eyebrows furrowed in confusion.

"You expecting somebody or something?" he asked, lifting his head off the bed, just as confused as me.

"Hell no. The only person I know in Dallas is you, the landlady, and Lil Todd," I said, pulling back the covers to find my robe so I could go investigate.

"Let's ignore it, then," Jock said, reaching out to grab one of my titties.

"Nah, I'm going to look through the peephole," I said. Shit, I wanted to know who the fuck had the audacity to be knocking on my door. I wrapped my robe around me and rushed through the living room. I crept over to the door and quietly looked through the peephole. I didn't see anybody out there. I slumped my shoulders in relief. *Maybe they had the wrong door,* I thought, but just as I turned to walk away, they knocked again.

"Tst." I sucked my teeth, ready to curse somebody's ass out. This time when I looked through the peephole, all I could see was the long black barrel of a gun. I opened my eyes wide, and a flash of heat came over my body. I fixed my lips to call out to Jock and run. Before I could run, the door came crashing in. I tried my best to get my bearings and scramble away from the door, but I was not fast enough. The person seemed to be on my ass with one leap into the apartment. All of a sudden, I felt my head being yanked back by the hair.

"Ahhhh!" I screamed, trying to fight. But my hair was my weakness. Once someone got hold of it, I was at their mercy. The pain shooting through my entire head was unbearable as the man wrapped his hand up in my hair, using it to control me like horse reins. I immediately thought about my son sleeping in his room. We were about to die; I was sure of it. Jock came running out of the room in just his boxers when he heard me scream, and another dude drew a gun on him. Jock put his hands up in surrender. The one who grabbed me finally let me go, sending me flying to the floor.

"I guess your boyfriend doesn't watch his surroundings and who the fuck is following him. You didn't really think we would let you get away free and clear with a quarter of a million dollars, did you?" said the guy I recognized as Dray, Todd's cellmate, leveling his gun at me. I thought Jock had told me Dray was really a DEA agent and that he was not going to be a problem as long as Bobby Knight was out of the picture. It didn't seem like that shit right now; he was here for the fucking money and I knew it. As soon as I saw his face, I knew the deal. The real ultimate heist was about to go down right there in my living room.

Todd

Right after I got the news from Dray, I completely gave up on life.

I stayed in the hole because I acted like a fucking maniac every time they tried to let me out. After a few weeks of that shit, I just decided to ride my time out until they transferred me to the long-term prison where I would be serving out my life sentence. I still had a court date coming up, but that shit was just going to be a for-mality. The plea was already off the table, so I had no choice but to let my shit go to trial with a new court-appointed attorney.

Once I calmed the fuck down, I was set to be released out of solitary. The first day I got out of the hole, I received my mail call, which they hadn't allowed me to have while I was in segregation. Along with a letter, I also received a commissary receipt. Someone had put cash on my books, and it was a lot of cash. I examined the letter, and I could tell from the handwriting that it was from Shan-non.

"Huh." I let out a little laugh. This bitch had put money on my books as a guilt consolation, I guess. Then I guessed she sent me a

letter to try to cop a plea or explain herself. At first I started to rip
the shit up, but I decided to open it. Maybe she was writing to tell
me she was still going to someone who could help me the fuck out.
Maybe she was writing to explain how the fuck Jock knew about
the safe in our house. Or maybe the grimy bitch I had pulled up
out of the gutter was writing to say thank you for all the sacrifices I
had made for her bitch ass. I looked down at the paper, smelling
her perfume on it, and read:

Dear Todd,

*First let me just say me and Lil Todd are alive and
well, no thanks to your sorry ass. I am in no way sorry
about any of the things that happened. I have taken
the money and our son and moved on. How could you
ever risk my life by putting me in this situation? You
are and always will be a selfish piece of shit. Oh, you
don't think I know you had been fucking that bitch
across town and that she just had twins? You promised
me over and over again that you would go legit and
that I would never have to worry about you going to
jail or seeing other women again. Well, you lied, and
now I'm moving on with Jock. He was waiting for me
so he could give me the dick he has been giving me for
the last two years while you chased bitches around
Virginia. Me and Jock are together raising your son.
Your son who calls Jock Daddy. Well, as payback for
the little bit of shit you did do for me, like taking me
from my fucked-up mother, I left you some money on
your books. Yeah, it's about $300, which is what I*

think you are worth, you lying sack of shit. By the
way, Jock took all of the money out of the safe before
he told the police where it was. He set you up good.
Your best friend, a real man, with a real good dick. I
hope your life in prison is as miserable as you made
mine. You made me have low self-esteem. Good thing I
have Jock to tell me how beautiful I really am. Have a
nice life serving your life sentence.
Your wife,
Shannon

"Arrghh!" I screamed, causing other niggas on the tier to look up at my cell. I ripped that fucking letter into a million little pieces. How dare that bitch, after all I had done for her hoodrat ass! And that motherfucker Jock. We had known each other for years, since we were little niggas trying to survive. I had something for both of their asses. I still had people out there.

"They won't get away with this shit!" I gritted, throwing myself back on my bunk and covering my eyes with my arm. For the first time since I was a child, I let tears roll out of my eyes. It turns out I had been the victim of the ultimate fucking heist.

I had been robbed of my money, my wife, my son, my pride, and my entire life.

Shannon

After they fucking tied us up, Dray started his shit.

"Damn, baby, you are more beautiful than I remember," Dray said, holding his gun on me while he forcefully kissed my lips.

"Mmmm," I groaned, turning my face away.

"You don't mind me kissing you, do you? I mean, you've fucked for what you wanted all this time—your husband's best friend and Bobby Knight—and let's not forget you set your own husband up. It just doesn't get more grimy than that, baby girl," Dray continued.

"Yo, man, leave her the fuck out of this. Take the fucking money and get the fuck out!" Jock barked, fighting against the telephone wire binding his hands. Before the words were fully out of his mouth, a gun went slamming into his head, immediately drawing blood and causing a gash over his eye.

"Ahhh!" Jock screamed out.

"Now, don't talk," Dray said, like he was getting off on the power.

"So, Ms. Marshall, where is the money?" Dray asked.

"I don't have it here," I lied.

"Well, you don't fucking have it in a bank either," Dray snapped, lifting his gun menacingly.

"I have it put away," I said sarcastically. Shit, at this point if he was going to kill me, he was just going to kill me.

"Okay, well, I'm waiting to hear where that is," Dray said snidely.

"I bet you are," I retorted.

With that, Dray pointed his gun at Jock and shot him in the leg.

"AHHHHHH!" Jock let out a screeching, animallike scream, his head falling to his chest as he tried to catch his breath from the pain. Blood was pouring out of Jock's leg. I started sobbing when I heard Lil Todd start crying upstairs.

"Please! Let me get my son," I pleaded with Dray, looking him in the eye to appeal to any mercy he may have.

"Baby girl, all you got to do is tell us where the money is so we can get the fuck up out of here. See, I don't have a beef with you. I had the beef with Bobby Knight, so his money belongs to me— you know, payback, restitution," Dray growled, his eyes looking all fucking crazy. He was a DEA agent, but obviously he wasn't sticking to no fucking code of honor right now.

"The money is in a safe in the closet," I surrendered, because my son was screaming and I was so scared he would open the door and run downstairs and see what was going on. It wasn't worth it.

"Go," Dray said, nodding to his partner. The man left. I heard the silenced gun go off as he shot the fucking lock off the safe. I jumped, hoping he didn't try to hurt my son.

"There's no money in here!" he called out.

As soon as Dray turned his head to respond to his partner, I heard voices screaming, "POLICE! POLICE! Drop the weapon! Drop the fucking weapon!"

My jaw dropped when all these cops came trampling up in my apartment. I was really confused as hell now.

Dray turned toward the cops who were rushing in and raised his gun. Before he could get a shot off, like ten of the cops who were filing in the door let off shots on his ass. I heard Lil Todd crying louder at the top of the steps. All of the screaming and chaos must've scared my baby almost half to death.

"Oh my God! Please don't shoot my son!" I screamed, closing my eyes as tears flowed out of them like a river. The other guy who had been with Dray came running out when he heard the shots, and the police officers shot him too. The remainder of the cops came rushing in and started barking orders.

"Call an ambulance! Untie them! Get the kid!"

I was glad they had an ambulance called for Jock, because he looked like he had lost a lot of blood. The cops finally untied me and started asking me questions. One of the cops who walked over to me I recognized from Norfolk. He was one of the fucking cops who was always after Todd.

"Ms. Marshall, we followed Jock all the way here, and you're lucky we did or you'd be dead. Andre Burkett was an undercover DEA agent who was not satisfied that you'd gotten away with the money he felt he was entitled to. When he didn't get his way, he went AWOL from his team. Luckily, Jock led us to you, and we figured out that Agent Burkett was coming after you," the cop said. He noticed the look on my face. "I am Sergeant Labeckie from the Norfolk Police Department gang and narcotics unit. Ms. Marshall, you have the right to remain silent. Anything you say can be used against you. . . ."

I just stared at him in shock. When Dray's partner said there was no money in the safe, I knew immediately Jock had turned the tables on me.

I sat in my jail cell waiting for the count. "Marshall, mail," the fat female CO who I hated called out. I grabbed the letter from her hand. I had been locked up for weeks with no mail, no commissary money, nothing. I ripped open the letter and read it:

Dear Shannon,

I guess the fucking joke was on you. I heard through the grapevine that Jock turned on your ass. I had to laugh. I guess you should've been more careful about who you gave your pussy up to. If I had gotten out, you would've been sitting pretty right now. Instead, you are being charged with conspiracy to commit armed robbery and accessory to murder. You must be kicking the shit out of yourself right now. I hope you rot in jail, you bitch! By the way, the judge put the plea back on the table for me, so with good behavior I will be out in seven. I hope you grow old and fucking die in prison, you grimy bitch. You will always remember the end re-sult of the ultimate heist!

Love your husband,

Todd

I folded the paper, hung my head, and sobbed and sobbed until I was completely dried out of tears. The next day when my lawyer visited me, I told him where he could go to find his fee. He was the same lawyer who had gotten Todd off so many times. A bitch wasn't that stupid. Money for a rainy day was a must. I had to get out because I definitely had revenge to exact on a few motherfuckers.

Robyn Banks

DE'NESHA DIAMOND

Prologue: The Jackal

New York. July 2, 1985 . . . the last job

The moment night falls in the East Hamptons, me and my dawgs—Rawlo, Mishawn, and Tremaine—load up into our black GMC van and ride out. Rawlo, the wheelman, knows exactly where we're headed and the safest route, so we're not to draw any suspicion. In the back, the rest of us are sliding on our black gear so that we can blend effortlessly into the night. We're old hats at this thing, and we run every job like a well-oiled machine.

"We're coming up on it now," Rawlo says, the usual alert that tells us that we have five minutes until we arrive at our destination. In all honesty, that's when my adrenaline really kicks in. There's a certain high niggas in our profession get when the shit is about to go down—a lot of times because it is a huge chess game being played out between us and whatever whack security system our target has set up. I don't mean to brag, but my reputation speaks for itself. There hasn't been a security system invented yet that I haven't been able to hack or maneuver around. Lately, these new computer programs have me longing for the days when all a nigga needed was a good ear on a combination lock safe.

Maybe I'm just getting too old for this.

Rawlo turns off the main road, and in less than a minute, we're parked and the engine is shut off. "Time," he calls.

We all look at our watches.

"Nine-thirteen," I announce. There's a series of beeps around me. We have twenty-five minutes.

Mishawn slides open the side door, and he, Tremaine, and I jump out. Each of us carries our own black tool bag as we hunch over and do a half-mile run up through a wooded area and through a soft security spot on the east side behind the Donovan estate. From here you can hear and smell the ocean, and there's a cool breeze whipping a few branches against my face, back, and hands. When we get through, we see the Donovans' sprawling crib sitting high on a hill. It never fails to trip me out just how some of these rich folks live. After studying the blueprint of this place for the past two weeks, I know almost every nook and cranny of this twelve-thousand-square-foot home and wonder what it would be like to provide something like this for my own family.

Maybe one day.

Two minutes later, we're in through the back door, and I go through my handy black bag and disable the code keypad in less than ten seconds. This is simple. The heavy-duty shit is going to be upstairs, closer to where Gary Donovan hides all his most prized possessions.

"Let's go. Let's go," Tremaine whispers, rolling his hands along after I close up the keypad.

We hustle up the stairs to the handsome library / study where we come up against the only variable that we don't know. Where's the safe? We spread out, checking under mirrors and picture frames.

"Are you sure it's in this room?" Mishawn asks, sounding frustrated.

"That's the intel," I tell him. "Guzman has never been wrong before."

Hector Guzman is the big boss man who usually hires me for these high-end jobs. It doesn't bother me in the slightest that we've never met in person. He sends his people—I send mine. Never the two ships shall meet. In this business, the less you know about someone the better off you are. No meetings. No phone calls. He gets word and my money to me through the proper channels, and I get his products to him the same way.

Now, just because I've never met Guzman doesn't mean that I haven't heard stories about him. And what I've heard loud and clear is that he's not the man to be fucked with. This Colombian nigga got connections all over the damn place. Violent. Ruthless. And some call him downright medieval when it comes to torturing muthafuckas who try to jack him, which brings the irony of him always hiring me to jack other people.

A few times when we roll up onto an item that we're extracting, it occurs to me and a couple of my boys that we could probably make more by keeping the shit to ourselves and doubling our money on the black market. I'd be lying if I said that I haven't been tempted. But I'm a man of my word, and a man's word means everything. Even to a thief.

I step back and survey the room again. What am I missing?

"We got fifteen minutes," Tremaine announces.

I scan the room again, and then my eyes snag on the wall-long bookcase. I cock my head and wonder at the possibility of a hidden compartment. "Start looking for a lever." The three of us move to the bookcase and start moving books as quick as we can but without throwing them off the shelves. Finally, I pull back on a fake book; there's a soft *thump*, and the edge of the bookcase moves forward.

"Hot damn. We found it," Mishawn says, sounding relieved.

"Was there ever any doubt?"

"Yes," they both answer, and then chuckle.

We pull and swing the bookcase forward, and sure enough behind it is probably the largest safe I've ever seen in a private residence.

"Damn. You sure you got enough time to get in that muthafucka?"

"Watch me." I rush up to the big iron box and start checking it over for outside wires (there are quite a few) and then take a peek at the kind of lock I'm dealing with (there are more than one of those too). I unzip my bag, crack my knuckles, and get down to work. The wiring is a little tricky only because I think Donovan hired some second-rate electricians who weren't fit to hook up a VCR. Once I get past that, Mishawn settles down next to me and helps me hook up the electronic password decoder.

"Who in the hell has a sixteen-digit code?" he asks, shaking his head.

"A man who's trying to protect his shit," I answer.

"Ten minutes," Tremaine says. "We're not going to make it."

"Chill the fuck out, man. Don't you see that he's working?"

Tremaine huffs and starts pacing like a caged tiger in a zoo.

Two minutes later, we get through the first lock with three minutes to go.

"He's right. We're not going to make it," Mishawn says, looking at his watch.

"Ye of little faith." Three minutes later, we are in and staring at the mother lode.

"Baby, wake up."

My six-year-old baby, Robyn, peels her eyes open, and then a groggy smile hooks the corner of her lips.

"Daddy."

"Shh." I place a finger against my lips to let her know that she needs to keep her voice down so that we don't wake her mother. That's the last thing I want to do since I'm not even supposed to be here. I sneak over here whenever I can, but it's just a secret between me and my little girl. "I brought you something," I tell her.

"Really?"

Immediately Robyn's bright hazel eyes light up. I have said the magic words. I quickly reach over to my black bag and pull out a brown, fluffy teddy bear. "It's the same one you told me about at FAO Schwarz."

"Ahh, Daddy. You got him," she says, grabbing the bear and wrapping her small arms around him. "I love him. I love him."

"Is he the only one you love?" I lean back with my hands on my hips.

"Oh, no. Daddy, I love you too." To prove it, she drops the bear and launches her small body into my arms.

"Daddy loves you, too, pumpkin." I squeeze her tight and love how she still smells brand-new, with Ivory soap clinging to her skin. "All right, now. Let's get you settled into bed." She quickly scurries back beneath the sheets, and I hand over her precious new teddy bear. "Now, are you going to take good care of him?"

"Forever and ever," she promises, beaming up at me. "I think I'm going to name him Fred."

"Fred?"

"Like Fred Flintstone," she says like the answer is obvious.

"I'm going to hold you to that," I tell her, and then lean down and place a quick kiss atop her forehead. Just then, before I can grab my bag, Robyn's bedroom light clicks on.

Damn.

"I see that you're still breaking and entering into people's homes."

"Mommy, Mommy. Daddy is here," Robyn exclaims.

"I can see that," Sandra says sweetly from the door. "Jonathan, can I see you in the living room for a minute?"

I exhale a long breath and finally turn to see the love of my life, arms crossed and looking like she's just two seconds from ripping me a whole new asshole. "Sure. I'll be right there." I turn to my sweet Robyn and press another kiss on her face. "I'll see you later, sweetheart."

"Promise?"

"I promise. Now get some sleep." I grab my bag and then follow her mother's thick curves into the living room. Just watching her hypnotizing hips switch back and forth has me weighing the odds on making a play to get her into the bedroom. I should have married her when I had the chance.

I barely have one foot in the room before Sandy turns on me.

"What the fuck do you think you're doing?"

"Now, Sandy, calm down."

"Don't tell me to calm down. I told you not to come around here anymore. You're not welcome."

"Come on, Sandra. She's my daughter."

"Correction: She used to be your daughter. You lost all parental rights when I found out what you do for a living."

"What? It's not like I'm a drug dealer or something."

"No. You're a thief. You rob banks, people, jewelry stores—you name it. I'm not raising a child of mine to think that that bullshit is okay. And you can't keep breaking into this house to try and see her at all hours of the night."

"What are you going to do? Put in a new alarm system?"

"No. But the next time I catch you in her room, I'm going to call the police."

I cock my head at the empty threat. "No, you won't."

She closes her eyes and sucks in a long, patient breath. "Jonathan . . . one of these days you're going to get caught."

"That's not going to happen."

"Thieves always get caught—especially serial thieves with God complexes. Jesus Christ! Just look at your family history. Your father *and* grandfather served long bids in prison. I don't want my daughter—"

"*Our* daughter," I correct her.

"*My* daughter," she spats heatedly. "I can take care of Jordan myself."

"Jordan?"

Sandra thrusts out her chin. "I had her name legally changed when I married George."

No shit. Her words are like a kick in the gut. "But Robyn was my grandmother's name."

"Like I said, I don't want my daughter having anything to do with you or your family. You're free to go out there and risk your neck if you want to, but I will not have it affect my daughter."

"Is there a problem in here?"

Great. Now we woke up asshole.

Sandra pulls the belt of her robe tighter as her husband, George Hayes, shuffles into the living room and then wraps an arm around my girl.

"What the hell is *he* doing here?"

"Nothing," Sandra says, leaning into him. "Jonathan was just leaving." Our eyes lock. "Weren't you?"

My gaze swings back and forth between her angry glare and his desperate attempt to look Johnny Badass. But I know straight off that there is no point in attempting to reason with their united front. "Yeah. Sure, you're right. I was just leaving." Gripping my black duffel bag tight, I head toward the front door. Just when my hand lands on the doorknob, my little girl's voice floats out to me.

"Bye, Daddy."

I turn my head to see her standing in the hallway. "Bye, baby."

Chapter One

On the west side of Atlanta, I pause outside a closed auto shop for half a beat, check to make sure my team is in position behind me, and then allow my adrenaline to take over when I kick in the side door and shout, "Everyone on the ground! Move it! Move it! Move it!"

Like a soldier, I hustle into a warehouse with my government-issue Glock, my heart pounding like a jackhammer. My team of DEA agents floods in behind me. A large group of hands goes up in the air. A couple reach out for their weapons on one of the tables loaded down with bricks of cocaine.

"Don't even think about it!" I bark with my weapon trained on the Big Poppa look-alike in the center. "Get your ass on the fucking ground!"

Seeing the never-ending parade of agents spilling into the shop behind me, everyone starts acting like they know English and get their asses down. But like always, there's one stupid muthafucka hidden somewhere we don't count on, and a shot is fired off. This one goes whizzing by my head. I jerk my arm upward and squeeze the trigger. At the same time, at least twenty other agents react, and a barrage of bullets turns the brother on the second floor into Swiss cheese. He jerks around a bit before spilling forward and flipping over the railing. The brother hits the concrete floor with a loud *bam!*

Internally I wince at the gruesome sight, but externally I keep my game face on all the way through cuffing and loading the twenty-three members of the Marseille cartel. With just one glance around the shop, I estimate that it's perhaps our biggest bust to date. After a fifteen-month investigation, I'm glad this damn case has come to an end. Maybe I'll be able to get some sleep. At the same time that we moved in on this operation, agents in Columbus; Mobile, Alabama; and Dallas, Texas, were synchronized to shut down the other arms of this organization.

"Hey, Rambo-ette! Great job!" Agent Elliott Baker rolls up on me and smacks me hard on the center of my back.

"Thanks."

"Yeah. 'Get your ass on the fucking ground.' Classic." He winks and then rolls his eyes.

Undoubtedly he thinks that because he's six-two, well built, and reasonably cute that my ass likes him. But he's wasting his time.

Elliott and his small party of knuckleheads—agents Aaron Pitman and Eric Thompson—chuckle around us.

"Yeah. Whatever. I got my muthafuckin' point across, didn't I? They got their asses down," I say, turning my attention away from the black vans pulling away with our arrests to glance at the forensic team snapping pictures.

"Yeah, maybe you should have let big man stay in his seat. It took seven of us to help get his ass back up," Pitman tosses in. "I swear I don't know what these big muthafuckas be eating some-times—whole grocery stores?"

Agent Thompson twists his face. "Who gives a fuck? These assholes are slinging poison in the street, and your ass is worried about their muthafuckin' diets? What the hell is wrong with you?"

Pitman shrugs. "I'm just saying."

I've had enough. "As entertaining as I find this conversation, I'm about to roll out."

"Yo, Hayes. Does that mean you're not joining the boys for a celebratory drink over at Flint's tonight?"

"What? Just so I can watch you pussies toss your cookies after a couple of shots of Jägermeister?"

The boys club immediately erupts into laughter.

Elliott grins while his gaze skims over my stacked five-eight frame and heart-shaped ass as if he's considering making a pur-chase. "You know, Hayes, you always talk a lot of shit for a girl."

"So do you," I snap back.

More laughter.

Elliott shrugs the barb off because trash talk is just a way of life in this business. "A'ight. I'm going to let you have that. But you know you owe the boys a round for the last rain check."

"Fine. Damn. Stop your bitchin', man. I'll catch you on the flip side at Flint's." That shit seems to make his night, because his eyes light up like a six-year-old on Christmas Day. I shake my head as I walk away. Elliott has been trying to get into my panties for two years and takes each rejection like a personal challenge. Momma was right—men love what they can't have.

It's not like there is something wrong with Elliott. Far as I can tell, he's a nice guy. It's just that I don't believe in fucking people I work with. It'll only cause problems when I toss their ass to the curb, which I will eventually do because I bore easily. It's my MO.

Two hours later, I exchange my DEA clothes for my usual wardrobe of tight blue jeans and a basic white T-shirt. To soften my look, I let my thick, wavy hair hang loose to the center of my back. Of course it gets attention the second I walk through the door.

"HAYES!" everyone shouts the minute I enter. The place is packed.

I flash them all a brief smile and then thread my way up to the bar.

"Looking good, Hayes," a few male colleagues comment as I pass them by.

Mitch, the bartender and owner, plops down my first shot of the night without even waiting for me to order it. "First one is on the house," he reminds me. It was his usual way of paying back the men and women in military or law enforcement.

"Thanks!" I toss back my shot without a second thought. The instant jolt of alcohol is like an electric charge to the heart. "Damn. I didn't realize how much I needed that."

"Another?" Mitch asks.

"Don't stop until I tell you to," I tell him.

Just when I start to turn around, Elliott, Aaron, and Eric surround me like a pack of wolves. Outside the job, these boys are my dawgs. We hang tough on poker night, Monday night football, and, of course, after-work drinks at Flint's.

"Glad to see that you could finally make it, partner." Elliott's hand smacks the center of my back like he's trying to crack the motherfucker wide open. I don't flinch because I know he only does that shit to try getting a rise out of me. "After having a bullet whiz by my head and my life flash before my eyes, believe me, I needed a drink."

"Yeah. It would've been a damn shame to toe-tag the prettiest thing on the team."

The compliment is so awkward that everyone, including the bartender, laughs at that shit.

Elliott's mocha complexion deepens to a dark burgundy. "Yeah. Whatever. A brother is a little tipsy."

"Already?"

He couldn't have been here more than twenty minutes before me. "I told you your ass doesn't know how to handle your damn liquor. I don't know why you're always running up in here trying to hang with somebody."

"He's been a lightweight since high school," Eric cuts in. "You'd think that his ass would've built up a resistance by now."

We all get a laugh over that. For the next two shots, the conversation turns, like it always does when talking with men, to sex.

Eric holds the court. "I'm telling you, man. I was waxing that ass like a full-time job." He pumps his hips and pretends to be smacking a bitch's ass. "I mean, pow! Pow! I was up in there. You hear me?"

I just shake my head. "I don't see what the big damn deal is. Didn't Big Joe and 'em smash that girl a couple of weeks ago?"

"Yep. Yep." Elliott and Aaron cosign and then laugh and point at a red-faced Eric. "Big Joe said she's a hotel hooker at the Marquis downtown."

"Well," I say, impressed. "That's a step up from an out-and-out streetwalker like you had on New Year's Eve."

"It wasn't New Year's Eve," Aaron corrects me. "It was his birthday."

Elliott chimes in, "Actually, it was New Year's Eve *and* his birthday." He looks over at Eric. "Hell, I'm starting to think that you spend half your paycheck on hookers."

We all crack up while Eric shoots his middle finger at us. "You know what? Fuck all y'all. I'm a brother with needs, and I like dealing with bitches who are straight up with their shit. That's all I'm going to say. I ain't got to deal with bitches trying to trap a brother with a baby or some trick, whining about how I'm responsible for her rent or getting her hair whipped and dipped just because she gave me some pussy. Cash on the table is up front and honest, and I always leave with a smile on my face."

"All right. I respect what you're saying," I say.

"Oh. Is that right?" Elliott laughs. "What about you, Jordan?"

I cock my head. "What about me? I know you don't think I have to pay for sex." I stand up from my stool and strike a pose. "Look at me."

Elliott takes his time, doing just that, licking his lips as well. "How come you ain't got a man hitting that shit on the regular? I mean . . . shit. You're fine as hell and got a little sense about you. I would have thought that a nigga would have snapped you up by now."

"Thanks. I think." I roll my eyes.

"You ain't answered my question." He places his hand on my knee, which immediately causes my eyebrows to jump. "Don't you ever get . . . urges?"

Aaron and Eric act like they've suddenly became interested in the bar's decoration as they start looking around like they don't hear shit.

I lean toward Elliott with the biggest smile I can manage. "Oh, I get urges all the time."

"You do?" His gaze drops to my full lips.

I can tell his ass is fucked up by the way he's struggling to keep his eyes open. "Uh-huh." I inch closer. "You want to know what I do then?"

"What?"

I lower my voice to a throaty whisper. "I ease back on my big old bed, spread my legs wide, and peel open my fat pussy." Eric and Aaron think they're slick, but I see their asses leaning closer. "I take my fingers and test the waters for a little bit by stirring them around underneath my pink clit until I hear it go"—I pick up my drink and stir my finger around so that it starts to slosh around the glass—"and then . . ."

After a beat of silence, Elliott asks breathlessly, "And then what?"

I lean back. "And then . . . nah. You can't handle that shit." I wave him off and turn around on my stool. "Mitch, hook me up with another."

"Awwww, man." At least twenty brothers who had been listening start hissing and booing.

"Damn, Jordan. You're just going to leave me hanging?"

I look down at his pants and see his dick trying to bust out like the Incredible Hulk. "Nah, man. I ain't trying to give Mitch here more shit to clean up off his floor tonight."

"That's cold," they all chorus, shaking their heads.

I toss back another drink and then hop off the stool to make a run to the little girl's room. "Save my seat." I walk through the main bar area, but as I glide through the pool hall, I start to feel a heavy gaze on me from somewhere in the room. I ignore it and go into the bathroom to empty my bladder.

On the way back, however, I feel it again and take a look around. Leaning over a pool table holding a cue is hands down the finest brother I've seen in I don't know how long. Large, sexy eyes; plump, juicy lips; broad shoulders; and biceps I want to use as pillows.

His green eyes lock on me over the white ball a second before he cranks a shot and breaks the triangle of balls at the other end. He doesn't look to see how many of the solid or striped balls scatter into pockets, because his eyes are still molesting my curves.

Shit. I have to remind myself to breathe. I try to pull my gaze away, but it's damn near impossible. The brother's green eyes are like a powerful magnet, and it's either him or this whiskey that's got my body tingling.

Finally he smiles, and two dimples wink at me. He stands up so I can peep out his whole six-foot-three frame. The man has to be solid muscle. I can't find an extra inch of nothing on his ass.

"Damn." I manage to shake this trance off and push one foot in front of the other until I return to my stool at the bar.

Elliott doesn't miss a beat. "I was beginning to think you fell in."

When I don't answer but keep my eyes toward the back of the bar, he starts looking around. "What is it?" Elliott turns to see who has caught my attention.

Almost on cue, Mr. Sexy waltzes out of the pool hall and spots me at the bar. I can't help but smile. "I think my eggs just lined up."

Elliott takes one look at the dude and frowns. "Aww, shit. Don't tell me you go for the gangster type," Elliott complains in my ear.

Mr. Sexy sits down at the other end of the bar and gives me a look that says I have to meet him the rest of the way.

"All right. I won't tell you." I get back up from my stool.

"Is she going down there to *him*?" The peanut gallery behind me explodes with laughter, but I don't pay them any mind because I have my target in sight.

"Buy you a drink?" I ask, taking the seat next to him. I don't know what he's wearing, but damn he smells good.

"You want to buy *me* a drink?"

Shit. The muthafucka even sounds good. A deep, smooth bass that gets my clit thumping in my panties. "Is that a problem?"

"No. But usually it's the man who buys a woman a drink."

"If it makes you feel any better, you can buy the next round," I tell him.

He cocks me a smile, showing two perfect rows of white teeth. No. It's definitely not the alcohol that got me feeling this dude. "All right. You got a deal."

"Mitch, you want to hook my boy up?" I ask without pulling my gaze away. "By the way, the name is Jordan."

"Jordan? That's different." He nods, still trying to play it cool.

"And you are?"

His smile stretches even wider. "Keston."

"Keston? That's different." I smile while my gaze continues to eat his fine ass up. Thank God I have on silk panties tonight and not cotton.

"What will it be?" Mitch asks.

"I'll have another Heineken." Keston doesn't look up either. When Mitch walks away, he asks me, "Like what you see?"

"So far," I admit. "You got a wife, Keston?"

"Do you have a husband?"

"I asked you first, slick."

He pauses just long enough for me to suspect his answer will be a lie. "No. And you?"

I return the favor by waiting equally long. "No."

He laughs, and honest to God it's the sexiest shit I've ever heard. "So"—he leans in closer to me—"how do you want to play this out?"

"The usual. I get you drunk, take you to a hotel, and then fuck your brains out."

Still smiling, Keston whips out his car keys. "Fuck the beer. Let's go."

Chapter Two

Alvaro Guzman Jr. sits behind his handsome mahogany desk with his hands braided and his hard gaze burning holes into everyone in the room. The Colombian drug lord is infamous for his explosive temper. Undoubtedly, someone in the room is just seconds from getting maimed, shot, or stabbed for this latest fuckup. Alvaro means for his erratic temper to instill fear in his men, but the truth is, the new Colombian king is nothing more than a spoiled child. His father, God rest his soul, is the one who built the Guzmans' vast drug trade to what it is today. Some speculated that Junior would run the organization into the ground within two years. So far it's been sixteen months.

"What happened?" Alvaro asks in a menacingly calm voice. "How is it that the government seized a half billion dollars of MY MONEY?!" He slams his hand down onto the desk, causing everything and everyone to jump.

Visibly trembling in his white linen suit, Alvaro's right-hand man and childhood friend Delmar steps forward with his forehead slick with sweat. "At the moment we're not sure, but I got our best people on it." He runs a hand through his greasy hair.

Alvaro's brows stretch up. "Our best people?" He laughs. "These wouldn't happen to be the same best people who lost my shit in the first place, would it?"

Delmar swallows and shifts his gaze back around the room.

"Half a *billion* dollars," Alvaro barks. "Half a fucking billion dollars!" His fist hits the desk again. The desk jumps and everyone else jumps as well. "I want to know how this happened. *Now.*" He opens the top drawer of his desk and pulls out a chromed 9 mm, a favorite of his that Father bought for Alvaro's eighteenth birthday. "You, Delmar." He points the gun. "You tell me what you think happened. We're boys, right? I can trust you to be honest with me."

Delmar's large Adam's apple bobs up and down in his throat.

Seeing the fear in his best friend's eyes, Alvaro strolls casually from behind his desk and then up to his friend. He wraps his free arm around his neck. "See, I know that you would never lie to me, my friend. So tell me." He presses the gun against the center of Delmar's chest. "How could such a monumental fuckup happen under your watch?"

Sweat rolls from Delmar's greasy hairline and then nests in his guff-looking day-old beard. "I . . . I suspect that we had a breach . . . somewhere. A mole, I believe."

"Ah. A mole," Alvaro repeats with his eyes growing blacker. "But, my friend, what does this matter? Do I not pay law enforcement handsomely enough to look the other way? I mean, tell me. Am I a cheap bastard or something?"

"Of course not. You're most generous—more than generous."

"Then why are they *fucking* with my shit?" Alvaro's arm tightens around Delmar's neck while the barrel of his gun damn near cracks his breastplate.

"It's not the local police. It's the goddamn DEA. Somehow they got a man on the inside and hit those three states."

Silence.

Delmar is trembling so bad that he looks like a human earthquake. If he survives this bullshit, his men aren't ever going to let him forget this humiliation.

Finally, Alvaro sucks in a deep breath. "You mean to tell me, amigo, that I don't have eyes and ears in the DEA? Is that what you're telling me?"

"I . . . well, yes, you do. But I don't know if they knew about this bust." Delmar senses that he'd said the wrong thing when the other men turn their faces away. Some even shake their heads. "But I will find out, Alvaro. I promise. There has to be some reasonable explanation."

During the next long silence, Delmar just goes ahead and closes his eyes. In his mind, he pictures his six-month-old son, sucking on his wife's tit this morning. They'd looked so beautiful and peaceful when he'd left them. Had he known that it was possibly the last time he'd see them, he would've taken the time to kiss them good-bye.

"I'll tell you what else you'll do," Alvaro whispers. "You'll get me my shipments back."

Delmar finally reopens his eyes. "Excuse me?"

Alvaro laughs. "C'mon, amigo. You've known me for a long time. When have you ever known me to stutter?" He removes his arm from around Delmar's neck, but the gun stays put. "I want it back—all of it."

Delmar's mind races to how such a request can even be possible.

Alvaro winks. "You're my right hand. You'll make it so, *sí?*"

"*Sí.*" Hell, there isn't any other answer. To deny Alvaro is to deny life, and knowing how fucked up Alvaro can be sniffing his own shit, chances are that his amigo wouldn't stop at just putting a bullet in his head. His son and his wife would undoubtedly receive courtesy bullets as well.

"Good. Good." Alvaro finally removes the gun from Delmar's chest only to swing it left toward Felipe and pull the trigger. Everyone in the room jumps while their colleague's lifeless body propels backward and crashes into a glass table. "That'll be all."

Delmar is sure that he pissed a little bit in his pants, but he bows to Alvaro and quickly rushes out of there, wondering how he's going to steal a half billion dollars' worth of drugs back from the DEA. "*Dios me ayuda.*"

Chapter Three

No lie. I came the moment Keston's lips touched mine. It started in his car when I sucked on his beer-and-peppermint-tasting tongue and slipped my hand down the front of his pants and discovered the anaconda that snaked halfway down his thigh. This man is a walking, talking fantasy.

One-night stands are tricky. You don't want to bring some unknown brother to your house, hung or not, and you don't want to roll over to his crib in case he's one of those crazy muthafuckas with a basement that you'll never walk out of. So as a compromise, we head over to the closest hotel—in this case the Marriott Marquis. A little fancy and expensive but neither one of us wants to drive to a dive on the outskirts of the city.

At the front desk, dude pulls out a roll of cash that could choke a fucking horse. Just great. I'm a DEA agent about to hook up with a possible drug dealer for a quickie. Any thoughts of backing out of this shit disappear the moment he turns toward me and flashes those sexy dimples.

"Enjoy your evening," the perky blonde behind the counter says, handing Keston a pair of card keys.

"We intend to," he says with a wink.

I blush. Fuck. I haven't done that shit since junior high.

We don't even have the patience to wait to reach the room. The second I enter the small glass elevator, Keston pushes me up against the glass and starts slowly grinding against my ass while reaching a hand down in front of me and squeezing my pussy. There's a few people milling around in the bars and restaurants below, and more scandalously, they can see us. That shit gets me off.

"You know that I'm going to bust this shit wide open, don't you?" His warm breath rushes up against my ear and causes my nipples to look like giant marbles sitting up in the center of my chest.

"You got the dick," I pant. "But do you know how to work it?"

He flips me around and looks me dead in the eye. "You're about to find out."

A minute later, we're in the room, ripping off each other's clothes. He's so fucking strong that when he yanks off my jeans, my body is jerked up in the air for a few seconds. "Goddamn. You're a fucking brick house," he says, admiring my frame.

I'm about to say something smart back, but that's just when his boxers hit the floor and I'm introduced to that big-ass cock in person. "Oh . . . shit."

A sexy grin hooks the side of his lips as he gives his fat cock a few good strokes. "I sure hope that you ain't thinking about backing out now."

Eyes still wide, I shake my head and watch that chocolaty monster grow a few more inches in his hand. I reach out and run my fingers along the entire length, loving the way it feels like silk. As a rule, I don't put shit into my mouth until I get serviced first. Why the hell should I put in a five-star performance on a two-star nigga? Reluctantly, I pull back and inch my body to the center of the bed. His gaze tracks me while I slide my legs open and give him a good look at the strawberry and cream I got waiting on him.

"Nice," he says casually, but he doesn't just dive right in. Instead he pulls up one of my legs and starts peppering kisses along the bottom of my foot while his dick rubs against my thighs. *Oh, shit. I got myself a freak.* I'm stunned for a few minutes until he sucks in my big toe and makes me cum right on the spot.

"Holy shit," I pant, blinking stars from my eyes. I'm just mildly able to recover before my beloved freak dips his tongue on the small spot behind my right knee. I shoot off again. *What the fuck?* All along my body, Keston zeroes in on all my G-spots. There's quite a few that I didn't even know I had. By the time he settles in to feast on the honey bubbling up around my clit, my mind is blown and my shit is sensitive.

"Wait a minute. Wait a minute." I try to inch away because I need to catch my breath, but he makes it clear that he's not having any of that.

"Where are you going?" He chuckles, pulling me back and then spanking the hell out of my clit with his tongue.

"Aaaaahhh." I grab his head and try to push it away, but he's stubborn as an ox and doesn't move an inch. I try to wiggle away again, but he has my ass locked down.

"Mmmm. Cum on my face, baby. Give me all you got." He licks, smacks, and moans like a starving man, and when he plunges his fingers into my pussy and starts stirring it around, I nearly black out. *This muthafucka ain't even fucked me yet.*

"I bet you ain't had no nigga eat this pussy right, have you?"

"N-no."

He plunges his tongue in so deep that he literally cleans all four walls. *Holy shit.* Fuck a freak. He's a certified pussy monster.

"I'm going to show you how the big boys do it, baby." He shoves two fingers in my pussy and then pushes a third one into my ass. Like a bottle rocket, I blast off, screaming a whole lot of *goddamns* and *oh my Gods.*

When I finally start pulling air into my lungs at a normal rate, this nigga climbs up and starts coating his dick with the pussy juice that is streaming down my leg.

"Come and get you some of this candy, baby." He's still gazing at me like I'm T-bone steak, so I know my pussy is just getting a small break while I try to impress him with my head game.

Dizzy, I sit up and reach for his iron-straight shaft. My mouth waters while I run my tongue down the side. It might just be my imagination, but he even tastes like chocolate. I don't stop at the base of his cock. I keep going until I teabag his nuts, sucking each one into my mouth lovingly.

"Awww. Shit. I see you got game." He chuckles.

Smiling, I work my way back to the head and immediately give him a couple of jawbreakers to start him off. He jumps and sucks in a breath. When I set a good rhythm, Keston pulls my hair back away from my face so that he can watch me work. Within minutes, precum starts to drip from the tip, and I gobble it up with as much gusto as he showed me.

Clearly he's not completely the man of steel, because his legs start to tremble and shake the bed. "Ssss. Get it, baby. It's in there for you." He switches hands on my hair and starts pumping his hips.

I can deep throat only about half his dick, but it's enough to squeeze the head and get him to call on Jesus for a few seconds. I slide my hands around his waist and then drop them lower to get a good grip on his firm ass. Just when I think that he's about to blast off, he pulls back. His dick springs out with a *pop* and then swings like a pendulum in front of my face.

"Get in position."

I blink stupidly at him.

"Any position you want," he says, grabbing his cock and stroking it. "Just make sure your ass is comfortable."

Given his size, I figure it's best to just take him in a half-doggy-style, where I'm up on my knees but my shoulders lie flat so I can play with my clit while he squeezes into my wet pussy. I'm scared and excited at the same time. I've never had a dick his length and width. I'm hoping this shit feels good and not like I'm about to have a baby.

Keston sidles up behind me, leans down, and plants a big-ass hicky on my right ass cheek. "You ready, sweetheart?"

More honey drips from my pussy and slides all down my hand.

"Give it to me." I wiggle my ass and then try to push up on the dick myself.

"A'ight, Ma. Calm down. I got you." Keston slaps my ass, and while I wince from the slight sting, he slides into my glazed pussy. Immediately, my mouth drops open into a perfect circle as inch by inch I try to take all of him in. After a while, I feel like this brother has worked his way to the back of my throat. "How you doing, Ma?"

"Ooooh." That's all I can manage to get out.

"Awww. You like that?" He doesn't make me take him to the balls, but he starts stroking and opening my ass cheeks so he can watch his work. "Shit. You got the kind of pussy a nigga can fuck up and fall in love with."

Meanwhile, I'm mentally climbing the walls, struggling to catch my breath and just absolutely loving the magic this man is working in between my legs. *Where in the hell has this man been all my life?*

In no time at all, he has my pussy smacking, squishing, and making all kinds of funky noises while I'm moaning, groaning, and downright talking shit myself. Now that he's gotten me wide open, I'm taking him straight to the balls, and the bottom of my pussy is threatening to fall out. "Oh God. Oh God."

Keston keeps bucking his hips. "Your pussy falling, baby. Are you about to cum?"

"Y-yeeessssss."

"Did I tell you that you could cum?"

"W-whaa . . . ?"

Without warning, he pulls out and plops onto his back. His dick is completely glazed with our sex juices. "C'mon over here and clean me up, Ma."

Eager, I crawl to him and sink my mouth down over his shaft. Chocolate and honey. I'll be lucky if I don't go into diabetic shock.

"That's it. That's a good girl." Keston pulls my hair up into a ponytail with one hand and reaches over to slide his fingers into my pussy with the other. "Make sure you get every drop," he says.

While my tongue is mopping him up, Keston finger-fucks me to another orgasm. I scream out while his dick is halfway down my throat. I gag, choke, and spit all over his shit. Even then there's no rest. He pops me on the ass and instructs me to climb up. Now that I've been stretched open, my body swallows him easily. Once I'm on top, Keston crams his finger with my pussy juices on it into my mouth and orders me to suck and buck at the same time.

Beneath my bouncing breasts, I peep out the big-ass smile spread across his face and know that he is having just as much fun as I am. It's blowing my mind how much we're synching together. Our bodies act and feel as if we've known each other our entire lives.

For the rest of the night we fuck like dogs—literally. I'll get a nap in and then we'll go again. I've never met a man who has this much energy. Keston is always careful not to cum until he's ready. When he does, it's a full load blasting all over my flat abs and tits. It's hot, sticky, and sweet.

"How do you feel?" he asks, massaging his cum into my skin with the bottom of his dick.

"Wonderful." And it ain't a lie. Shit. I feel like a brand-new woman with my pussy still creaming like a muthafucka. After that, I just pass out. Vaguely I think I hear a cell phone going off. Keston answers it, mumbles a couple of words, and then curls back against me with his sausage dick resting between the buns of my ass.

When I wake up the next morning, the bed is empty and there's money on the table. "No, the fuck he didn't."

Chapter Four

"*The return of the Jackal? Law enforcement is baffled by a string of bank robberies in the Atlanta area leaving the calling card of the Jackal, the eighties bandit that's still at large and wanted by the FBI. The thief—or thieves—targeted what were once described as the impenetrable vaults at the Wells Fargo branch downtown. Early reports estimate the robbers getting away with more than ten million in cash. . . .*"

Jonathan Banks shuts off the television with his remote and turns with a smile toward his life-long friends Rawlo, Tremaine, and Mishawn. "The Jackal. When was the last time you heard that name on the evening news?"

"Looong time," Rawlo says, nodding with an equally large smile before tossing down his cards. "I fold." He pushes back his chair and moans and groans as he unfolds his arthritic frame from the metal chair. "I'm going to go take a piss."

"I fold too," Mishawn says, tossing down his cards. "I never understood why we all agreed to being called the Jackal in the first place. There's four of us. Shouldn't it have been 'the Jackals'?"

"I'll call." Tremaine pushes a couple of poker chips forward and looks downright pleased with his move. He looks up. "What? What's going on?"

"TREMAINE." Jonathan thumps the table and then points at Tremaine's ear. "Turn up your hearing aid. We're discussing something important."

"Huh? Oh. Hold on. Let me turn up my hearing aid."

Jonathan and Mishawn roll their eyes while Tremaine fiddles with the volume on his hearing aid.

"All right. Now what were you guys saying?"

"Why the hell do you always turn that damn thing down?" Jonathan snaps.

"My bad. My bad. I focus better when I don't have to listen to all that trash talk Rawlo be spitting. Now what are we talking about?"

"The Jackal," Jonathan says. "Our name was mentioned on the news."

Tremaine's brows dip. "What the hell for?"

"Some copycat robberies going on around town," Mishawn says. "I guess we're supposed to feel flattered."

"What, you're not?" Jonathan asks. "We finally got some people out there respecting how the real game is played. None of that smash-and-grab bullshit these young cats be doing nowadays. I mean, anybody can just run into a bank and point a gun. Where is the damn skill in that?"

Tremaine and Mishawn bob their heads in agreement.

"The game is man against machine. In our heyday, how many people got hurt?"

"None," Mishawn answers.

"That's right. Wasn't no need to. We get in and get out. We got our money and they got insurance. Clean—no fuss, no muss. All we did was bruise a few egos who thought they were smarter than us."

"True. True," Tremaine says. "Those were the good old days."

Rawlo stomps out of the bathroom still spraying the Lysol can. "Yo, Jonathan, you got some chips up in here? A nigga getting hungry."

"Check the cabinets." Jonathan shakes his head. "That muthafucka be putting a hurting on my grocery bill."

Mishawn chuckles under his breath. "That's why I never invite his four-hundred-pound ass over to my house. He's like a human garbage disposal."

They all get a good laugh at that.

"What's so damn funny?" Rawlo asks, walking back over to the card table.

"Nothing," Jonathan lies. "Whose turn is it?"

"YOURS!"

"All right. Damn." Jonathan drops his hand. "Two pair. Aces high."

"Shit." Tremaine tosses down his cards. "Two pair. Jacks high."

"Better luck next time." Jonathan reaches out and drags all the chips back over to his side of the table.

"So who do you think it is?" Tremaine asks. They look at him, confused. "The new Jackal on TV. Who do you think it is?"

The boys all stretch back in their chairs. Rawlo's chair makes a loud crack, and for a whole second they wait to see if it will dump him on his ass. When it doesn't, his face splits into a wide smile.

"It could be anyone," Jonathan finally answers. "It's not like we have our ears on the street like we used to."

"True," Tremaine concedes. "Not like the good old days." A palpable silence drifts over the table. "I kind of miss it."

Everyone's head bobs just as the doorbell rings. Jonathan huffs out a long breath and gets up from the table, but his face lights up when he answers the door.

"ROBYN!" He throws open his arms, and his baby girl walks into his embrace with a wide smile.

"It's Jordan now. How many times do I have to tell you that?"

He groans and waves off her comment. "As many times as I've told you that you can be Jordan with your stepfather. You're Robyn when you're with me. Now come on in here." He gestures her into his small apartment and then closes the door behind her. "Your grandmother's name was Robyn."

"I know. I know." She waltzes farther into the cramped apartment and spots her play uncles at their usual poker table. "Hey, guys."

"HELLO, ROBYN!"

She cocks her head at them, and they all snicker. "You told them to do that," she accuses her father.

"I did no such thing." Jonathan waves her off, pecks her on the cheek, and then returns to his poker game. "So what brings you by?"

"The news," she answers honestly. "Everyone is buzzing about this latest robbery by someone—or a group of people—calling themselves the Jackal."

Jonathan turns a smug face toward his friends. "You don't say?"

Jordan walks over to the table and props a hand on her hips. "Don't play crazy. One thing older people do is watch the news."

Mishawn clears his throat. "We . . . might have heard something about it." He shrugs. "We didn't pay it no mind or nothing."

"Nope," the other men chorus at the table.

She eyeballs them. "Didn't pay it any mind?"

Four gray heads shake.

Seeing how hard she's studying them, Jonathan cracks up. "What? Surely you don't think we're running around town robbing banks again, do you?"

The four buddies crack up.

"We'd have to change our names to the AARP bandits." Mishawn chuckles. His weak eyes are four times their normal size behind his thick bifocals.

"No worries," Jonathan says, winking at his daughter. "Your old man is still on his best behavior."

"Good." She leans over and places a kiss against his cheek and then turns back toward the door. "I gotta head on to work. I just came by to check on you." She turns, and on the back of her black jacket are the bright yellow letters DEA.

All the men at the table groan as if they can't believe that someone they love and care about is actually a part of law enforcement.

"It could've been worse," Jonathan whispers. "She could've been FBI."

"You ain't never lied," Rawlo says, shaking his head.

"You're still coming to the barbeque this weekend, right?" Jonathan asks his daughter.

"If I don't get called into duty, I'll be here."

Jonathan hops back up and follows her to the door. "Um . . . you know you can extend that invitation to your mom?" His eyes light up. "I mean, since she and your stepdaddy are separated now. No sense in her just sitting at home alone."

Jordan smiles and shakes her head. "I'll ask her."

"That's my girl." He leans in and plants a kiss against her cheek. "See you this weekend." He closes the door behind her and returns to the table, clapping and rubbing his hands together. "It's just a matter of time now, boys."

"Why not? You've just been waiting twenty-five years to get back with her momma."

"Yeah. Wasn't she the reason we retired in the first place?" Mishawn asks. "You thought you were going to win her back."

"I am going to win her back." He shrugs. "It's just taking a little longer than I thought. Just you wait and see."

Chapter Five

During the short drive to my field office, I can't help but laugh that my dad and his old hanging buddies thought I believed that they had gone back into the bank-robbing business. Uncle Tremaine is as deaf as a stump, Uncle Mishawn is legally blind, and Uncle Rawlo, God bless him, isn't exactly in the best of shape to be breaking into anything.

I pull in a deep breath and then laugh. Overall, it hasn't been easy growing up with the secret that my father used to be a famous bank robber / jewel thief. When I was younger, I wanted to blab to everyone who would stand still. That was when it seemed kind of cool. When I decided to get into law enforcement, it made me nervous when the government ran a background check.

Jonathan Banks has quite a criminal record, though he never went to jail for being the Jackal. That's amazing in itself. Despite the fact that the statutes of limitations are up for his eighties shenanigans doesn't mean I've stopped looking over my shoulder, and it certainly doesn't mean that it can't come back and bite me on the ass. My mother doesn't like that I've maintained a relationship with my father. She thinks that it's somehow a big slap in the face to my stepfather—the man who raised me. I would love to point out that was a choice she made because my father always wanted to be there, but it's not worth fighting over. I like to keep that crazy drama between them.

And now that Mom and George are separated and talking divorce, I see renewed hope in my dad's eyes, and it's kind of contagious. Then again, maybe all children want their parents to get and stay together.

I whip my ride into my usual parking space at the field office and hustle into the office, because I have a thing about always being on time. And sure enough, as I rush to my office chair, I see Elliott leaning against it and tapping the face of his watch.

"I don't know what you're talking about," I tell him. "I'm on time." I look down at my watch. "In fact, I have two minutes to spare. Now get off my desk." I shoo him away and plop down in my chair.

"We have twenty minutes before Benson goes in for a press conference regarding last night's raid."

I wince. "Are we going in there with him?"

He nods. "What are you going to do? It's part of the job."

"Twenty minutes. I guess that gives me enough time to work some of those reports you passed off to me last week."

"You haven't done those yet?" He plants his ass on the corner of my desk while I boot up. "Soooo . . . you left the bar pretty quick last night."

"Catch that, did you?" I try to keep a smile from creeping across my face. Despite the money on the table, I can't deny that I had one hell of a time.

"Awww. It was that kind of evening, huh?" There's a tightness in his voice.

"A lady never kisses and tells," I answer, and since I know what his follow-up will be regarding me being a lady, I wave a finger in front of his face. "Don't say it."

He tosses his hands up. "All right. Fine." He gets up from my desk and returns to his own in the next cubicle. But two minutes later, he stands up and looks down at me. "Soooo . . . Are you seeing that dude again?"

I roll my eyes upward. "Why? What's it to you?"

He shrugs. "Nothing. Can't I be concerned about you? I mean . . . what do we even know about this dude?"

"I know that he can fuck. Does that count?"

Elliott's face fell. "I . . . uh . . ."

Aaron popped up. "You guys ready to go down to the press conference? We have to stand behind the special agent in charge and look official and everything." He looks at Elliott and frowns. "What's wrong with you?"

I stand up from my chair, smirking. "I think a cat got his tongue."

We head outside where a podium and an American flag have been set up before a truckload of drugs confiscated in last night's raid. There are a few members from the local press snapping pictures and filming, and there was one reporter from CNN.

Dressed in our official DEA jackets and hats, Elliott, Eric, and Aaron line up behind the podium while the special agent in charge, Rodney Benson, and Henry Dobson, director of the FBI Atlanta field office, take to the podium and thank the press for coming.

"Last night at approximately eight-thirty, the DEA, in conjunction with the FBI and the local police department, conducted a raid at Clark's auto shop. Our agents recovered ninety pounds of cocaine. At the same time, field agents in Mobile, Alabama, and Dallas, Texas, also moved in on connected networks that we believe to be part of the Guzman cartel. The total street value estimated on the drugs is believed be somewhere around five hundred million dollars."

Alvaro hits the MUTE button on the remote and smacks a hand against his tense forehead. "My. Fucking. Drugs." He sucks in a long breath and then starts rocking on the edge of his chair. "This shit is not happening." He finally hops up and nearly tips over his glass of orange juice onto the three perfect lines of coke on a silver tray, otherwise known as his breakfast. "DELMAR!"

Storming through his two-story Mediterranean-style Miami home, Alvaro goes looking for his right-hand man. It's already past nine, and his ass should have been here by now. "DELMAR!"

Finally, Delmar appears, running down the hallway. "Yes, Alvaro. You called?"

"Of course I fucking called you. When the fuck am I going to get my drugs back? Those damn government agents out in Atlanta have my shit all over the news."

Delmar sucks in a long breath. "I'm on it, Alvaro. It's going to take a little time for—"

"Time?!" Alvaro whips out his beloved chromed gun and starts waving it around. "Let me tell you something, amigo. You don't have any fucking time, goddamn it." He wipes the end of his nose with the back of his hand and accidentally fires the gun.

Delmar jumps and then clamps a hand over his ear. Blood trickles and oozes through his fingers. "Shit. Fuck."

Alvaro's eyes bug out a bit, and for a moment it looks as if he's about to apologize. But then he seems to remind himself that he needs to exude strength. "Stop your damn bitching and get me my muthafuckin' drugs back. You hear me? I don't care how the fuck you do it—just get it done."

Still holding his ear, Delmar clamps his jaw tight and nods. "As you wish."

Chapter Six

Saturday morning, I arrive at my childhood home out in Alpharetta, a suburb of Atlanta, dressed in pink shorts and a matching spaghetti-strap top. Frankly, I think I'm looking kind of cute. I use my key to enter the house. "Mom! Are you ready?"

"Here I come."

I glance up toward the top of the stairs just as my mom appears in an outfit better suited for church. "We're going to a barbeque, not a revival."

She glances down. "What? You don't like this?"

I can't help but shrug. "It's . . . a bit much. Don't you have like a pair of capris or something?" When my mother frowns, I just rush to the top of the stairs. "Here. I'll help find you something to wear."

"I don't know," she complains. "Maybe I should just stay home. I really don't feel like going anywhere anyway."

"You're not going to stay home and mope around the house feeling sorry for yourself."

"But what if George calls?"

"When was the last time he called?" I ask gently.

She doesn't answer.

I turn around and see her sad face. I immediately go to her and wrap her into my arms. It's strange to see my mother this vulnerable. She has always been so strong. I like to think that I inherited my strength from her.

"Okay. I'm okay," she says, sniffing and pulling out of my embrace.

"You sure?"

"Yeah." She nods and flashes me a smile. "Let's find me something to wear and get on over to your friend's barbeque. I think it's sweet of them to invite your mother. Are you sure I don't need to bring something? We can run to the store and pick something up in the deli."

"No, no. That won't be necessary," I say, suddenly trying to avoid her gaze. No way am I about to tell her that I am taking her to my father's barbeque. She would flat out refuse to go. But if I can just get her there, then who knows?

"No, Mom. It's just a come-as-you-are kind of thing," I say, and then rush to find her something to wear. In the end, I hook her up in some nice white capris and a blue top. At least it's something that will show Dad that she's maintained her nice curves over the years. When we make it to Dad's crib in the heart of Atlanta, she's already frowning suspiciously.

"Who's giving this barbeque?" she asks.

"Huh?" I park the car and quickly jump out of the vehicle. The smell of barbeque has saturated the air, and George Clinton and Parliament Funkadelic's "Knee Deep" is on serious blast. People are milling about out front of the apartments dancing or bobbing their heads to the music.

Mom climbs out of the passenger side and has to jog just to catch up with me. "Jordan, hold up. What's your big hurry?"

"Oh, nothing. I'm just ready to eat me some good barbeque." I ring Dad's doorbell and then turn to face her. "Now, I want you to be nice," I tell her.

"Nice? Why do I—"

Dad jerks open the door.

"Jonathan?" Her eyes nearly bug out.

Dad's face splits into a big-ass smile. "Sandra. You came!" He steps out and sweeps my mother into his arms. "I was afraid that you wouldn't come."

Mom's gaze cuts over to me, and I give her a guilty shrug. "Surprise?"

"Robyn." Dad turns and then sweeps me into his arms as well. "I got my two favorite girls back. Life is good." His smile is wide, and his eyes are so bright I'm praying that Mom will just be on her best behavior.

"It's . . . um . . . good to see you again," she says stiffly, pushing out of his arms and cutting me with another look that promises an ass chewing later on.

"Well, y'all come on in." He steps back and allows us to come inside. The music is still bumping as we push our way inside. The place is crammed with wall-to-wall visitors. Frankly, I didn't know my father had so many friends.

"GUESS WHO'S HERE?" my father shouts over the music as it changes to "Flashlight."

"ROBYN!" they all shout.

My mom cuts me another hard look. "Sorry. Dad just insists."

"Soooo . . . can I get you two ladies something to drink?" Dad asks, still grinning. "Sandra, I know you don't drink, so I made a batch of sweet tea."

"No. I think I'm good. *Jordan* and I aren't staying long. We—"

"Mom." I elbow her.

"What?"

Be nice, I mouth to her. She clamps her jaw together for a minute and then returns Dad's smile. "I guess one glass won't hurt."

"I'm on it." He winks and takes off toward the kitchen.

Suddenly, I'm aware of the floor moving, and for an insane moment I'm thinking we're having an earthquake until I see Uncle Rawlo in the middle of the living room getting his groove thang going with Ms. Davis from next door. Watching him bump and shake his four-hundred-pound body all around her ninety-five-pound one has everyone else in the room pointing and laughing. Ms. Davis seems to be having the time of her life until she gets too close to a hip swing and is sent flying across the room.

That shit cracks me the hell up. I turn to see Momma smirking as well, and I feel a little better about bringing her to the party. "Having a good time?"

She wipes the smile off her face but not from her eyes. "We'll talk about this later."

In the dining room, there's a poker game going, of course I can tell by the way Uncle Tremaine is focused on his cards and not the argument going on around him that he has his hearing aid turned off. He's kind of cute like that.

"I see the gang is all here," Momma says, pulling a deep breath.

"Not everyone. I don't see Uncle Mishawn."

"Oh, Jordan. These criminals are *not* your uncles," she hisses.

"I know." I shrug my shoulders. "But I kind of think of them that way."

I get another eye roll for that one.

"Here you go." Dad returns. "One sweet tea and one root beer," he says, handing me a brown bottle.

I laugh. "Dad, I drink the real stuff now."

"Not at my house you don't," he answers sternly.

No matter how hard I try, I'm never going to be more than just his little girl. So I drop the subject and pull a long chug of my icy-cold root beer. "Ahhh. Thanks, Dad. Where's Uncle Mishawn?"

"Where else? Out on the grill. Every barbeque he just takes over my shit."

"Well, he got it smelling good up in here," I tell him.

"That's because he got his son out there helping him. Otherwise he would've probably burned the place down by now. Don't tell him, but his eyes aren't what they used to be."

"His son?" I frown while I search through my memory Rolodex. "Since when did Uncle Mishawn have a son?"

"Since thirty years ago when his baby momma kept it to herself and married some other dude with health benefits and a retirement plan."

"There's nothing wrong with a woman wanting to settle down with someone with a little more security."

"There is if she doesn't love the man," Dad challenges.

Seeing that they are gearing up to rehash an old argument, I decide to exit stage left. "I'm just going to say hi to Uncle Mishawn," I tell them, but I might as well have been talking to a brick wall for all the attention they paid me.

I melt into the crowd and dance to half of Rick James's "Bustin' Out" before I make it out onto the balcony. "Hey, Uncle Mishawn, I—" I stop cold when my eyes zero in on the man standing over the grill next to Uncle Mishawn. "You. What are you doing here?"

Keston blinks at me with the same look of surprise on his face, but before he can answer, his father cuts in.

"Hey, Robyn!" Mishawn lights up behind his large glasses and quickly rushes over to give me a hug. "Glad you could make it." He steps back. "I hope you brought your appetite, because me and my boy are putting a hurting on these ribs."

My tongue nearly falls out of my head. "*You're* Uncle Mishawn's son?"

"*You're* Robyn Banks?"

Chapter Seven

R ibs, hamburgers, and hot dogs sizzle on the grill while Keston and I continue to stare at each other as if we're ghosts that just popped up in each other's lives. However, my body doesn't think that he's a ghost. My tits start tingling, and my clit is thumping so hard in my panties I'm afraid that someone is going to notice.

"I take it you two know each other?" Uncle Mishawn asks, swinging his head back and forth between us.

"We've . . . met," I tell him. "Briefly."

Keston finally blinks out of his trance and slides on an easy smile. "I don't know about it being brief," he says.

"Ha-ha." I roll my eyes and then flash Uncle Mishawn a quick smile. "I'll leave you to your work. You make sure that you save me one of those burgers." I plant a quick kiss on his cheek and then turn and rush off the balcony.

"Whoa, Robyn. Wait up." Keston chases after me, but I keep it moving. Of course this would be the time I can't spot my mother so that we can get the hell out of here.

Keston grabs me by the arm and pulls me back. "Yo, wait up, Ma. Where's the fire?"

"Anywhere you're standing." I snatch my arm back and roll my neck.

"Is there something wrong?" He actually has the nerve to look confused.

"Are you fucking kidding me? You left two hundred dollars on a nightstand, asshole."

Keston looks around. "All right. All right. Lower your voice."

"Fuck you," I say, backing up. "We don't have shit to talk about." I try to turn away, but clearly this fool doesn't take rejection lightly. His arm snakes out and grabs mine again, but out of reflex I flip his big ass over and he hits the floor with a *bam!*

People jump out of the way, and for a few seconds everyone freezes.

Keston, lying on his back and blinking up at the ceiling, is clearly trying to review in his head what just happened. Seeing him dazed and confused, I cross my arms and smile down at him. "You shouldn't grab women like that."

"Point taken." He finally attempts to get up, checking for broken bones along the way.

The crowd now feels comfortable about laughing and pointing at him. To show that he's a good sport, Keston holds up his hands and smiles at everyone. "Ha-ha. Chuckle it up." He turns those adorable dimples toward me. "Does that make us even now?"

"Hardly." I roll my eyes and go search for my mom.

"Robyn, wait up," he calls after me, but this time he doesn't make the mistake of touching me. "Robyn!"

"My name is *not* Robyn."

"What? But . . . ?"

I knock on the bathroom door. "Mom, are you in there?"

The door opens and Uncle Rawlo steps out, spraying the Lysol can.

"Good God." I pinch my nose.

Rawlo smiles. "Y'all might want to wait a few minutes before going in there."

No shit. I turn away with my nose hairs burning and my eyes watering.

"Moooom!" I knock once on my father's bedroom and then walk right in. "Oh my God."

"Jordan!" My mom springs away from my father and then pulls the sheet up over her face.

Mouth open, I shift my gaze over to my father. I can't believe this shit. "Dad?"

"Hey, baby." He cocks a smile. "Um, me and your mother are a little busy at the moment."

"Oh my God! Oh my God!" My mother grabs a pillow and piles it on top of her covered head. "My baby girl is going to think I'm a ho!"

"Nonsense," my father tries to reassure her.

"I . . . I was just about to leave," I stutter.

"So soon?" My father frowns. "But you just got here."

"Exactly," I say, still trying to take in the scene. "You surely didn't waste any time."

"What can I say? I still got the magic touch. Ain't that right, Sandra?"

"Does she still have the door open?" she croaks from behind the pillow. "Oh my God, I'm so humiliated."

"Now, baby. There's nothing to be ashamed of." Dad turns and tries to hug her through the piles of pillows.

"Don't worry. I'm leaving." I start backing out.

"I'll make sure your mother gets home okay," Dad volunteers.

Whatever. I keep backing up until I close the door to *The Twilight Zone.* When I finally turn to leave, Keston blocks my exit like a big brick wall. "Cool parents."

"It's not what it looks like."

His brows dip together. "Oh. Because it looks like they were fucking."

"Never mind. I don't have time to explain it." I march around him, suddenly needing some air. The crowd in the living room seems to have grown even larger. The music is bumping, and people are jamming all up on each other. Daddy and his boys really know how to throw a party.

"C'mon now. Are you going to make me chase you all the way out to your car?" he asks, following me. "I'm trying to apologize to you. And seeing how we're sort of like cousins, you'd think that you'd cut me a break."

"Cousins?" I turn on him. "Boy, I don't know you."

He shrugs. "Well, more like play cousins since my father is your uncle Mishawn. Sooo . . ."

· I laugh dead in his face. "I like your nerve."

He steps toward me, licking his bottom lip. "There's a helluva lot I like about you. The main thing being how fucking wet you get when I'm sucking on those fat titties."

I try to swallow but my mouth is fucking dry. *Goddamn. It's fucking hot in this bitch.*

He risks moving closer and linking his fingers through the belt loops on my shorts. "Stop playing hard to get. You've made your point. I fucked up. I'm sorry. Now how do we start this shit over, Jordan . . . Robyn . . . whatever the hell your name is?"

"Start over?" My gaze dips to his plump, juicy lips, and then my head starts filling up with all the nasty images from the night at the hotel.

"Surely you can give a brother a second chance."

"Robyn!"

I jump and swivel my head toward Uncle Mishawn.

"I brought you that burger you wanted."

He hands me a plate and then pinches my cheek. "Keston, you take care of my girl here. She's like family."

"I was just telling her that." He tosses me a wink and then cuts me a comical look that makes it almost impossible to stay mad at him.

"All right. All right. I give up," I say.

"Good. How about we find us a spot out on the lawn?"

I roll my eyes but there's a smile on my face as we thread our way through dancing bodies. At least the music has changed up from the seventies and skips to the nineties with Montell Jordan's "This Is How We Do It."

We find a pair of empty lawn chairs off in the corner of the backyard where a lot of kids are just running around in circles telling bad "your momma" jokes.

"Your momma's teeth are so yellow she spits butter," one boy spats.

"Your momma is so bald that you can see what's on her mind," a tough tomboy spats back.

Keston and I share a smirk as we settle into our chairs. "Kids," he says, shaking his head.

I roll my eyes. "Don't act like you ain't ever played that game."

"Who, me?" He presses a hand against his chest and tries to give me his puppy-dog look.

Laughing, I shake my head. "Innocent is not a look you can pull off."

"No?" Keston's dimples deepen. "Huh. I'm going to have to work on that."

For a few minutes we just sit there and grin at each other. I can't seem to stop the flow of memories of our one night together from crowding my head. That chest, those abs, those hips, and that fucking *dick*. I start to hand-fan myself, and Keston hops back up. "You hot? You want me to get you something to drink?"

I glance around. "Yeah. If you can sneak me a real beer, I'll owe you big."

"Cool." He winks. "And I'm going to hold you to that." He turns away, and I watch his fine ass as he walks away.

"Oh, Jesus." I start fanning myself and then notice that every woman in the yard is clocking his every move. When their gazes drift over to me, there is definitely haterade in the air. If I wasn't around, I get the distinct impression they'd be pushing a whole bunch of titties in Keston's face.

"Here you go." Keston hands over a cold Bud before settling back into his chair. "Sooo . . . why don't we back up since we put the cart before the horse last time? What's your story?"

"My story?" I ask before taking a big bite of my burger.

"Yeah, the woman with two names. I'm not even sure what the hell I'm supposed to be calling you."

"Jordan," I tell him. "Just my father and his friends call me Robyn."

"Why?"

I shrug. "Well, I was born Robyn Jordan Banks, but after my

mother married my stepfather, she had it legally changed to Jordan Hayes. It was probably done just to piss off my father."

"Ah. The games women play," he says, bobbing his head.

"Excuse you?"

"Nah. I'm just saying that . . . you know." He shrugs. "When shit doesn't work out with a female, it's always about getting revenge on a brother. And if there's a kid involved, fucking forget about it. Suddenly you can't come around unless there's an officer from the court around, or you got to sign over your whole paycheck for the next eighteen years just for the kid to be able to come around your people."

I cock my head at him. "Sounds like you're speaking from experience. You got kids?"

He shrugs. "One. A little girl. I ain't seen her since she was two years old. Her momma got pissed off because I cut her off."

"What? You stopped paying child support?"

"Nah. Nah. I cut off her dick payments. Shit wasn't working out anymore. I sat her down and told her that I'll always care for her but that I wasn't feeling it anymore. Shit. I thought I was doing the mature thing in just being up front with her. Right?"

"Were y'all married?"

"Engaged."

"For how long?"

He thought about it for a minute. "I don't know—about two years."

I nearly choked on my burger.

"What?"

"So you just had her playing house?"

"Nah. It wasn't nothing like that. . . . It just never felt right.

You know, we got engaged when she told me that she was pregnant, so I thought the thing to do was to propose and make our shit legit. But . . ."

"It never felt right," I help him out.

"Right." He shakes his head. "I guess you think that makes me some kind of asshole."

"I didn't say that."

"You didn't have to. It's written all over your face." He laughs. "Damn. Doesn't a brother get any brownie points for stepping to her and just telling her the deal? I wasn't cheating on her or nothing like that. I kept it real."

"Well kudos, I guess." Shaking my head, I take a deep pull from my bottle of beer.

"So let me guess. You would prefer for a man to just lie and stay in a relationship he knows ain't working?"

"I didn't say that."

"Like I said, you don't have to. Your face is about to twist off."

"Nah. It's just . . ." I bounce my shoulders. "It just seems that every dude I meet has all these kids and baby mommas everywhere. It's like an epidemic."

"Ahh." He leans back. "You're one of *those*. Are you about to start preaching now?"

"No, no. I'm just saying."

"What you saying? That you don't want to have my baby?" he challenges.

The question unexpectedly shuts me down, because the very idea of having this man's baby isn't a complete turnoff. "Look. Let's just squash this. I don't know what I'm saying."

"A'ight. Cool." He finally takes a bite of his own burger, and for a few minutes we just chill and watch folks dance and talk around the yard. When we finish eating our burgers and are just picking over the potato chips, Keston asks, "So what do you do?"

"For a living?"

He bobs his head.

I cock a smile because I know what's about to happen. "I'm in law enforcement."

His face falls. "No shit?"

"No shit. I'm a DEA agent."

"Whooo." He plops back in his chair and starts cracking up. "I wasn't expecting that shit. Motherfucking DEA?"

"Is that a problem?"

Still laughing, Keston shakes his head. "Nah. Nah. It's . . . uh . . . cool. I guess." He keeps going like he can't stop.

"You're sure? You're not involved in any illegal activities I should know about?"

"If I am, do you seriously think I'd sit out here and tell you about them?"

It's my turn to laugh. "No, I guess not." I rake my gaze over him again. Despite his thuggish good looks and tats, Keston still strikes me as not being all that he appears to be. "What about you? What do you do?"

"A little bit of this and a little bit of that," he answers with a smirk.

I cock my head. "Now that's not fair. I told you what I do for a living."

"Well, you'll know better next time." He laughs.

Uncle Mishawn tries to push another burger on us, but we wave the offer off and decide to join the people dancing in the living room. No surprise, Keston busts out some good moves that instantly get me hot, so I start freaking his ass right back. It doesn't even matter that we are doing this in my father's living room. We are in our own little world.

By the time R. Kelly's classic remix of "Bump 'N' Grind" comes on, I'm thinking that I could really fall for this guy. That shit is scary.

Chapter Eight

Two weeks later . . .

"Impossible?" Alvaro spats, glaring at Delmar. "I've been waiting weeks for you to get my drugs back and you tell me it's impossible?" he says, and then wipes the cocaine residue from beneath his nose.

"Alvaro—"

"Shut the fuck up!"

Delmar snaps his mouth shut and draws in a deep breath. For weeks now he had been plotting and planning on just how to get his boss's shipment back. It doesn't matter that their organization was back up and running in the three states the DEA hit. In fact, that had been the easy part. In the grand scheme of things, the busts are just mild hiccups considering the amount of weight they are moving day to day, week to week, and month to month. They were far from bankruptcy, but Alvaro refused to let it go. As far as he was concerned, the government's interference was a major slap in the face.

Slowly, Alvaro stands from behind his desk, clutching his 9 mm. What is left of Delmar's right ear starts tingling.

"Take a walk with me," Alvaro commands as he heads toward the back glass doors that lead to the pool area.

Delmar casts a worried look to the other men in the room, but they carefully ignore meeting his gaze. He has no choice but to push his fear aside and fall in lock step next to his old friend. Once they're outside, they walk slowly around the pool.

"You know . . . I don't like this word. Impossible." Alvaro sniffs. "No one should know this better than you, amigo."

"Yes, Alvaro, but—"

"No, no." He holds up a finger. "No buts. I don't like it. Telling me something is impossible is like telling me no. You know I don't like that either."

Delmar swallows nervously.

"I've been more than patient with you. It's been two weeks, and I still don't have my drugs back. Because we're friends, I feel comfortable telling you that you're starting to piss me off."

Delmar's ears start tingling again. "I'm sorry. That is not my intent."

"I should hope not. I'd hate to have the pool boy scoop you out of the pool tomorrow."

Delmar takes another deep breath. "Forgive me, old friend, but I'm just trying to point out the level of difficulty involved in stealing drugs from the DEA. It's nothing more than a suicide mission. All people within the agency keep telling me the same thing. Those headquarters are guarded too well. It'll be like breaking into Fort Knox."

Alvaro stops walking. "Are you telling me that you can't get my drugs back?" Alvaro's hard stare turns into black ice while he starts waving his gun around.

Once again, Delmar clamps his mouth shut and tries to prepare for either pain or death.

"It's protocol for the DEA to house or store the drugs until the trials, correct?"

"Yes, amigo. But like I said, those facilities are usually well guarded."

"But I imagine they would need all the drugs to be transferred to one location."

"Yes, but—"

"Has that already happened?"

"Well, I don't know."

"Don't you think you should find out? Because it seems to me that the best time to snatch back what is rightfully mine is to intercept the drugs during transport."

Delmar opens his mouth, but then quickly shuts it when he realizes that his stoned boss has actually made a valid point.

A wide, sinister smile creeps across Alvaro's thin lips. "You see, amigo? Nothing is impossible."

Delmar smiles, though he still has a bad feeling about this.

"Get on the phone, find when those drugs are going to be transported, how many cars are going to be guarding, and then hire the best people you can find and get me my *fucking* drugs."

Chapter Nine

K eston Bishop is hands down the best fucking lover I've ever had. I've never had a brother who brought his A-game every single time. I broke my own rules and allowed him to start spending the night at my place. I even let his ass have a small corner on the bathroom counter where he could leave his toothbrush, shaving cream, and electric razor. A few times, I've even got up in the morning and cooked his ass breakfast.

Me. I don't do that shit.

"Move your pussy over this way," Keston coaches after twisting my ass up like a pretzel and then hitting me off from the side. "Ah. Shit. That's it."

He ain't lying. He's hitting my spot so good that it feels like my pussy has turned into liquid candy. It doesn't matter because Keston is going to clean me up with that greedy-ass tongue of his after a while.

"Are you loving this shit, baby?" he asks above the sound of our bodies slapping together.

"Y-yeeessss." Shit. Doesn't he know it's hard for me to breathe?

"Then how come I don't hear you telling me how much you like this good dick?"

"Baby, I . . . I love this good dick."

"LOUDER!"

"I LOVE YOUR FUCKING DICK!"

"Now that's what a nigga likes to hear." His hips shift into overdrive, and he pounds me so deep into the mattress I'm going to start coughing up foam in a minute. I start to feel that familiar drop in my belly, and I try to hold my breath to prepare for this next orgasm, but there's just no way to prepare for this mother-fucker, which seems to explode everywhere, from my toes to the ends of my hair.

Behind me, Keston is chuckling about the amount of candy I'm coating that sweet dick with. When he releases my legs, I pop up and get on my job tongue-bathing him down. "Ssssss. Shit, baby." Like always, he brushes my hair out of my face so he can watch me work. It's all right. I like when he watches me. It feels like there's a spotlight on me and I'm working to impress.

Maybe it's in the back of my head that I don't want him to feel like he ever needs to sit me down and tell me that he's not feeling me anymore. I can see how a woman might go a little insane if she's told that she is being cut off from dick privileges with Keston. It's been only a couple of weeks and my ass is straight addicted. When we're not together, I'm constantly looking and checking my phone for calls or text messages. And if there's a night where he can't come over, I'm wondering why and whether there's another girl in the picture. That can be a strong possibility. I don't have any real claim on him, and, hell, it ain't like we ever had a conversation about the shit.

Sinking my head down as far as I can go on his cock, I squeeze the muscles at the back of my throat for as hard and long as I can. Keston tenses up while the head of his cock starts pulsing and drizzling precum down my throat. I want him to lose it and blast off, but he's not finished playing with me, so he pulls out and rubs his wet dick all over my mouth.

"What's your rush, baby? We have all night." He slaps me on the back of my ass and then lays down flat. "C'mon, Agent Hayes. Climb on up here and twerk that fat ass on this dick you claim to love so much."

I climb up into the backward cowgirl position, taking my time burying that thick, silky pole of his into my still-creaming pussy. Inch by inch, I swear to God I'm falling deeper in love. When I reach the base, I take a few seconds to rotate my hips to adjust.

Keston hisses and settles his hands on the bottom of my ass. "Twerk it, baby."

"Like this, baby?" I lean forward and squeeze one ass muscle at a time to make it pop. "You like that, Daddy?"

"Fuck. You know I do." He slaps my ass. "Keep it going."

Pop. Bounce. Pop. Bounce.

His hissing grows louder, so I speed it up.

Pop. Bounce. Pop. Bounce.

"Hold on. Hold on," he says, trying to control this situation.

But I want him out of control—sort of how he does me when he unleashes that fat tongue of his on my pussy. I want him to cum when I want him to cum.

Pop. Bounce. Pop. Bounce.

"Ahhh. Wait."

Pop. Bounce. Pop. Bounce.

"Jor—dan." His toes start curling.

Pop. Bounce. Pop. Bounce.

"FUCK!" Roaring like a lion, Keston's hands clamp down hard on my hips. He cums so hard that I can feel his hot cum seep out the front of my pussy. "Shit."

I start to climb off him, but he stops me. "Don't move. Shit. Please don't move. You got my shit all sensitive."

I laugh because I know he's just mocking me. That's what I usually say when he has worn me out. I roll off of him, give him a quick peck on the cheek, and head off to the shower. A minute later, he's in there helping me scrub my back and a few other places. But being naked around each other can last only so long. Somewhere in between the second rinse cycle and splashing on some baby oil, Keston has me pressed up against the bathroom tile, trying to blow my back out.

Whatever vitamins this brother is on, I hope that he never stops taking them. Not to mention he has the sexiest fuck faces I've ever seen. He always bites his lower lip and stretches his upper lip so high it touches his nose. And when he starts growling, I always start cumming.

"Take this dick. Take this dick."

"Give it to me. Give it to me."

My shower proves to be too small to do all we want, so we return to the bed, dripping wet and still a little soapy. But at some point I black out and then wake hours later snuggled under him and the room dark. It's so comfortable, lying pressed against him like this, that I find myself hoping that I'm not just living some brief fantasy that's going to vanish as fast as it appeared.

"Are you awake?"

I jump at the sound of his deep voice and then laugh at myself.

"I'm going to take that as a yes." Keston chuckles and then plants a kiss at the back of my head. "Good. Now that you're awake, maybe I can get some sleep. It was a little hard to do with all that snoring you do."

"What? I don't snore."

"I don't know who told you that bullshit." He chuckles, pulling me close. "Baby girl, you be mowing down some serious trees. For real."

My face is blazing with embarrassment. "Stop lying." I reach back and smack him on the leg. "Why the fuck you playing me like that?"

Keston's chest rumbles and shakes the bed. "Settle down, Ma. It ain't like I brought up all those silent-but-deadly fart bombs you be letting go in the middle of the night."

"WHAT?" I grab a pillow and whip around and smack him dead in the face. "Stop lying."

Keston cracks up, putting up very little defense as I hammer his head.

"Take it back," I demand, even though I'm laughing as hard as he is. "Take it back."

He holds out as long as he possibly can before finally throwing up his hands. "All right. All right. I take it back." He wrestles the pillow out of my hands. "It looks like someone can't take a joke."

"I can take a joke. That just wasn't funny." I mush him on the head.

"I don't know. I was laughing." He rolls me beneath him and then starts raining kisses all around my neck. "Damn, girl. I just can't get enough of you."

A lazy smile floats across my face while his large hands drift farther down my body. Just when I think he's about to peel me open again, I hear a cell phone ring. The kissing stops as we both groan and pull apart.

"Is that you or me?" I ask, rolling toward the right side of the bed.

"I think it's me," Keston answers, leaning over the bed and swooping up his pants to grab his cell phone. He takes a quick look at his caller ID and huffs out a long breath. "I gotta roll."

"Now?" I frown as I watch him climb out of the bed.

"Afraid so." He jumps into his boxers and jeans so quick I'm wondering if there's a fire somewhere he has to put out. "Sorry, baby. Maybe we can hook up tomorrow night or this weekend."

"But . . . I don't understand. What's so important that you have to leave at . . . three o'clock in the morning?"

"Business."

"Business?" I cock my head. "What kind of business?"

Keston jams his T-shirt over his head and then grabs his white Nikes. "Just business, baby girl." He leans over. "Give me a kiss so I can run." I hesitate, so he kisses me instead and even tweaks a nipple. "I'll catch up with you later." He bolts for the bedroom door.

Stunned, I sit in bed for a moment, but then I hop out of bed naked to storm after him. "KESTON!"

"I got to go, baby," he says, still not breaking his stride.

"Fine. Go. But you can still tell me what kind of business you have to take care of in the middle of the night."

"Look, baby. We can talk about it another time." He opens the front door. "I promise." He turns to me and kisses me again.

"Later." He races outside and hops into his chromed out black Escalade.

I'm stuck holding the door and watching him as he pulls out of the driveway. I have a bad feeling about this. And when I get those feelings, I'm never wrong.

"Shit. I knew his ass is too good to be true."

Chapter Ten

"Cancer?" Jonathan's fingers slip on the button of his shirt as he stares at Dr. Ryan. "Are you sure?"

"I'm afraid so," he says, and then returns to pointing at the X-rays on a light board. "I'm also sorry to tell you that . . . it's inoperable."

Jonathan's shock widens.

"Maybe if we had caught it a year ago, we may have stood a chance."

Jonathan nods while the backs of his eyes begin to sting. "I understand. How long?"

The doctor pauses for a second and then pulls in a deep breath. "I don't know. It could be anywhere from six months to a year." He clicks off the light board. "I'm sorry, Mr. Banks. Is there anyone here with you today that you need for me to talk to?"

"No. No, I came by myself today." He clears his throat and resumes buttoning up his shirt. "Thank you, Doctor."

"Again, I'm sorry." The doctor turns away and leaves him to finish getting dressed.

Six months to a year.

That shit keeps replaying in his mind while he drives his '98 Cadillac back to his crib. That and a long list of regrets. The number one being that he never married his childhood sweetheart. Now he doubted whether her divorce would even be finalized before he kicked the bucket. Instead of going straight home, Jonathan stops by Opulence jewelry and starts looking at rings. Even the smallest thing he can find has a price tag that could choke a horse.

"Is there anything I can help you with, sir?"

Jonathan shakes his head. "Nah, nah. I was just looking." He turns and heads out of the store. However, the rings are still on his mind two hours later when his buddies show for their poker game.

On the television, reports of the Jackal striking again runs on the ticker tape on CNN. Shaking his head, Jonathan shuts it off.

"Can you believe that cat? Stealing all our moves?" Mishawn asks, running a hand through his thinning gray hair.

"You know what they say: imitation is the sincerest form of flattery." Jonathan cocks a smile and starts dealing out the cards.

"That's just bullshit," Mishawn huffs. "How come they can't get their own moves? Using our calling card with the jack of spades. C'mon, son."

Jonathan laughs. "This shit is really getting to you, huh?"

"I can't believe that it's not bothering you guys. We're talking about our reputations here," Mishawn says.

Rawlo finally jumps in, shrugging his large shoulders. "Aw. It's no big deal. It's like Jonathan says: At least this dude or dudes aren't just doing those smash-and-grabs. These cats are hitting them where they live—in those big vaults. Shit. Ten million here.

Twenty million over there. These muthafuckas are stacking some serious bank."

Jonathan laughs as he tosses back a long swig of beer. "Yeah. They didn't have that kind of dough back in the day. I remember that one bank we hit out in Rochester, New York, and all that motherfucker had in it was like twenty grand. Big-ass double-steel motherfucker and it just had some damn chump change jiggling around in it. Y'all remember that shit?"

Everyone's head bobs at the table except for Tremaine.

Jonathan slaps his cards facedown on the table and rolls his eyes. "TREMAINE!"

Tremaine glances up.

"Turn your damn hearing aid up!"

He frowns. "What?"

"TURN UP YOUR FUCKING HEARING AID!"

"Oh, wait. Let me turn up my hearing aid." Tremaine reaches behind his ear and fiddles with the volume. After a loud piercing sound, he asks, "Now what are you guys talking about?"

"Nothing. Forget about it," Jonathan huffs while Rawlo and Mishawn crack up.

"Then why in the hell did you tell me to turn up my hearing aid? Shit. I gotta concentrate so I can win back some of my money. I got doctor bills, you know."

The boys laugh at him.

Jonathan takes in the scene with a dose of nostalgia. Damn. When did they all get so old? They are all gray-haired. One is blind, one is deaf, one is morbidly obese, and one is dying of cancer. Is this how he'd pictured their golden years? Day after day, playing poker and eating chips? How sad.

"Sooo . . . how are things with you and Sandra?" Rawlo asks, changing the subject.

That pulls Jonathan out of his depression. "Good. Good. We're taking things day by day."

"So are you two officially back together?"

"I like to think so, even though she's still dealing with some un-finished shit with that asshole she married."

"Divorce?" Rawlo asks.

"Fingers crossed."

"Then are you going to make an honest woman out of her?"

Jonathan nods and hopes that no one notices the tears gathering in his eyes. *Six months to a year.*

"Are you going to play?" Mishawn asks Jonathan over the thick rims of his glasses.

"Oh. Sorry. I'll bet ten," he says, and moves two red chips forward. "Can I ask you guys something?"

"Shoot," Rawlo says, and then adds, "I'll call."

"Do you guys ever regret retiring when we did?"

"Hell, yeah." Mishawn tosses down his cards. "I fold."

"If I remember correctly—and I believe I do—you were the one who gave everyone their pink slips," Rawlo reminds him. "Your turn."

"I know. I know." Jonathan shrugs. "I guess what I'm getting at is do you guys ever miss it? The danger? The adrenaline?"

"Don't forget the money," Rawlo and Mishawn echo at the same time and then laugh.

Tremaine turns up his hearing aid again. "What's so funny? What did I miss?"

Mishawn leans over. "Jonathan is asking whether we ever miss being the Jackal."

"Oh, hell yeah!" Tremaine grins. "It was the only damn thing I was ever good at, and it beats the hell out of what we do now. No offense, guys. I call."

"No offense taken," Rawlo says. "I know exactly what you mean. Hell. If I knew the cost of living was going to spike like it has, I would have stacked a little more cash instead of spending most of mine on bitches and hos. Now my monthly pharmacy bill runs more than my rent."

"Hear, hear," Mishawn and Tremaine cosign.

"And let's not forget doctor visits. Between copay, coinsurance, and deductibles, I feel like I'm the one being robbed," Rawlo finishes.

Everyone grumbles and bobs their head again.

Jonathan sets his cards down on the table. "Then why don't we do something about it?"

The boys freeze while their eyes roll toward Jonathan.

"Do something like what?" Rawlo asks.

Jonathan can't stop the smile spreading across his face. "Do something like . . . get back into the game. Why not? One last score."

Four sets of eyes start shifting around the table.

"What? What's the problem?"

"The problem," Tremaine says slowly, starting to crack up, "is that we're old. Just look at us. We're not exactly as quick and nimble as we used to be. Every twenty minutes, Rawlo has to take a piss, Mishawn can't see for shit, my hearing is shot, and arthritis is wearing all our asses out."

"I didn't say there wouldn't be some . . . challenges." Jonathan pumps his shoulders. "I was just thinking that it would be . . . kind of fun."

The boys fall silent while they shuffle poker chips around.

"Ain't nothing wrong with a little fun every now and then," Rawlo says, and then slowly Mishawn's and Tremaine's heads start to nod.

"What are you thinking about hitting?"

A big smile spreads across Jonathan's face. "I have this one jewelry store in mind."

Chapter Eleven

In a nice suburb in Gwinnett County, the DEA, along with the local police department, move in on a two-story brick McMansion. With the agents' shields up and guns pointed, Elliott barks out the command, "Everybody get down on the floor!"

Two large brothers in the living room reach for their weapons and come up shooting. Before I can squeeze off a shot, the sound of a baby crying catches my ear. I pivot and sure enough there is a woman standing behind us holding a baby with one hand and a .38 in the other. "Put down your weapon!"

The woman doesn't even seem to be concerned about her child as she squeezes off a shot. The bullet goes wild, but I aim for her left shoulder and pull the trigger. The woman jerks back, drops the baby, and smashes into the wall. I don't know why this crazy shit always surprises me, but it does.

When the action calms down, we make seven arrests and find drugs stashed everywhere—the couches, the freezer, the mattresses, and even in the toy bins. This shit doesn't make any sense.

"Cheer up," Elliott says, noting my long face. "It's not like you shot the baby."

"Yeah. I know. Not that his momma gave a damn." Which is true. At no point when she was screaming and yelling about what sons of bitches we were had she inquired about the safety of her child, who was steadily screaming at the top of his lungs. We couldn't even get an answer out of her on who we should call to come and take care of the baby, so Family and Children Services were called.

Much later, we stroll into Flint's to toss back a few much-needed whiskeys, and I find myself questioning how much longer I can actually do this fucking job.

"Why are you so quiet?" Elliott asks, already looking a bit tipsy.

I shrug my shoulders. "Just thinking."

"About?"

Drawing a deep breath, I turn and look him straight in the eye. "About whether it's time for me to hang up my boots."

Elliott's face twists with surprise. "Are you fucking kidding me?"

"No," I say, shaking my head.

"C'mon, Hayes. It was just a bad day."

"I'm starting to have a lot of bad days. And that can't be good." I feel a little better getting that off my shoulders. "I think it's time to start looking into something a little less stressful."

Elliott keeps shaking his head as Mitch sets another drink down in front of us. "You're trippin'. You're an adrenaline junkie like the rest of us. We either do this or join the military to be shipped out to Afghanistan. We're not the kind of people who can just settle for a nine-to-five. We need excitement."

"I don't know. It's all starting to feel hopeless to me. The more drugs and criminals we take off the street, the more there are to take their place. It's an endless cycle. The war on drugs is a joke, man."

"And what are our options? To fucking give up? Make all the shit legal so crackheads and junkies can take over? You really think that's the answer?"

I shake my head.

"So what are you saying?"

"I don't know. I just fucking know that I'm getting tired of this bullshit." I toss back my shot and then relish the burn. "I need a break from dodging bullets."

"Then you're in luck. Tomorrow we're babysitting a transport down to Columbus. Should be a walk in the park."

"Oh, goody-goody. I get to sit and listen to you bump your gums in a car for about six hours."

"Damn. You really are in a pissy mood." He cocks a slick smile at me. "Does that mean that things between you and Mr. Thug ain't working out too good?"

"Get your nose out of my business, Elliott."

"What?" He chuckles. "Clearly something ain't right. I'm just trying to figure out what it is. I share shit with you."

"Oh, yeah. About that: stop."

Elliott throws his head back and laughs. "That's fucked up, partner. Fucked up." He turns toward Aaron and Eric. "Y'all hear my partner over here?"

"What's up?" Eric asks, switching stools so he can flank my left side.

"Jordan still thinks it's cool for her to listen and chuck in her two cents when it comes to other people's private business, but she wants to keep her shit under lock and key."

Eric shrugs. "Same old, same old. She's been doing that shit for years. Why is that bothering you now?"

"Thank you, Eric," I say.

"Oh, I ain't saying that it's right. I'm just saying that you do it. You always keep one foot in and one foot out of the boys' club."

"No. The problem is that y'all bitches gossip like teenagers. And since I don't want my business all over the department, I'd rather keep my rat trap shut."

"Fine. You don't want to tell details—you can be general. Like, are you still seeing old dude? We got a pool going."

"What?"

"Don't worry," Elliott says. "I've already lost. I thought ole boy was just going to be a one nighter. He didn't look like a deep conversationalist. Were those prison tats all over his body?"

"No, they weren't prison tats, asshole."

He shrugs me off. "I think Aaron has you down for three weeks. So if you can hang in there until this weekend, he'll win about fifty bucks."

Aaron glances around Elliott's shoulder and gives me a sheepish smile. "I'll split it with you if you want."

I look over at Eric. "And what did you pick?"

"I gave y'all a week."

"I don't believe you guys."

"What are you getting so mad about? You made some bets in the past. It's not like we're so far off base here. I mean, what is the longest relationship you've ever been in?"

"None of your fucking business."

"So hostile. You ever think about going to anger management?"

Instead of responding, I flash them my two middle fingers and tell them, "And rotate."

"It's not your fault," Elliott continues. "Children of divorce usually have trouble with intimacy. I read that somewhere."

"I don't believe I'm having this conversation."

"I think it's true."

"For your information, smart-ass, my parents were never married."

"Oooh." They all twist their faces like they're sucking on lemons.

"What?"

"That's even worse," Aaron chimes in.

"You know what? Fuck y'all and the horses you rode in on. Why the fuck should I be listening to y'all anyway? None of you are with anybody either."

"My parents divorced," Elliott admits.

"Mine too," Aaron says.

"Me three," Eric pipes in.

"Fuck." I hop off the stool and drop a twenty on the bar. "Keep the change, Mitch."

The boys just laugh at me behind my back. "All right. I guess this means that you'll just miss out on our vast knowledge about relationships."

"Thank God," I shout, and storm out of the bar. Before heading home, I decide to swing by my father's place. He had mentioned having a doctor's appointment, plus my uncles would be there. Perhaps I can interrogate Uncle Mishawn about his son. It's a little sneaky but probably worth it.

I knock and wait while I hear things being moved around on the other side of the door. *What the hell are they doing?* When Dad finally answers the door, he looks a bit sweaty and out of breath.

"Hey, Daddy. What are y'all doing in here?" I have to push on the door, because it looks like he isn't about to invite me in.

"Oh, nothing." He glances over his shoulder and then finally steps back to allow me in.

Frowning at his odd behavior, I step inside and glance at the dining room table where my three play uncles are sitting around with their cards and poker chips. Still something seems a bit odd about their behavior. "Is everything all right?"

"Oh, yeah. Everything is fine." Dad smiles broadly.

I glance back at the table.

"Great," Rawlo says, giving me the okay sign.

"Wonderful," Mishawn adds.

"Couldn't be better." Tremaine grins even though his hearing aid is whistling loud enough to wake the dead.

"Well," Dad says, grabbing me by the arm. "If that's all, we need to get back to our game." He starts to shove me back out the door.

"Whoa. Wait a minute." I snatch my arm free. "Why are you trying to get rid of me?"

My father's face almost turns into the color of eggplant. "What? No. I just thought that . . . you know, that you had to go."

"Uh-huh." I move past him and head over to the dining room table. Everyone suddenly sits up straighter and flashes me wobbly smiles. *They are definitely up to something.* "Sooo . . . who's winning?"

"Huh?" Tremaine asks.

"Uncle Tremaine, I think you need to turn your hearing aid down a bit."

"Oh, yeah. Right. Hold on." He rubs his finger behind his ear until the whistling stops.

I cast my gaze around the table and notice that everyone is trying their damnedest not to look me in the eyes. "Uh-huh." Lastly, I turn toward my father as he takes his seat at the table. "Sooo . . . how was your doctor's visit today?"

His eyes fall as well. "Fine."

My heart skips a beat. "What did the doctor say?"

"Nothing." He clears his throat. "I'm as healthy as a horse." He flashes a fake smile at me, and I weigh whether I should press him for an honest answer, but there is a chance that he just doesn't want to discuss this in front of his friends, so I decide to let it go— for now.

The table is quiet, and no one seems to be in any hurry to resume the game. "Mind if I join in?"

"What?" My father finally looks up at me. "You know the rules. No women allowed."

"That's a stupid rule." I notice a notepad on the floor. "Oh, Uncle Mishawn, you dropped something." I go to pick it up, but Mishawn moves faster than I've seen him move in years to swoop down and pick it up.

"I got it."

"What is it?"

"Nothing." His magnified eyes blink up at me.

I can't help but laugh. "It's clearly something, Uncle Mishawn. Let me see it."

"No. It's . . . personal."

"Personal?" My gaze moves around the table again. Everyone still avoids my gaze.

"Okay. I'm not stupid. You guys are up to something. You might as well tell me now."

"There you go," my father says, throwing up his hands. "Always suspicious, just like your mother. That's why no women are allowed to play—you always just mother hen us to death."

"All right. All right." I throw up my hands too. "You guys don't want me around. I can take a hint. I'll go."

It might just be me, but they all suddenly look relieved.

"I guess . . . I'll just call and check on you a little later," I tell my dad.

He bobs his head, gets back up from the table, and starts escorting me toward the door.

"You guys stay out of trouble."

"Who, us? Get into trouble? Why would we get into trouble?" they chime awkwardly together. So much so that it causes the hair on the back of my neck to sit up and my eyes to narrow.

"You sure you guys aren't up to something?"

"Nope. Just playing poker," Rawlo says.

"Yeah. It's not like we're sitting up here trying to figure out how to rob a bank or anything," Uncle Tremaine spouts.

Everyone's head turns toward him.

"What? I just meant it as a joke." He shrugs.

"Ooookay." I look at my dad but he's waving off the comment.

"Don't pay Tremaine any mind. You know he has a warped sense of humor." He takes me by the arm and firmly ushers me out the door.

"I . . . I guess I'll just call you later," I tell him.

"All right. Talk to you later. Bye." He slams the door in my face.

What the fuck?

Chapter Twelve

After my father slams his door in my face, I figure I'll go check on my mother. Things have been a little weird between us since the barbeque. I didn't know whether I should ask if there's something going on with her and my dad or if she's going to try and wait it out with my stepdad. However, the minute I enter the house and have to duck from a vase hurtling toward the door, I think I have my answer.

What the fuck?

"GET OUT!" my mother screams at the top of her lungs.

"Mom?"

"Sandra, please just let me talk to you for a minute," George pleads.

"I DON'T WANT TO HEAR ANYTHING YOU HAVE TO SAY!"

I rush into the living room to see my mom snatch up another crystal vase.

"HOW COULD YOU?" She sends the vase flying at my step-dad, who shows remarkable ability to duck out of the way. "YOU'RE NOTHING BUT A FUCKING LIAR!"

"Mom, what's going on?" I rush over to her and try to shield her just in case George charges. Of course, I've never seen him do such a thing, but then again I've never seen my mother this angry either.

"Sandra, baby. Please just let me explain."

"Explain what? That for most of our marriage you had a second family living on the other side of town that you've been supporting with *our* money?"

"What?" I turn my stunned gaze toward my stepfather, who was definitely no player. If anything, he looked like a dull-as-dishwater accountant.

"Yes, George. Tell Jordan here about all her secret brothers and sisters that you've conveniently forgot to mention."

"Sandra, baby. I know that you're upset."

"You're fucking right I'm upset." She tugs in a deep breath. "Here I thought all these years that I married a good, respectable, and *settled* man only to find out that he's been making a fool out of me for twenty-five years."

"Is this true, George?" I ask.

He hedges. "I'm sorry," he says almost pleadingly. "I didn't mean to hurt anyone. It just . . . happened."

"And when were you going to tell me about it? Why did I have to find out about it through a private detective?"

"You hired a private detective?"

"I knew something was going on. It only took me TWENTY-FIVE YEARS to figure it out."

I turn and wrap my arms around my mother. "Calm down."

"No. No." She pushes her way out of my arms. "Tell her. Tell

Jordan how many children you have by that home-wrecking bitch!"

George blinks guiltily at me. "Six." He clears his throat. "I have six children by Lynette."

"HOW DARE YOU SAY THAT BITCH'S NAME IN MY HOUSE!" Another vase is picked up and thrown.

George ducks, but a little too late and he gets whacked right in the forehead. He's knocked backward and hits the floor with a loud *thump*!

"Mom!"

"FUCK HIM."

"George . . . I think you should go," I tell him, still trying to hold my mother back.

He pulls himself off the floor. "Look. I know this hurts, but the fact is that me and your mother were never able to have children of our own. And we've tried."

"So that makes it cool for you to go knock up another bitch?" I ask, trying to follow his reason.

"No. It's just that . . . Look. I love you, Jordan. But the fact of the matter is, you're someone else's daughter. And every time I look at you, that's who I see."

"Wait." I stop him. "Now this shit is my fault?"

"Oh, it's everybody's fault," my mother hollers. "Except the motherfucker who can't keep his dick in his pants. GET OUT!"

He opens his mouth to say something, but now I'm tired of him too. "George, leave."

George's face falls.

"And I want a fucking divorce! Since there's nothing keeping us together, you can just go marry Ms. Loose Pussy who you've been taking care of all these damn years."

"George, please. Just go."

He actually looks remorseful, but I can't begin to understand this mess he's made of their marriage. And I doubt after he walks out of that door that I'll even try.

"All right. I'll go."

"And don't bring your sorry ass back here!"

George's gaze drifts back over to me, but he finally turns and heads for the door. Once we hear the front door slam, my mother completely falls apart.

"It's going to be all right," I whisper, wrapping my arms back around her.

"No. It's not. I wasted all those years."

"Shhh. All we can do is move forward," I tell her. "If you need to cry, just get it all out."

My mother hangs on to me. "I should have married your father. He was the only man who truly loved me. He still loves me."

I can't help but smile. There's still that part of me that wants my parents to get together. Later, after serving her half a pot of chamomile tea, running her a bubble bath, and putting her to bed, I clean up all the broken glass in the house and finally head back to my place. During the drive, I can't help but think about my jacked-up family and wonder if Elliott and the boys had a point.

Do children from broken marriages have a disadvantage when it comes to developing relationships? I didn't tell my partner what my longest relationship was because I don't know. Two months? Three?

I park in my driveway and shut off the engine. I sit there for a

while thinking. Is there something really there between Keston
and me, or is it just lust and a warm body in the bed? Do either of
us even have a clue as to what we're doing?

I scoop my cell phone out of my pocket. No missed calls. No
text messages. For all I know, I'm just a booty call to him. Drawing
in a deep breath, I climb out of my vehicle. However, I freeze the
minute I enter the house and the scent of roses catches my attention.

"Surprise," Keston says, standing up from the dining room
table. "I was just thinking that this was going to turn into dinner
for one."

I close the door behind me, and after picking my mouth up off
the floor, I have to ask, "How did you get in here?"

"I have my ways." His sexy-ass dimples wink at me.

"I don't believe this." I move closer to the twinkling candle-
light.

Keston clears his throat. "I figured that we've moved to a point
in our relationship where I can show you how I throw down in the
kitchen."

"So your skills extend farther than a grill?"

"What can I say? My mother raised me right."

Still smiling, I set my duffel bag down on the couch and then
peel out of my DEA-embossed jacket before I head over to the
table. "I ain't going to lie. It smells good. What is it?"

"Chicken marsala. Do you like Italian?"

I don't think my smile can stretch any wider. "I love Italian."

"Perfect." He leans over and captures my lips in a kiss.

Oh. He's pulling out all the stops. "Let me just go wash up and
I'll be right back."

"Need any help?"

"No. If you go back there in that room with me, our food is going to get *really* cold."

"All right, then. You better hurry up." He pops me on my ass and sends me on my way.

I take a quick ten-minute shower and change into my one black dress. Keston whistles the moment I walk into the room.

"Turn around and let me see you." He holds up my hands so I can spin around. "Hot damn. Our dinner still might get cold," he says, pulling me close.

I laugh and push him away. "I would have never pegged you as a romantic."

"As long as you keep that shit between us, it's all good."

"What? Afraid someone is going to ask you for your player's card?"

"Hell, yeah. A brother always has to take that shit serious. Once it's gone, you can't get it back."

We share a laugh as I run my hands down the hard muscles of his chest.

"Hungry?" he asks.

"Depends on whether we're talking about food." My hands drift lower and brush against the hard length running down his leg.

"Mmmm. Dessert comes later." He winks and then turns to pull out a chair for me. "After you."

Blushing like a schoolgirl, I ease into the chair. Slow jams on the stereo, flowers, and white wine—it looks like Keston has gone all out to make this a special night. I'm simply blown away because I've never had anyone go through so much trouble.

"You're going to fuck up and make a bitch fall in love."

"Maybe that's the goal."

I cock my head and try to weigh whether he's serious, but Keston has a serious poker face that I haven't been able to crack yet.

"What, you ain't never had a brother treat you like the dime that you are?"

"Will it make me look pathetic if I say no?"

He shakes his head. "It just makes me incredibly lucky."

"Boy, you really know how to turn on the charm." I reach for my glass of wine. "I'm trying to feel you out."

"There's nothing to it. I'm just a brother that's feeling you. Ain't nothing wrong with that, is there?"

"No." I hold his gaze. "Do you think all this means that we're not going to discuss what it is that you do for a living?"

"Is that still bothering you?"

"Only when you have to sneak out of my bedroom at three in the morning."

He leans back in his chair. "I don't recall me 'sneaking.' I seem to remember telling you that I had to go."

I nod. "All right. Since you're being up front and honest, what do you do for a living, Mr. Bishop?"

His lips curl. "I'm not at liberty to say at this time."

Surprised, I blink at him. "What kind of shitty answer is that?"

"It's just the truth, babe. The real question is whether you can deal with that."

"What if I say no?"

"Then we have ourselves a real problem."

I reach for my glass of wine and try to stare him down, but his poker face never changes. "Do we have a problem?"

I glance down at my half-eaten meal and my glass of wine before making a decision. "I guess not."

His sexy dimples return, and the next thing I know we're in the middle of the living room floor—him trying to blow out my back and me scratching his.

"After tonight, baby, you belong to me. You got that? This pussy is mine. Don't you give this pussy to no other nigga, you hear me?"

"N-no." Hell, I would agree to give him my soul as long as he doesn't stop stroking me so deep.

"I knew your ass was the one for me the minute I laid eyes on you," he whispers raggedly. He reaches up and tilts my chin toward him. "Look at me."

In between my sighs and moans, I manage to peel my eyes open and meet his intense gaze. "From now on, whenever we're making love, I want you to look at me. You hear me?"

I nod.

"Aw. Shit. This pussy is so tight." His hips pick up speed. "You feel me girl?"

"Yes."

"I don't fucking hear you."

"YES!"

"That's right, baby. All this shit is yours. Any time you want it." He drops his head and pulls a nipple into his mouth. "Are these titties mine, baby?"

"Yes," I pant.

"I can have them any time I want them?"

"Aw. Fuck yes."

He hooks my legs high over his shoulders and drills me until the bottom of my pussy falls out. After that, I'm sure my ass is straight talking in tongues. He has taken me to a whole new level. Yesterday, I would've bet cash money that I was just in love with his dick and mad head game, but today I believe I'm falling in love with the man.

After watching my mother fall apart today, I know that nothing can fuck a bitch up more than falling in love.

Chapter Thirteen

The next morning I wake up with the sound of birds chirping outside my window. I smile and roll over in bed only to find that I'm in that bitch by myself again. *What the fuck?* I sit up, turn my head, and breathe a sigh of relief when I see there is no money left on the nightstand. Still I'll be hurt if Keston crept out of here again in the middle of the night.

I climb out of bed and wrap the top sheet around my body and then go and see if he's really gone. He isn't in the bathroom, so I storm down the hall. I start to call out his name and then stop abruptly outside my home office.

"What are you doing?" I ask.

Keston hits a key and hops up from my laptop. "Oh, morning. You're up."

"Are you looking at my stuff?"

"What? No. I was just checking something out online," he says before spreading on a smile. "You're up early."

"The bed was empty."

"Sorry about that." He walks over to me and wraps his arms

around my waist. "I didn't think that you'd miss me. Did you have fun last night, baby?" He dips his head and nuzzles kisses down the side of my neck.

"Yeah," I answer while fighting like hell not to melt into his arms. I'm not quite sure that I buy his explanation.

"C'mon. Why don't we take a shower together and then maybe afterward I can fix you some breakfast?"

"Ah. The cooking spree continues."

"I'm still trying to impress you," he says. "C'mon."

My eyes fall back to my laptop, and I have to fight the urge to just run over there and double-check behind him.

"What's the matter, baby?"

I tilt my chin up at him.

"You're acting like you don't trust me."

My stomach muscles clench into a tight knot. Now that the romantic glow from last night has dimmed some, I'm struggling against my basic instincts to not trust anyone.

Keston whispers, "Come on. How about that shower?" He kisses me again until I can slowly feel my defenses melt away. *Maybe I'm just being paranoid.*

I allow him to take me by the hand and lead me back to the shower where we play just as much as we try to get clean. After that, I really don't have too much time for breakfast or I'm going to be late for work.

"Are you sure?" Keston checks. "It's just going to take a few seconds for me to scramble us up something," he asks while grabbing his things as well.

"No. That's all right. I'll just pick up some coffee on the way into the office."

He bobs his head, and together we walk out of my house and lock the door. "You know, you never did tell me how you got into my house," I remind him as I hop into my SUV.

"What? You think your dad is the only one who knows how to get around alarm systems?"

My heart drops for a second, but then I remember that with him being Mishawn's son, of course he'd know all about the Jackal. "All right, then. How about you put your stalker tendencies on ice and only enter my apartment when I open the door?"

He stretches his brows. "I think I can do that."

"Good."

I smile. "See you later tonight?"

"Sounds like a date. I might even take you to one of those fancy restaurants downtown."

"Oooh. I get to put on some more girlie clothes." I wink.

"Yeah. As long as dresses are as short and tight as the one you wore last night."

"You got it. Can I drop you off somewhere?"

"No. My car is just up the block. I'll see you tonight." He leans into the SUV and plants a soft kiss on my lips.

I sigh and breathe him in. "See you tonight." I pull out of my driveway. My smile remains in place for a few blocks while I replay last night in my head. Yesterday was bad but last night was beautiful.

"I don't fucking believe it," Elliott says, tapping his watch. "You're actually two minutes late."

"Bullshit." I glance at my watch but see he's right. "What the fuck ever. What are you going to do, write me up?"

"Ah. I see it's going to be that kind of morning."

"What, the kind where you work my last nerve?" I ask, laughing.

"Aw, shit. Is that a glow I see?" Elliott starts shooting an invisible gun at me. "I guess that means that you and the thug kissed and made up?"

"Fuck you very much and stay out of my business. We got transport duty, right?"

"Yep." He sighs and pushes off his desk. "It's you and me and our boys Eric and Aaron."

"The four amigos." I suck in a long breath. "All right, let's get down to the evidence department. The faster we get there, the faster we can get back."

"Go on ahead. I'll meet you down there. I just have to make a quick call."

I tap my watch. "Make it snappy." I laugh and walk off. Halfway to the evidence department, I catch up with Aaron and Eric.

"Yo, Hayes. What's up?" Eric says, giving me daps.

"I'm hanging in there," I tell them. "Who volunteered us for this babysitting job?"

Aaron laughs. "Hell, I thought you did."

"Hell no. I'd rather kick in doors than have to listen to Elliott try to sing along with the radio for hours on end."

"Then it must have been your partner because it certainly wasn't us."

We make it over to the evidence department in time to see Agents Peterson and Jeffries sign out the department's record bust of cocaine while a team from the tech department loads up the van.

"Is everybody ready to rock and roll?" Aaron asks, sliding on his shades.

Peterson and Jeffries turn and start exchanging daps. "So you guys are our babysitters today?"

"Yep. We're just waiting on my partner," I say.

"The wait is over," Elliott announces, strolling up behind us. "Let's do this."

I turn toward him and slip on my shades. "You drive."

Jeffries and Peterson climb into the black van while Elliott and I climb into one black Taurus and Aaron and Eric hop into another. The minute we pull off from headquarters, I ease my seat back and kick my feet up on the dashboard.

"Comfortable?" Elliott laughs.

"Just drive. I didn't get that much sleep last night." I clear my throat. "I figured that you would understand."

"Aw, shit. Was that a snippet about somebody's sex life, Ms. I-Don't-Kiss-and-Tell?"

"Fuck you, Elliott."

"Nah. Nah. You had your chance, but no. You're into thugs and gangsters. You don't like us square, hard-working niggas."

"Cut it out."

"What? I'm just peeping your game. It's all good." He shrugs his shoulders. "Women always want the bad boys and then be crying foul when they run all over you."

"I'll spare you. What's this square shit? Your ass bounces from chick to chick. Your ass needs to be on a leash just like the rest of the dogs. Don't even play me like that."

"Who? Me?"

"Yes, you, so go on with that bullshit."

"I think you got me confused. I've been trying to get you to give me the time a day for a minute. What's the deal?"

"Are you kidding me?"

"Nah. Come on. I want to know what's up."

"Man." I shake my head and plant my feet back down. "You know I don't have nothing against you. It's just that we work together. That shit would be awkward and fucked up."

He starts shaking his head. "You're just punking out now."

"No. Real talk," I tell him, sliding up my shades. "I don't want to bruise your ego. You're my boy and all, but that office romance shit never works out. Not in our line of business anyway. Fuck. We're together all the time as it is."

Elliott just twists his face.

"You know I'm right."

"It doesn't mean that I have to like it." There's a loud screeching noise, and we both jerk our heads to the left. "WHAT THE FUCK?"

Out of nowhere, a car careens into us and sends us barreling into the concrete guard wall. Given our speed, we immediately spin back out like a toy top. The second we stop, I glance up to see another car blowing its horn and heading straight toward us.

"Oh, shit." I try to brace myself for the impact, but there's no time. The next thing I know, my head bounces off an air bag and my entire body erupts with pain.

Head ringing, I'm vaguely aware of the sounds of rapid gunfire. *What the fuck?*

Dizzy, I glance to my left and see Elliott's head twisted at a weird angle and his head drenched in blood.

"Elliott?" I croak, and reach out toward him.

He doesn't move.

I give him a good shake and then check his neck for a pulse. *Fuck. He's dead.*

My mind reeling, I hear more guns firing, people screaming, and car horns blaring. To top it off, the pungent smell of gasoline starts wafting into the car.

Get out of the car! I try to move but can't. Then I remember my seat belt and struggle to unsnap it. Once it releases me, the pain in my chest doubles. *Get out of the car!* I grab the door handle, but it doesn't move. After ramming my shoulder against it a few times, I finally realize that the window is broken, and I can climb out. I ignore the sharp glass stabbing my hands as I push my way out of the car.

Once I succeed in planting my feet on the ground, my knees threaten to drop me.

"Ma'am, you should stay put," someone calls out to me, but I wave them off and start toward the sound of gunfire.

I retrieve my gun from my holster, and despite my blurry vision, jog up a few feet to see Agents Peterson and Jeffries being tossed out of the van and onto the highway.

"FREEZE!" I lift my gun and start shooting at the tires.

The perps peel off, running over a body in the road.

"Fuck. Goddamn it." I lower my weapon and run toward the other smashed-up Ford Taurus. It's not until I get closer do I realize that the body the van ran over was Aaron. "Shit. Shit." I draw closer to the car.

Still strapped in the passenger seat, Eric is shaking and blowing blood bubbles. "Eric, oh, God. Don't move. You're going to be okay." I turn and shout to the people hanging back, "SOMEONE CALL nine-one-one!"

Eric tries to speak.

"Shh. Eric, don't talk. It's going to be okay. I'm going to get you some help." I whip my head back around. "GET HELP NOW!"

"What . . . happened?"

"I don't know, buddy. Don't worry about it. Just try to relax. Everything is going to be okay." *I hope.*

Chapter Fourteen

Alvaro watches the late breaking news on CNN with an expanding smile. The carnage and different eyewitness reports make him wish that he had been there to see the shit go down for himself. "That's right, you slimy muthafuckas. You don't fucking mess with Alvaro Guzman's shit." He pumps a fist against his chest as if it declared him king of the jungle.

"Delmar!" he shouts. "Delmar, get your ass in here!" Chuckling to himself, he turns to head back over to his desk where he proceeds to chop off a few more lines of coke.

Delmar rushes into the room, looking tense and nervous. "You call for me, boss?"

"Yeah, come on in here, amigo." He waves him in. "Impossible, huh? Just look." He points to the television. "Does that look impossible to you?" He starts laughing again.

Delmar turns toward the television and watches a few minutes of the breaking news. Finally he relaxes a little. "You were right, Alvaro. Nothing is impossible."

"Damn right. From now on, this is how we handle our business. Without fear and with big-ass cojones." He grabs his balls and gives them a good shake. "After today, everyone will know that we're not the ones to be fucking played with. It's all about respect," he shouts. "C'mere, you." He stands back up and waltzes over to Delmar to embrace him in a big hug. When Delmar hesitates to hug him back, Alvaro frowns. "What's wrong? This is a time to celebrate!"

"Mind if we join in?" a voice booms behind them.

Alvaro and Delmar turn to see Hector Guzman standing in the doorway.

"Ah, Uncle Hector!" Alvaro's arms sweep back open as he strolls over to give his father's only brother a welcoming hug. "What a surprise. I didn't know that you were coming here today."

"It was an unplanned trip." He glances over his nephew's shoulder to look at Delmar. "I hope that I'm not interrupting anything."

"No. Don't be silly. You know I always have time for you. C'mon in." He sweeps an arm toward the television. "Surely you've heard the great news. I have dealt a powerful blow against the federal government. From now on, they will think twice about who they're fucking with," Alvaro declares, bright-eyed.

"So you're proud of this disturbing news?" Hector inquires sternly.

Alvaro's smile shaves off a few inches. "Disturbing news? I don't understand."

Delmar's gaze shifts from the uncle and the nephew to the four brick walls that masquerade as Hector's bodyguards. He doesn't like the way this looks.

"Alvaro, I know a great deal has been placed on your shoulders to fill your father's shoes."

"Yes. But I have risen to the occasion. Except for that minor hiccup when the DEA breached a line of our operation. But today, I struck back," he brags.

"You call that fiasco today taking care of things?" Hector's cool voice starts to rise. "This atrocious public display of violence in the middle of a major fucking city is the way you chose to handle a situation?"

Clearly confused, Alvaro's mouth drops open.

"Tell me, Nephew. What do you think the government is going to do about this bold heist that you've chosen to pull off in broad daylight?"

"Do?" Alvaro blinks.

"Yes. Do." Hector steps toward his nephew, and Delmar thinks he actually sees steam rolling off of him. "Do you think they're just going to accept this backhand slap? Do you think the public will accept it? Do you want to know what *I* think?"

Alvaro steps back.

Hector continues without waiting for an answer. "*I* think that in response to your childish act, the federal government will make our lives a living hell."

"But . . . but . . . they stole from us."

"Yes. A mild inconvenience. Nothing more and nothing less. We win some and we lose some. Nine times out of ten, we win more than we lose, no? *This*"—he points to the television—"will demand the attention of local police. *This* will demand the attention of Homeland Security. *This* will demand the attention of the president of United States. The public will demand that they do something. Americans don't like the idea of major drug wars breaking out in the middle of a major city."

Hector steps back and drags in a deep breath. "The key to our success, Nephew, is the ability to remain invisible." He points to the television again. "Does this look like we're invisible to you?"

At a loss for words, Alvaro shakes his head.

"*This* is the work of a clown," Hector says. "*This* is the work of a fool. *This* is the work of a child."

As Alvaro stares up at his uncle, his eyes start to glisten with tears. "Sorry, Uncle. I didn't—"

"You didn't think," Hector thunders. "And now I have to do the thinking for you." He walks past Alvaro and moves to his cocaine-covered desk. "What's this?"

Alvaro starts stuttering. "It . . . it's just a little pick-me-up."

Exhaling an impatient sigh, Hector turns back around to face his nephew. "You have disappointed me greatly today. I can't help but think that your father is rolling around in his grave. How much of this do you do a day?"

"What? It's nothing." Alvaro tries to wave off his uncle's concern. "I just do it on special occasions. Isn't that right, Delmar?" He turns to his childhood friend.

Delmar keeps his mouth shut and his eyes glued straight ahead of him. He knows better than to get involved in a family squabble.

"Do you think that your father and I built this organization off our blood, sweat, and tears just so you can shove it all up your fucking nose?"

Alvaro jerks back at the rebuke. "Now wait a minute, Uncle."

"No. You wait," he says with chilling effect. "You're nothing but a child pretending to be a man. And I'm not going to let you run this organization into the ground. Let me ask you something. How far do you think that van is actually going to get?"

Alvaro frowns.

"Do you not see that there are helicopters in the sky? Both the government and the news media? And even if by some miracle they are able to shake the helicopters, how much do you want to bet that the van has a GPS or homing device on it?"

Alvaro's eyes widen.

"Your stupidity will lead police straight to whatever safe house or warehouse you have your men going. They're better off dumping it and making a run for it. And on top of that, whatever eyes you have working on the inside will probably be closed to you now that it's been reported that three DEA agents were killed on the scene."

Alvaro finally swallows the large lump in his throat. "I'm sorry, Uncle. I didn't think—"

"That's right. You didn't. But don't worry. I'm relieving you of your responsibilities."

"What? You can't do that."

"I absolutely can and I just did." Hector turns.

"But this is my birthright. My father left me in charge."

"The Lord giveth and I taketh away. I will clean up *your* mess, and you can go back to your drug habit." Hector heads toward the door.

Alvaro glares at him and starts to shake uncontrollably. "I can't let you do this." He reaches into his waistband and pulls out his 9 mm. "I am the boss!" He lifts and aims the gun at Hector's back. Hector's men are late going for their own guns.

Without thinking, Delmar whips out his gun and splatters his childhood friend's brains all over the room.

Slowly, Hector turns around. He glances at his nephew and then over to Delmar. "Looking for a job?"

Delmar swallows and then nods.

"Good. You're hired. Come with me."

Relieved that he won't be eating a bullet, Delmar smiles and steps over Alvaro's dead body, then follows Hector toward his new future.

Chapter Fifteen

I'm banged up pretty badly, but I'm going to live, which is more than I can say for Elliott, Eric, and Aaron. In a small room at Northside Hospital, I watch the constant coverage of the DEA heist loop over and over again on CNN. The thugs who had hit me and my men were captured just two hours outside of Atlanta.

"Stupid, stupid, stupid." I shake my head. Tears pour from my eyes while images of my partner and friends float through my head.

My parents rush to the hospital and refuse to leave my side.

"You could've been killed," my mother sobs over and over again.

"I'm going to be all right," I try to comfort her, but the effort seems useless. Uncle Rawlo, Tremaine, and Mishawn soon all fill the room to express their love and concern.

"Baby girl," my dad chokes. "Don't you ever scare your old man like that again."

I remember taking hold of his hand and squeezing it, but soon after, the painkillers take over and I drift off to sleep. When I wake up, I'm holding Keston's hand.

"Hey, you," he says, smiling down at me. "You sure do have a funny way of passing a brother a rain check."

I laugh and try to speak, but my dry throat just has me coughing.

"Shh. That's okay. Just try to relax. I'm not going anywhere."

"My parents?"

"We're right over here, sweetheart."

I turn to my right to see both my mom and dad still next to my side. In that moment, I feel surrounded with love and drift back to sleep. The next day, I am released with a clean bill of health. No broken bones, just sore as hell. There is a small argument about who should come home with me. Keston wins but not without my mother promising to call often.

"I really like your parents," Keston says when we pull off in his black Escalade. "They're really cool people."

"Thanks."

He reaches for my hand, and I give it to him. "Do you feel like talking about what happened?"

Silence.

"Do you remember what happened?"

I suck in a long breath and weigh whether I want to answer that question. To answer it means that I have to relive it, and I'm just not up to it at the moment. "Can we just talk about something else?"

Keston glances over at me for a long moment and then finally flashes those dimples at me. "Sure. Not a problem. You just sit and relax, and I'm going to take care of you." And that's exactly what he does. From cleaning to cooking and even helping me in the shower, Keston reveals his tender side.

"I think that I can get used to this," I confess when he climbs into bed with me.

"Hmmm. I just bet you could." Gently he pulls me close.

When the lights go down and I'm curled up next to him, hot tears surface and trickle down my face. *Elliott, Eric, and Aaron. Why am I the only one to survive?*

"Shhh. It's going to be all right," Keston reassures me, kissing my wet face.

He pulls me closer, and I feel his heartbeat as well as his stiffening hard-on. But he doesn't make a move to satisfy his lust. He just holds me and listens to my tears as I drift off to sleep.

Hours later, I hear a phone ring and then Keston pulls away from me.

"Hello?"

I try to hear who he's talking to, but instead there's just an "I'm on my way," before he clicks off. He sighs and then slowly tries to extract himself from me. Instinct tells me to feign sleep while he gathers up his clothes and then creeps around the room. When he finally heads toward the bedroom door, I sit up and click on the light.

Keston freezes in his tracks.

"Where are you going?"

Forcing on a smile, he turns back toward the bed. "I have to run out. But don't worry—I'll be back before you get up in the morning."

That shit isn't about to fly with me. "What do you mean you have to run out?" I glance over at the clock. Sure enough, it's three. "Why the fuck do you always have to leave at three in the fucking morning?"

"Jordan, calm down."

"Nah. Nah. Don't tell me to calm down. For once I want some goddamn answers, and I want them right now! Where the fuck do you go every night? Why are you always creeping around?"

Keston sighs and tries to pacify me. "Look. Clearly you're upset."

"You muthafucking right I'm upset. You're keeping something from me, and the shit ain't cool no more."

His strong jaws clamp tight while muscles start bulging on the side of his neck. "Look. We've already been through this shit before." His phone starts ringing again. He doesn't bother answering it. "I'll be back. Just go back to bed, chill out, and we can discuss this at another time."

"No. No. Fuck that shit." I storm toward him. "Too much weird shit has been going on since you popped up. You're either sneaking into my house, hopping onto my computer, muthafuckas spring out of nowhere trying to kill my ass. My friends are dead and—"

"Whoa. Whoa. What the fuck are you saying?"

"Just what do you think I'm saying? You keep drug-dealing hours. Was it *you* who set me up the other motherfucking day?"

"WHAT? How the fuck you going to think some foul shit like that?"

"Well, shit. Since you don't answer nobody's muthafucking questions, it leaves me to think all kinds of things."

"I don't fucking believe that I'm hearing this shit." His eyes darken while he pulls in deep breaths.

"What the fuck are you getting all swoll for? I'm just asking you a goddamn question."

"No, what you're doing is accusing me of some bullshit—and you fucking know it."

"Then clear your name. Tell me what you do and where you're going. I'll shut the fuck up."

"Look, Jordan—"

"Don't 'look, Jordan' me, Keston. Answer my questions."

"Questions or accusations?"

"Take your pick. Did you have anything to do with that heist? Huh? You were all up on my computer that morning. Did you find out about me transporting that shipment?"

"HOW THE FUCK ARE YOU GOING TO SAY THAT SHIT TO ME?" He storms toward me so fast that I have to back the hell up. "What we've shared these past few weeks don't mean shit to you? Is that it?"

"Yeah, it means something. It means that you're a good fuck. Anything outside of that is a goddamn question mark. I don't know you." I rake my gaze up and down his fine ass, but I'm determined to hold my ground. "And don't throw Uncle Mishawn up in my face either, 'cause it ain't like he raised your ass. You just popped up out of the blue one fucking day. Shit. You don't even look like his ass. Maybe y'all should get a DNA test."

"I don't believe I'm hearing this shit."

"Believe it. And as much as I love Mishawn, his credentials should give me pause anyway since his ass is a crook."

"So is your father!"

"My father wasn't out there trying to kill my ass."

"And I was?"

I toss up my hands. "Clear your name. That's all I'm saying."

His phone starts ringing again. He ignores it.

"Answer the fucking phone."

"I'm out of here." He turns and storms away.

"Aw. Maybe I got this wrong. Maybe that's your other bitch on the line."

Keston keeps moving. "You're sounding real stupid right now."

"And you're looking real foul," I say, dogging his heels. "Even now you're blowing all this smoke in my face about trust and you can't even trust me with whatever the fuck you're hiding."

"I'm out of here," he announces, still shaking his head.

"What the fuck? You're really not going to tell me?"

"I told you that I can't!" He reaches for the front door.

"Keston, I swear to God, if you walk out of this fucking house, don't you dare even *think* about walking your ass back in here."

His hand freezes on the door. "I don't like ultimatums."

"And I don't like secrets," I snap back. "Whatever the fuck it is, just tell me and we'll fucking deal with it." The tension between us grows so thick it feels like I'm choking on it. "Keston." I try softening my tone. "I can't deal with not knowing who you are. I don't want to believe that you had something to do with that heist yesterday." Tears start stinging the backs of my eyes. "Just tell me who you really are."

He turns toward me, his face still angry and hard as stone. "You know who I am. I'm a man who loves you."

I shake my head at his stubbornness. "How can I believe that?"

"Haven't you felt it?" His phone starts ringing again. "I gotta go." He jerks open the door and strolls out.

"Keston!" I march up to the door. "Keston!" He just straight up ignores me as he climbs into his SUV. "KESTON!" He starts up his ride and pulls out of my driveway. "I meant what I said! If you leave, don't come back!"

He gives me a look that says "message received," and I instantly want to take my words back. Instead I just stand there, hugging myself while I watch him drive off.

Fuck.

Chapter Sixteen

I stay walled up in my apartment for the next three days waiting and trying to will Keston to call. In between that, I try my best to deal with this survivor's guilt I have over this week's heist. News reports claim that the men arrested are still not talking and have lawyered up with the best money could buy. I try not to obsess over the case, but I stay glued to CNN on my couch.

The director at the DEA headquarters finally calls this morning and requests a meeting. That means I have to get up, take a shower, and face the world. The minute I'm in the parking lot, I'm overwhelmed with anxiety. I'm almost at the point of just starting the car back up and going home when I suddenly find the strength to put my life back together.

"Hayes!" a few colleagues shout the moment I enter the building. I also get my fair share of sympathetic looks. Somehow I put on a brave face and march to the office of the agent in charge, Rodney Benson.

"Agent Hayes," he says, standing up. "I'm glad that you could make it. Would you care to take a seat?"

"Yes, sir." I step into the room, and immediately FBI director Henry Dobson stands up. My hackles rise as I suspect that I'm about to be interrogated more than questioned about my health and well-being.

"Agent Hayes." Dobson thrusts out his hand, and we exchange a firm handshake. After the formality I take my seat.

"I'm going to cut straight to the chase," Benson says as he braids his fingers together on his desk. "There's been a few details brought to our attention regarding Monday's heist that we're hoping you can help us put to rest."

"I'll do my best," I say, shifting in my chair.

"Before you and Agent Baker left the department to escort the federal evidence to Columbus that day, there was a call placed from your desk phone to a residence in Miami." He pauses for effect, and I wait to see where the hell he's going. "Do you know about this call?"

"I can't say that I do. I don't recall making any call that morning," I tell him. "I arrived with my partner waiting for me at my desk. We talked for a minute, and then we headed down to the evidence department."

The two men share a look.

"What?" I ask suspiciously.

Agent Benson pulls another deep breath. "It's who the home belongs to that has raised some red flags."

"Okay." I wait to see if he'll continue, but when he doesn't, I'm forced to ask, "Who does the home belong to?"

"Alvaro Guzman," he answers. "At least it used to."

"Guzman . . . as in the Guzman cartel?" I ask.

"That will be the one," Dobson says, folding his arms and staring me down. "You want to tell us why you'd be calling a drug kingpin just minutes before you're to escort our record drug bust down to Columbus?"

I shake my head. "I told you. I didn't call anybody that morning."

"Are you disputing the phone records?" Benson asks.

Suddenly I feel like I need a lawyer. "I'm saying that if there was a call made, it wasn't by me. I told you I came in, talked to my partner, and then went to the evidence department."

"With your partner?"

"Yes, well . . ." I think about it for a minute.

Dobson leans in. "Well what?"

I hesitate.

"Agent Hayes," Benson says patiently. "If you know something pertinent to this developing case, I suggest you speak up now. Shit is rolling down from the top on this thing—fast and furious—and it's raining on my head like a monsoon. So talk."

I stare at him and try to find my tongue. "Elliott," I finally manage to push out of my mouth. "He said that he needed to make a call. I went ahead with Agents Pitman and Thompson to the evidence department. He joined us maybe three minutes later." The room falls silent while two sets of eyes blaze holes in my head.

"So your story is that your dead partner made the call?"

I swallow. "He must have." I drop my head, thinking some more. "Just like he was the one to volunteer us for the escort in the first place."

The two men exchange looks, but I'm not sure either one of them believes me. I don't want to believe it myself. *Elliott—a dirty agent?* I rub a hand against my forehead, feeling a major migraine coming on.

"Of course, you know this is an ongoing investigation," Benson says. "And I'm afraid that at the moment I have to suspend you until further notice."

"Excuse me?"

Benson tosses up his hands again. "I told you. The shit is heavy. If nothing else, we need to show the public that we're taking this whole fiasco seriously."

I glare at him. "That makes me look like I'm guilty of something."

"Are you guilty of something?" Dobson asks.

I cut my eyes toward him, mainly because I don't appreciate being double-teamed. "No."

Dobson shrugs. "Then there's nothing to worry about."

I clamp my jaw together while heat blazes up my neck. "Then does that mean I'm free to go?"

Seeing my anger, Benson leans back in his chair. "Look, Hayes. Mind if I call you Jordan?"

I don't answer.

He reaches for a manila folder on his desk. "You're a great agent. Your record speaks for itself. Frankly, I'm inclined to believe you, but I have to check under every stone on this one. I hope that you understand that. I have three dead agents on my hands here. I have to answer why."

"Then you're looking under the wrong stone." I stand up and remove my badge from my back hip pocket and remove the gun from my holster. "Do me a favor," I say, setting both items on his desk. "Keep those. I won't be needing them back."

"Agent Hayes, that's not necessary."

"Maybe not for you." I turn and walk toward the door, but before I head out, I add, "I've had enough of this shit." Without another backward glance, I stroll out of there.

Chapter Seventeen

A half-moon hangs in the middle of a black inky sky while the high humidity nearly makes it impossible to breathe. The night has an ominous feeling to it. The new Jackal checks the time and frowns. Twenty minutes. In and out. However, tonight there's a lot weighing down on the Jackal's mind.

Maybe it's time to get out of the game.

Maybe.

Tonight's job is a multimillion-dollar estate in Alpharetta, Georgia. There is no why to it. It's just an impulsive job to fill time. The Jackal ignores the voice, warning that this is a bad idea. It isn't until the alarm goes off that his premonition is confirmed.

Running like a bat out of hell, the Jackal covers the four blocks to the hidden SUV in record time.

"Are you sure that you still want to do this?" Rawlo asks, poring over the sketchy plans he and his boys have spent the last couple of weeks drawing up. When Mishawn, Jonathan, and Tremaine's gazes jump up at him, he holds up his hands. "I'm not saying that

I'm backing out, it's just . . . this is starting to look like an awful lot of work."

Jonathan stands up and stretches out his sore back. "Of course it's a lot of work. It's always a lot of work. What's the problem?"

"Nothing," Rawlo says, almost defensively.

"Well, I don't mind admitting that I'm starting to have second thoughts," Tremaine says. "It's been a long time since we've done this. What if we get caught? I don't want to spend my golden years in the slammer."

"So what are you saying?" Jonathan challenges, tossing down his pen. "What happened to all that talk about fun and adventure?"

Mishawn pipes up. "Are you even sure that you can bypass their alarm system? Technology has definitely advanced since our heyday."

Jonathan puffs up his chest. "Are you doubting my skills?"

"A little bit, yeah," Mishawn says testily.

Two seconds later, the group of friends are in a full-scale argument until there's a knock on the door.

"Fine. Let's just call it off." Jonathan storms toward the front door and then blinks in surprise. "Sandra!"

The boys behind him immediately start scraping things off the table—a bit loudly.

"Is this a bad time?" Sandra asks, trying to look over Jonathan's shoulder to see what's going on.

"Huh . . . just a moment." He shuts the door in her face and then rushes back to the table to help put everything away. "Hurry. Hurry."

"Why did you answer the door before we put it up?" Rawlo asks.

"Will you stop your bitching and hurry up!"

Sandra knocks again.

"Just a minute!"

When they get everything swept back into a large blue bin, the boys quickly take their places at the table and break out the playing cards.

"Sandra, come on in," Jonathan pants, out of breath.

"What on earth are you boys doing in here?" she asks, inching into the house carrying a casserole dish.

"Hey, Sandy," Rawlo greets with a wave.

The rest of the boys follow suit with heys and what's ups. She smiles and waves back at them. "Hello."

"What you got there?" Jonathan asks. "It smells good."

"Oh, just a chicken-and-rice casserole. While I was making one for Jordan, I figured I'd just make another one for you. I hope you don't mind."

Jonathan shakes his head. "Now, why would I mind that?" They stand there and grin at each other until Mishawn coughs and clears his throat.

"Do we need to leave?"

When neither of them answers, the boys take the hint and start prying themselves out of their chairs. "Looks like this game is heading over to my place, boys," Mishawn says.

They all chuckle as they say their good-byes and head out the door.

Once they're gone, Sandra folds her arms and asks, "So what were you guys really doing?"

Jonathan shrugs while he heads toward the kitchen to put away the casserole. "Nothing. What makes you think that something is up?"

"Is that a real question?" she asks, following him. "I know you. And I definitely know when you're lying." She stops and leans against the refrigerator. "You can either tell me now or I'll go and take a peek inside that blue bin in the dining room."

Jonathan blinks.

"Aha!" She waves a finger at him but doesn't erase the smile from her face. "You'll never change, will you?"

"Actually, I've changed a lot. It was just all too late," he admits, moving in close.

"I don't know. Lately I'm of the mind that it's never too late." She loops her arms around his neck. "We've all made mistakes."

"Are you talking about us or that peanut-head husband of yours?"

"Soon to be ex-husband," she reminds him.

"Sooo, does that make me Mr. Rebound?" he asks.

"No." She shakes her head and draws a deep breath. "I don't know whether you'll believe me, but . . . I've never stopped loving you. I resented what you did. I was always afraid that you'd land in jail and leave me to raise a kid on my own."

"Security was always important you," he says. "I realize that. Admittedly, a little late."

"And now?"

"And now?"

She cocks her head at him. "C'mon. You can tell me. I watch the news. And you know who's splashed all over it lately? The Jackal."

Jonathan laughs. "Oh, please. You don't seriously think . . . ?"

"So you mean to tell me that if I go peek inside that bin, I'm not going to find plans of you and your buddies' next hit?"

He clamps his mouth shut.

"Yeah. I thought so." She starts laughing. "You have to give it up," she says. "If we're going to try again, then you're going to have to stop."

Jonathan's lips curl into a smile. "You want to try again?"

"Why not? Better late than never."

Jonathan draws her body up against his and pulls her sweet lips into a long kiss. Sandra moans and tightens her arms around him. After all these years, the time just feels so right. But if he is going to do this, then he needs to be up front and honest with her.

"I have a few things I need to tell you," he says.

Sandra braces herself at his serious tone. "What is it?" She steps out of his arms. "You're not seeing someone else, are you?"

"No." He shakes his head. "But I'm not who you think I am."

She laughs. "You're not?"

"Well, I'm not currently who you think I am. I'm not the Jackal who's all over the news. None of us are."

Sandra folds her arms. "Really?"

"Really." He takes her hand. "And if you go look in that bin, you will find some plans of me and the boys looking to get back in the game. But we haven't pulled a job, and it doesn't look like we're going to either—which is probably a good thing since I haven't figured out how we're going to get Rawlo through the ventilation system."

Sandra laughs. "Are you for real?"

"Afraid so." He shrugs. "I think we're just a group of men who miss the action. The adrenaline shot. The danger."

"At least Jordan got it honestly."

"Robyn," he corrected.

Sandra starts to argue but finally gives in. "Robyn."

Jonathan pulls her face into another kiss, but there's one more thing that he needs to confess. "If we're going to try this, there's something else I have to tell you. Something I haven't told anyone else."

"It sounds serious."

"It is." He takes in a deep breath. "I went to a doctor last week. I'm sick."

"How sick?" Sandra asks suspiciously.

Jonathan hesitates again. "It's not good. I have cancer. He says that it's inoperable and I . . . The doctor gave me about six months to a year."

"What?" She tries to pull away. "Is this some type of sick joke?"

"No. I'm afraid not." He drops his head. "And like I said, I haven't told anyone. I don't want anyone *treating* me like I'm sick. I don't think that I can stand that." He glances at her. "I think it's what really got this foolish notion in my head about pulling one last score. But I know now I'm just fooling myself. Those days are long gone. I need to concentrate on the here and now." He picks up her hand again. "I'm hoping that's me and you."

"I don't believe it," Sandra says, shaking her head. "I won't believe it. We'll get a second and a third opinion. We'll fight this."

Jonathan smiles tenderly. "I don't want you to have false hope. That's not fair to you."

"And I don't want you to just lie down and die," she insists with a new fire lighting her eyes. "This was just one doctor, right?"

"Yes, but—"

"No buts." Sandra shakes her head. "We're going to fight this, and we're going to win."

"I love you," he confesses. "I've always loved you. And one of these days, I'm going to put a ring on you. But I think I have to get a job first."

"Ring or no ring, I'm your woman."

Chapter Eighteen

Cloaked in black, the Jackal climbs into the black SUV four blocks away. Not until the vehicle is rolling does the mask come off and the criminal breathes a sigh of relief.

"So how did you do?"

I jump at the bass booming from the backseat and nearly swerves the car off the road. Heart pounding, I glance up into the rearview mirror and meet a pair of familiar brown eyes.

"What are you doing here?"

"Pull over," he barks.

I hesitate.

"Now," Keston commands calmly.

Drawing a deep breath, I pull over and wait. When the silence stretches for too long, I start getting nervous. "Aren't you going to say something?"

"What would you like for me to say?" he asks evenly.

"I don't know. I guess you can tell me what tipped you off." I glance into the rearview. "Or how long you've known."

"It has more to do with your DNA than anything you did. And since there are just a small group of people who even know about our fathers' past criminal activities, the chances of anyone else putting the pieces together is slim to none."

I nod and fold my arms. "So now what?"

"You mean now that you have to admit that you haven't exactly been honest about who you are?" he challenges.

I toss up my hands. "All right. You got me. I grew up listening to my father's tales about him and my uncles doing all these daredevil heists. He used to show me newspaper clippings of the places they hit, and it all sounded exciting. He left the world guessing as to who he was." I shake my head as I reflect on those memories. "I used to love how he snuck into my room in the middle of the night—even though it used to drive my mom crazy."

"So you wanted to take his place?" he asks.

"I guess at first I wanted to see if I could do it," I admit. "It was stupid and I was scared. After all, there were four Jackals. But after the first job and the police didn't bang my door down, I guess I got a little more confident. I started planning bigger and bigger jobs and . . . It was never about the money. In fact, I've never spent any of it. Can't, really. My former job monitors agents' financial records."

"Former job?" Keston questions.

"Yeah." I draw a deep breath. "I sort of quit today. They're a bunch of assholes anyway." I feel a sudden rush of tears come on. "So now what? Are you going to call the police? Turn me over to the FBI?"

"Don't have to." He tosses something up to the front seat, and I turn and pick it up. To my shock I'm staring at an FBI badge. "You're fucking kidding me."

"Nope."

I whip around in my seat to stare into his face. "Are you arresting me?"

He doesn't answer.

My heart starts racing again. "You'd do that?"

"It's my job, isn't it?"

"Keston . . . I . . . don't believe this." Tears start trickling down my face. "I'll stop. I promise."

He shakes his head.

"Just like that?" I ask, incredulous. "What we shared means nothing?"

"It didn't seem to when you cut me out of your life," he says.

"I was angry. I didn't mean it," I say. "I've been waiting for days for your call. I love you."

"Humph. It's a funny time for you to admit that," he says dubiously.

"I know you don't believe me, but it's true. And it doesn't make sense because we haven't known each other that long. But I swear to you that I'm not lying."

His expression doesn't change. "Turn around and drive."

"Keston—"

"TURN AROUND AND DRIVE!"

I jump and then do what he says. My tears start streaming at a faster pace while my mind races. What will my parents say? My friends? My colleagues? The media? Funny, I had gotten so successful at pulling off these bank robberies that I'd long ruled out the possibility of ever getting caught. I thought I was too good.

After five minutes of silence, I take another glance in the rearview mirror. Keston's dark gaze is still blazing into me. "I want you to know that even though you're doing this, I meant what I said."

Silence.

I return my attention to the road while occasionally swiping my eyes.

"Get off at the next exit," Keston says, surprising me.

I glance back at him, but he's now avoiding my eyes. I get off at the next exit.

"Take a right at the light."

"Where are we going?"

Keston doesn't answer. He just continues to bark out directions until I realize that we're taking the back way to my house. "I wouldn't breathe a sigh of relief just yet if I were you," he says. "I still haven't made up my mind about what I'm going to do."

I nod, but I can't help but feel a flicker of hope that he's not going to turn me in. It's around midnight by the time we pull into my driveway and I shut off the engine.

We sit in the car another five minutes before Keston says, "Just so we're clear, I meant what I said the other day too. I love you, but we have ourselves in a pretty fucked-up situation."

"Does anybody else know about me?"

"Not that I'm aware of, but that's hardly the point, now, is it?"

"I guess not."

He nods. "Get out of the car."

I reach for the door and grab the bag from tonight's heist. When we climb out of the vehicle and march toward my front door, I'm still searching my mind for the right words. But the bottom line is that this whole thing is out of my control. I slip the key into the lock and enter the house.

"Have a seat," he orders.

I make a beeline for the sofa in the living room and wait. He follows and takes the easy chair next to the window. For another five minutes we just stare at each other as if we're waiting for someone to call or join us. When I can't stand the silence any longer, I ask, "So what are you going to do?"

"I don't know. I haven't made up my mind," he says honestly.

I try to look understanding while I fight myself not to start begging. Looking at him now, I'm reminded of the first night we met. He looked dangerous and sexy at the same time. It seems like no one in my life is who they appear to be. My father, my partner, my lover, and even myself. We're all masters of disguise.

Finally, Keston stands back up and walks over to me. "Stand up."

Nervous, I swallow the large lump in my throat and stand up.

"You love me?" he asks.

I nod.

"Look at me."

I force my eyes up and stare at him. For the first time, I can see so many different emotions written on his face. I'm stunned because up until now, he has always managed to keep himself calm, cool, and collected.

"Show me how much you love me." He lifts my chin and then lowers his hungry lips onto mine.

On contact, my mind is blown as I melt against his hard body. Until this moment, I hadn't realized just how hungry I am for his touch. We start tearing at each other's clothes. After I explode in his hot mouth, I run my tongue down the side of his neck while I rip the buttons off his shirt and expose the chest that I love so much.

Keston pulls my warm turtleneck over my head and then fills his hands with my firm D-cups. My hands fall to the front of his pants so I can massage the long imprint of his dick. Instantly my clit starts swelling and thumping in anticipation.

"C'mon, baby. Don't play with him. Show him how much you love him."

I'm more than glad to do that shit, because I miss this big muthafucker like nobody's business. I sink to my knees and unzip his jeans. While Keston rolls them down over his hips, I'm busy pulling his gorgeous cock out of his boxers. Shit. I'd almost forgotten how pretty his shit is. Going straight for the head, I stretch my mouth open wide and slide him all the way to the back of my throat on the first stroke.

Keston releases a long hiss and immediately starts to drip some of his salty tang on my tongue. "Fuck, baby. Nobody does this shit like you do."

For that compliment, I give a good jawbreaker and listen to him hiss and moan. Pretty soon I'm licking, slurping, and popping my mouth all up and down his dick, and then I lift that muthafucka up to service his balls with a good tongue-bathing.

"Aww. Yeah," Keston continues his praises even as he turns to sit down on the sofa.

I don't miss a beat, bobbing my head up and down and then running my tongue all around his shit.

"Stand up," he orders. "Get up here and put that shit in my face."

I quickly remove the rest of my clothes and go to stand over him on the sofa and then squat down to put my entire pussy right on his mouth. The second that fat tongue starts snaking all around my clit, my knees fold and I have to lean against the wall in order to hold myself up.

Once Keston gets hold of my pussy, he doesn't want to let it go.

He sucks, nips, and pulls on it until I'm just pouring honey down his throat. Every time I think I'm going to fall, he smacks me on the ass and tells me to stand back up. But soon it all becomes too much, and I tilt over and fall down on the sofa's thick cushion.

"That pussy looks like it's about ready," he says, standing up. "Is that pussy ready for Daddy to tear it up?"

"Oh, fuck yes."

"How do you want, it baby? On the sofa or on the floor? Get into position."

I climb up on my knees on the edge of the sofa and then brace my hands on the back of it.

"Is that how you want it, Ma?"

"Yes, baby." I twerk my ass up at him. "I want it all."

"Ask and you shall receive." He grabs the back of my ass and spreads my ass cheeks wide so he can get a good look at him entering my pussy from behind. My mouth sags open as he slowly eases into me. When he's halfway in, I start tightening up.

"FUUUUUCK." Keston grinds his back teeth together.

Pussy juice stars pouring down my leg. I reach down and start fingering my clit until I see stars. Soon after, Keston starts rotating his hips and sends me to another galaxy. When he's finally balls-deep, he hunches over and replaces the hand I have on my clit with his.

"You love me, baby?" he asks.

"Y-yes."

"Then let me hear that shit."

"I l-love you."

His hips pick up speed. "How much?"

"I love you with all . . . my heart."

His hand, hips, and dick intensify their rhythm. The sofa actually starts banging against the wall. The next thing I know, every cell in my body is cumming, and I'm screaming I don't know what up at the ceiling.

"Whoo. Look at you, baby," he says, pulling out and showing me how much I drenched his cock. He puts it back up against my mouth and orders me to clean him up. Once that's done, he lies down on the floor, and I saddle up in my favorite backward cowgirl position and start riding into the sunset. When Keston's toes start twitching, I know that it won't be long. Sure enough, he grabs the bottom of my ass and starts roaring. A second later, his warm cum gushes out of my pussy and makes a pretty mess.

We take a long shower together and then snuggle up in my bed. I want to go to sleep, but we still have some unresolved issues between us. Yet, I'm afraid to bring it up, because I don't want him to think that I just fucked the shit out of him just so I can avoid going to jail.

After a long while, it seems that he's learned the art of hearing my private thoughts.

"I'm not going to turn you in," he says.

Instantly, I sag with relief.

"But the Jackal is going back into retirement," he says.

"Absolutely," I say, and then cross my heart.

"And then me and you are going to get married."

"What?" I sit up in bed.

He pulls me back down. "You heard me." He nuzzles a kiss against my neck. "Someone has to watch you and make sure that you stay on your best behavior."

I don't know what to say. Married? Me? I'm thrilled and overwhelmed at the same time. "Are you sure?"

"Positive. Now lie down and take your ass to sleep."

I cup his face and pull his lips into a deep kiss. "I love you, baby."

"I love you too."

I lie down and fold his arms over me so that we can spoon. With so much shit going on lately, I can't believe that I've actually managed to find a little ray of happiness with this man. I'm almost too giddy to fall asleep. Before tonight, I didn't even know my ass wanted to get married.

I guess that it's never too late to change.

Chapter Nineteen

Keston's head pops up at the familiar sound of his cell phone ringing. For a few seconds, he actually contemplates letting the damn thing go to voice mail, but he knows that shit will only raise suspicions. He lifts his arm from Jordan and rolls over to pick up his phone.

"Hello?"

"What did you find out?"

"Hold on." He carefully climbs out of bed and heads toward the bathroom. He quietly shuts the door behind him. "Hello."

"Yes?"

"Everything is cool. She no longer works for the DEA. She quit, so I'm sure her access to her computer has been terminated."

"And you believe her?"

"There's no reason for her to lie to me. She trusts me."

"Just another trick out of your magic box?"

"Something like that."

"Still. It would have been nice to have a new set of eyes at the DEA office since my nephew fucked up my contact with Agent Baker."

"Sorry, she's a dead end. But if it makes you feel better, I'll keep a close eye on her."

"That sounds like far beyond the call of duty." He laughs. "Something tells me that you've fallen for her."

Keston doesn't answer.

Hector Guzman laughs. "All right, my friend. You can keep an eye on her for as long as you like. And what about that other matter?"

"The Jackal?"

"Yeah. Have you been able to get a lead on Jonathan Banks? Has he come out of retirement?"

"Nah. I don't think this new Jackal has anything to do with the old man."

"Humph. That's a shame. Jonathan was a great employee back in the day. Anyway, if you get anything on this new Jackal, let me know."

"Will do, Hector."

"All right. I'll be in touch."

Keston disconnects the call and then curses under his breath. He hates this bullshit, playing both sides of the game. He needs to tell Jordan the whole truth before this shit gets out of hand. He opens the bathroom door to go creep back to bed, but he stops short when he sees Jordan standing there with her arms crossed.

"Important phone call?"

"How long have you been standing there?" he asks suspiciously.

"So you'll keep a close eye on me, huh?"

He reaches for her. "Jordan . . ."

"Don't touch me." She steps back. "Who was that on the phone?"

"Just . . . work. Please, let's just go back to sleep, Jordan."

She shakes her head and steps back again. "You said no one else knew about me at the department, so who was that asking about the Jackal?"

He clamps his mouth shut.

"No more fucking secrets!" Jordan shouts. "All my fucking cards are on the table. Who the hell are you reporting my job status to? Why are they so concerned about my access to the DEA?"

Keston draws in a deep breath and wrestles with what to do.

"Goddamn it, Keston. Don't tell me all this shit is just a lie. Don't you fucking dare."

"It's not a lie," he finally says, shaking his head. "I just haven't told you the whole truth."

"Which is?"

"I am an FBI agent. An undercover agent. And for the last couple years, my department has been concerned about systematic leaks in a number of federal agencies. In that time, it seems some of the larger cartels were always one step ahead of us on busts, arrests, or even minor investigations. Then we got lucky when I was approached to work for Hector Guzman. So with my director's approval, I accepted the job. We thought it was the only way for us to find out about other dirty agents."

"Guzman?" Her eyes widen. "So I was right? You *did* set me up!"

"No, no," he says firmly. "That was not me. That had to be someone in your department—the leak I was looking for."

Jordan cocks her head. "You thought I was the leak."

Silence.

"I don't believe this." She laughs.

"You're telling me. I wasn't expecting to fall in love with a DEA agent-slash-bank robber."

Jordan turns and starts pacing around the bedroom. "This is quite a mess."

"It's complicated, but we can work this shit out. With you no longer at the DEA and breaking into banks, you and the Jackal will fall off everyone's radar." He walks over to her and takes her hands. "We'll get married, buy a big house, and fill it with lots of babies."

"And what will I do for my adrenaline fix?"

Keston pulls her close while pressing her hand against his hardening erection. "I don't know. I have a few ideas." He kisses her. "Let's go back to bed."

She takes a moment to study him. This is it. To trust or not to trust. Her heart and her head battle each other, but in the end she knows Keston is a once-in-a-lifetime thing. She can't see herself tossing it away like her parents and then living with regret for the next twenty-five years.

"Okay," she says, allowing him to pull her along. Once she's snuggled back against him, their hands start to explore each other once again.

"I love you so much, Jordan," he whispers in between kisses.

"Keston, can you do me a favor?"

"Sure, baby. Anything."

"Can you call me Robyn? I think I prefer it."

He chuckles as he pulls her close. "Sure, baby. Whatever you like."

Epilogue

Two years later . . .

Doctors don't know shit. Today Sandra and I celebrate our second wedding anniversary on the day Robyn and Keston are going to bring home my first grandchild, a baby boy, from the hospital. I'm already imagining all the fun things I'm going to teach him, and they have nothing to do with how to crack a safe or disable a security system. My boys—Rawlo, Tremaine, and Mishawn—and I never did get around to pulling the last job. We all decided that it was best how we left it: going out on top.

Right now, me and the boys' main job is getting this damn nursery together before Robyn and Keston come home from the hospital. But so far the instructions for the baby bed don't make any sense—in English or in Spanish.

"I think that we need a different type of screwdriver," Mishawn says. "I wonder if my son has any other tools around here."

I pull myself off the floor. "I'll go check the shed out back."

"I'll come with you," Rawlo says. "I need to see if he has another drill bit."

Together, we walk out the back door. "So how does it feel being a new grandfather?"

"It makes me feel old. What the hell do you think?" I laugh. We approach the shed and notice the padlock. We just laugh as Rawlo pulls out a small pin and five seconds later has the lock off.

"You still got it, man." I pound him on the back and then pull the door open. We frown as we enter the small shed crammed with miscellaneous junk. "Okay. Where would my son-in-law keep his tools?" I start looking around until I hear Rawlo crash and hit the floor. "Rawlo, man. Are you all right?"

He moans and groans, and I go over to see him struggling to get up. "What the hell did I trip over?"

I glance around on the floor and see a steel handle poking up. "What the hell is this?" I walk over and squat down. "Another padlock."

"What the hell would they have buried in the floor?" Rawlo asks, still struggling to lift his massive frame off the floor.

"You need some help, man?"

"Nah. I got it."

"Mind working your magic on this lock?"

"You sure?"

"We're looking for tools. There could be tools down here."

"Or, most likely, you're just being nosy." He waves a finger in my face.

"All right. Never mind." I start to walk away when Rawlo grabs me by the arm.

"But we should check to make sure."

"Uh-huh." I cock a smile to let him know that he's not fooling me. "Hit the lock."

"You ain't said nothing but a word." Five seconds later, the padlock comes off.

"Now let's see what's in this baby." I pull the metal door up and see a large blue tarp. "What the hell?" Squatting down, I start tugging at the tarp. "Holy shit." I stare at stack after stack of hundred-dollar bills.

"Is that shit real?" Rawlo reaches down and picks up a stack. "Fuck." He looks up at me, and for a few seconds we just stare at each other. "Where the hell would they get money like this?" he asks.

I notice a black box on the other side, so I stand and reach for it. Rawlo waits to look in the box as well. When I open it, I see piles upon piles of newspaper clippings. "The Jackal," I whisper.

"What? About us?"

I shake my head. "These are from a couple of years ago." Our eyes connect again. "They never did find that new guy, did they?"

"Not that I remember," Rawlo says. "Keston?"

I start to shrug when I notice a stuffed teddy bear buried in the tarp as well. "Fred."

"Who?"

I close the box and reach down for the teddy bear. "Hey, fella, I remember you."

"You want to clue a brother in?"

I laugh. "I bought Fred here for Robyn back when she was . . . I think like six years old. She named him Fred. Like in Fred Flintstone."

"Okay. So what does that mean? This is her stash? *She* is the Jackal? C'mon now."

Pride suddenly puffs out my chest. "It's possible. Like father like daughter."

"That doesn't rule out Keston."

I gasp. "What if they're a team? You know, like Bonnie and Clyde."

"Clearly with a happier ending."

The shed door squeaks, and we both look up to see Robyn. "What are you two doing out here?"

Rawlo tosses the money back down. "Um, I came out here looking for a drill bit. Your father made me pick the locks."

I turn toward Rawlo, stunned by just how fast he threw me under the bus. "Thanks."

"Don't mention it."

Robyn folds her arms. "Dad?"

"We did come out here looking for tools, but I think the real question is where did all this money come from?"

A small smile curves across her face. "I think you need to come to the house and meet your new grandson," she says smoothly, changing the subject.

"Okay, okay, but answer this: you or Keston?" Rawlo asks.

She hesitates.

"C'mon. You know our secrets," I urge.

"I know. Who do you think inspired me?" She winks and turns away from the door.

Rawlo and I turn and look at each other before I jump into the big man's arms and pump my fist in the air. "That's my girl!"

Available now wherever books are sold!

Hustlin' Divas
by De'nesha Diamond

In the first book of a fierce new series, meet Memphis's
hardest ride-or-die chicks as they fight along
with their infamous men to lock down the Dirty South.

Confessions
by Sasha Campbell

In this dazzling debut, Sasha Campbell delivers
a sexy, suspenseful tale of two women
whose marriages will be put to the ultimate test. . . .

Heartbreaker
by De'nesha Diamond, Erick S. Gray, and Nichelle Walker

Street lit's hottest stars bring you three
sizzling women out to rule the
game—and have it all—by any deadly means necessary. . . .

Turn the page for excerpts from these thrilling novels. . . .

From *Hustlin' Divas*

LeShelle

Datwon Jackson is standing in the center of Momma Peaches's cramped house, sweating like a runaway slave. Fear is a scent every Gangster Disciple killer thrives on, and we are all eyeballing Datwon's trembling ass while he takes his sweet time stacking money in front of our leader—and my man—Python.

I smirk at the weak-ass nigga. I know what the fuck is about to go down, and I can't wait for my man to deal with the weakest link in our organization. Had it been me, I would've toe-tagged his ass a long time ago. But he's Python's blood—who knows how he's going to handle this situation.

"Somebody shoot this dumb mutherfucka," Python hisses after taking one glance at the money stacked on the table and knowing that the shit is short.

An arsenal of handguns is lifted and aimed at Datwon.

I smile as I stand behind Python, ready for the shit to go the fuck off—which always happens when you get a bunch of niggas together.

"Whoa, whoa, whoa, mutherfuckas. Whoa." Datwon's eyes

bug out as he jacks up his hands. "Python, how you going to kill me? We're cousins, man!"

"Nigga, you're like my fifth cousin twice removed and shit. Ain't nobody going to be crying foul over that bullshit," Python sneers. His big, bulky, chocolate frame is littered with tats of pythons, teardrops, names of fallen street soldiers and, more importantly, a big six-pointed star representing the Black Gangster Disciples. Python isn't just a member of the violent gang; in Memphis he is the head nigga in charge. Everybody in South Memphis knows my nigga don't fuck around when it comes to his money, drugs, territory, and women—in that order.

The seriousness of the situation hits Datwon like a ton of bricks. The young nigga's face twists like he smells something nasty while his eyes manage to squeeze out a few tears.

That shit only angers Python even more. "Nigga, is you about to start crying and shit?"

The surrounding brothers snicker and cheese. It takes everything I have not to start instigating shit by yelling, *Put a cap in his ass.* This was a family situation. Everybody needs to fall back and let Python handle his.

Python snatches off his shades and rakes his black gaze up and down his cousin. Despite his hard-earned muscles, Python has a face only a mother can love. But the brother has presence, power, and mad respect. "If you going to be big, bad, and bold and steal from a nigga, then man up." He hammers a fist hard against his own chest. "Pump that shit out and meet Lucifer like a fuckin' soldier."

"I'm trying," Datwon cries. "But, Python, I didn't—"

Before Datwon can finish the sentence, Python snatches his

burner from the hip of his jeans and straight shoots his cousin in the foot.

"Aaagh!" Datwon hits the warped and dusty hardwood floor with a quickness.

Everyone jumps back and watches the family drama unfold like it was some shit on cable.

I smack a hand over my mouth to prevent myself from laughing out loud.

Python scratches at his scruffy face with the side of his gun as he walks over to his cousin and squats down.

Datwon grabs his bleeding foot and carries on with the theatrics. "C'mon, Python. You know I got a lil man and shit I gotta take care of. I'm planning on marrying his momma next week at the courthouse. Please don't kill me. I don't know why the shit is short. I'll get whatever is missing back to you. I promise. I promise. Just don't kill me."

"Nigga, quit all that hollering. You're embarrassing yourself—and me."

To Datwon's credit, he does attempt to quiet down, but then he starts snotting up.

"Lookie here, *cuz*. I'm going to be brutally honest with your ass. I don't think this is the business for you. You sloppy with your shit. Word is you bumping your gums to anybody who'll stand still long enough, and now you got Momma Peaches on my ass twenty-four/seven. A nigga like me don't need the extra stress. You feel me?"

Datwon whimpers.

"Now, I'm going to cut your ass a break, and in return I want you to keep your punk ass out of my face. If not . . . the next bullet"—he places the gun against Datwon's chest—"is going to hit where it counts. We clear?"

Datwon meets his cousin's black stare to see what most niggas usually saw: death.

"We clear?" Python presses.

"Clear." Datwon swallows the knot clogging his throat and damn near chokes to death.

Python nods and stands. "One of y'all niggas take this punk muthafucka to get fixed up. And the rest of y'all get this shit cleaned up. Momma Peaches is going to be here any minute, and she's going to be pissed if she sees blood and shit."

Niggas get busy as Python dumps his cash into a Hefty bag and then sweeps the shit over his shoulder.

I have to admit I'm turned on, watching my man do his thing. Nobody comes harder or keeps it more real than my thuggish boo. Every nigga up in this joint knows that shit—just as they know that it takes the baddest chick in the 901 to handle his ass. And there's no doubt about it: I'm that chick with the tightest pussy, the meanest head game, and the quickest trigger finger.

From the moment I'd laid eyes on Python, I wanted to be the Bonnie to his Clyde. Real talk there's something dangerous and sexy as hell about his ugliness. I ain't the only one. My nigga has five different seeds running around by five different bitches; all of them just as ugly as they daddy.

But none of that shit fazes me. Those little niggas were all on the scene before I claimed the throne as head bitch of the Queen Gs— the female gang that keeps the Disciples, or what most around here called 6 poppin': Sexed up and stress free.

I have only one true responsibility in life: looking out for my sixteen-year-old sister, Ta'Shara. We came up in the foster system. Nobody seems to know shit about what happened to our parents. Guess we're supposed to believe that we just sprouted out from under a rock or some shit. So for most of our lives, we moved from one home to another, watching people collect checks for taking us in. Shit changed when my booty rounded and my titties sat up. Suddenly I had to endure a few foster daddies and uncles who liked to play with my pussy and stuff my mouth with a different kind of lollipop in the middle of the night.

None of those muthafuckas paid attention to my tears or gave a shit that I'd gone to bed with my asshole bleeding. In fact, no one gave a shit until I saw one of them seriously eyeballing my little sister. I finally took action by slicing up one of those child-molesting muthafuckas while his ass was sleeping. Then suddenly *I* was the crazy one and had to be locked up in a group home.

For two years, I was separated from my sister. The hardest part was always wondering how Ta'Shara was or what she was doing. Would some doped-up muthafucka put her through the same hell I went through? Those couple of years was when I realized that I had seriously fucked up and had failed my sister.

How could I do my job looking after her from a damn group home?

However, that was where I had gotten my education in street politics. Drugs and boosted loot floated in and out of that group home like it was a fucking flea market. Despite all the heavy shit I could get my hands on, my drug of choice was weed—purple haze, to be exact. That shit made everything better: food, sex—just fucking life.

I first heard about the Queen Gs while lying in bed at that

place. This dyke bitch, Sameka, just straight raped this chick
Lovey with some metal dildo because she thought the girl jacked
one of her chains. Nobody helped the girl because no one liked her
big-boned ass. The next day, Sameka found her chain and realized
the shit wasn't missing after all. When someone suggested she
apologize to Lovey, Sameka smirked and claimed the bitch en-
joyed the shit.

And she must've, because to this day, Lovey is still Sameka's
main bitch. But back then, seeing the power that Sameka wielded was
mind-blowing to me. Bitches jumped when Sameka said jump, and
they jacked who she said needed to be jacked.

The only thing was, I didn't know how to go about asking to
join the Queen Gs. At first, I worried that I would have to let that
mean bitch rape or beat my ass. Turned out, I had great reason to
worry because that was exactly what happened. Four chicks held
me down and took turns beating my ass. Shit. I had to stay in bed
for damn near two weeks after that shit, but it was a small price to
pay for the kind of world that opened up to me after that.

Next thing I knew, I was flying high, boosting shit from Hick-
ory Ridge Mall for Momma Peaches's network and jacking cars
headed out to the Tunica casinos. It wasn't great money, but it was
enough to make sure I kept decent clothes on my back and something other than chicken in my belly.

When I finally left the group home and was placed with my sister at the Douglases in midtown, I felt like I'd been sent to another
planet. The biggest change was in Ta'Shara. She thought she was
good and grown and didn't have to listen to me anymore.

Where I had been hard and jaded, Ta'Shara believed her shit
didn't stink, with her straight As and being a star on the track

team. What really hurt was Ta'Shara thinking that I was crazy whenever I tried teaching her slow ass about how to navigate through the politics of the streets.

Ta'Shara just acted like she was above it all, not recognizing that it was my status that kept her safe—not only from the other Queen Gs but also from the Flowers and the Crippettes. But that was cool with me, seeing how my sister might actually have a chance of escaping Memphis's rat hole and actually making something of herself. If that happened, then maybe—just maybe—it would make some of the bullshit I've gone through worth it.

When I was rising up the ranks, I was a good foot solider, but I wanted more and set my sights higher. In order to do that, I needed to do something that would catch the HNIC's attention. That meant locking down Python, a nigga who got his name for all the damn snakes he has slithering around his house. Python's kryptonite is pussy—the tighter the better. He especially likes girls who have a different look. Ever since I can remember, people have told me I look like Chilli from TLC. Who knows, maybe I really had Indian in my family.

At sixteen, I got a fake ID so I could strip at Python's club, the Pink Monkey. From the moment I stepped out on the floor, I made sure I put niggas in a trance: winding my hips and popping my oil-slick booty like my damn life depended on it. But the Benjamins didn't start raining until I showed that I could swallow a big, long banana whole. That night, Python gave the order to bring me to his office. . . .

I was so excited. At the time, this was nothing more than a power move, if all went right. Of course, there was no guarantee that

Python wouldn't just fuck me and then put me back out in the stable, so somehow I had to make that first meeting memorable.

When I stepped into his office, it was smoky as hell. My weedology degree told me that Python was puffing on some blueberry AK-47. I was high before I even got to the center of the room. Up until that moment, I'd seen Python around the way, but never close enough to actually get a good look at him. But standing there in that room, staring into that face, I knew my life would never be the same.

I must've stood there forever while he inspected me in my string thong and white flower pasties. While he looked at me, I kept an eye on the red and silver corn snakes that swirled around his meaty arms and hands.

I knew then what I had to do. None of the girls liked Python's snakes, and to be honest, I wasn't too keen about them either. But on that day, I pushed all that bullshit to the back of my head and walked over to his chair unbidden.

"Can I play with your snake?" I asked in a schoolgirl voice that caused the side of his lip to curl. I'd never seen a smile that made someone even uglier, but for some reason the shit turned me on so hard that my pussy started swelling right before his eyes.

Python stretched out one hand and allowed one of his friends to slither up the center of my belly and then up between my breasts.

I smiled and locked gazes with Python, letting him know that I wasn't scared of a damn thing.

His lips spread wide as if recognizing that he'd finally found his ride-or-die chick. When he licked his fat lips, I saw that the nigga had had his tongue surgically forked to look like that of a snake. I couldn't wait to feel that shit smacking my clit. No doubt, he knew how to work it.

The corn snake slid up over one shoulder and then looped around my neck. Still, I didn't flinch. Python stood up, yanked down his baggy jeans, and showed me a cock that was long, veiny, and black as coal—all except the head. The head was more milk chocolate and looked like an overbaked muffin top. As he stared at me, precum started to drip from the tip.

"You got a pretty pussy," he said flatly. "But I want some ass."

That shit threw a monkey wrench in my plans. I was already wondering how I was going to stuff that fat head into my pussy, but my ass? Suddenly I remembered all those nights when I'd gone to bed crying, bleeding in my panties. I seriously didn't think I could do it.

But this was a chance of a lifetime. Becoming Python's girl meant no more menial carjacking and drug-muling shit.

"Whatever you want, Daddy," I said, wiggling my ass as if I couldn't wait for him to split me wide open. And that was just what the fuck he did—rammed into me raw and fucked me with no remorse.

If I'm proud of anything, it was of my ability to not shed a single tear. Instead, I should have won an Oscar for all the panting and moaning I did. Lucky for me, he had a quick nut that night and blasted off all over my back.

"You a good little soldier, Ma," he praised. But seconds later, I was shown the door.

For six months, I thought I'd ripped my asshole for nothing and went back to playing my position on the poles and doing a little drug-muling on the side until word started circulating that Python had put his latest baby momma, Shariffa, in the hospital because he caught her ass cheating. Nigga she was cheating with was found on the side of the road in a car that had so many bullets holes it looked like black Swiss cheese.

To this day, the Memphis police still had the case open with no leads.

Of course, everybody knew who sent that nigga to the devil's door. Just like every bitch in the Queen Gs was hyphy for the number-one position even before the ambulance showed up to take Shariffa to the hospital.

I'd hoped and prayed to catch Python's attention again, but I was never in a position where I could see him, much less be alone with him. But one night after my set at the club, there he was, wanting another go with my ass. Without missing a beat, I turned it up to him and then braced myself for a rough ride.

Python didn't disappoint. He turned my asshole into a crime scene and then hosed it down with a thick, heavy load. Determined not to have him just roll up on out of there, I washed him down and then gave him a sample of my mean head game and let him know how tight my pussy could grip his meat. I candy-coated that black cock from its head to its balls. The shit was crazy explosive.

I loved it. It was like fucking a dangerous beast that was trying to pound the lining out of my pussy. I fell in love with that muthafucka that night, and I promised myself that I would do anything and everything to become the Head Bitch in Charge—and I succeeded.

That was three years ago.

"C'mon, baby," Python says, pulling me out of my memories. He hands me the Hefty bag of money and then smacks me on the ass. "Get the molasses outcha ass. Momma Peaches is going to be here any minute."

"Okay, Daddy. Whatever you say."

From *Confessions*

Nikki

"It's ten o'clock and you're listening to Nikki Truth, the host of the most talked about radio show in the Midwest, *Truth Hurts*. As my listeners know, I don't believe in holding your hand. If you want my advice, then you better have the balls to accept the truth . . . even if it hurts. Caller, you're on the air."

"*Hi, Ms. Nikki. My name is Kimberly.*"

Obviously, Kimberly had been listening to my show, because everyone knows if I'm not referred to as *Ms. Nikki*, I have straight attitude. "Hello, Kimberly. What can I do for you?"

"*I've got a little bit of a problem.*"

I leaned forward on my seat, ready to hear what crazy drama was about to unfold. "I'm all ears."

"*Well, Ms. Nikki, I've been married to my husband for thirteen years, but for the last year our relationship has grown distant. I tried talking to him about it, even suggested maybe we get counseling, but he refused, saying nothing was wrong with our marriage. But I knew something wasn't right, because we haven't had sex in four months.*"

"Yep, that would do it. So what did you do?" I asked while adjusting my microphone.

"*Well, something told me my husband was messing around.*"

"Something like what?"

"*Like locking his cell phone, coming home at all hours of the night.*"

"Hmmm, those are definitely some signs."

"*Well, yesterday I waited for him to get off work and followed him to this house. When I knocked on the door, guess who answered?*"

"I hope for your sake it was a woman and not a man," I said with slight laughter, trying to make light of the situation.

"*Oh, it was definitely a female. He came up behind her in his underwear. I confronted him. He screamed at me and acted like we've been separated for years instead of still living in the same house!*"

"Okay, wait a minute. The brotha tried to pretend the two of you weren't even together?"

"*Oh, yeah, and I went off!*"

"Good for you, Kimberly."

"*I finally asked him to choose, and he told me on her front porch in holey draws and a dingy wifebeater, he was in love with the other woman.*"

"Ouch! Girlfriend, say it ain't so."

Kimberly breathed heavily into the phone. "*Yep, I'm afraid it's true. I was devastated. I got back in my car and drove home.*"

"Daaayum, girl! I wouldn't wish that kind of drama on anyone. So tell me, what did you do when he got home?"

There was a noticeable pause. "*Nothing.*"

"Nothing?" This female was stuck on stupid.

"*Ms. Nikki, that's the problem. I love my husband and I'm willing to do whatever I can to save our marriage. That's why I called. Be-*"

cause I need someone out there to tell me what I need to do to bring him back to me."

I shook my head and glanced through the glass at my producer, Tristan, who was shaking his head as well. There are some women out there who allow a man to get away with just about anything.

"Kimberly, honey, obviously you don't know anything about respecting yourself, 'cause if you did, instead of calling me, you would be packing his shit and burning it in the nearest Dumpster. Why in the world would you want a man who obviously doesn't want you?"

"He's the father of my kids." Don't you know she had the nerve to sound defensive?

"And that's supposed to make it right? Men can only get away with what women allow them to. He disrespected and played you in front of another woman. That's more than enough reason to dump his sorry ass." Tristan was going to have to do a whole lot of bleeping tonight.

"Hold up, Nikki. I love him, and I don't appreciate you talking negatively about my husband!"

"Excuse me, but it's *Ms.* Nikki to you, and if you love him that much, then why you even call my show? Next caller." I ended the call. Damn! I hate to say it, but women like her deserve what they get.

"Hi, Ms. Nikki. My name is Tasha, and my family thinks I need to leave my man."

Oh, Lord, not another. "Why is that?"

"Well . . . uh . . . a couple of weeks ago we were at my cousin Boo-Man's birthday party, and one thing led to another and my man hit me. I know he didn't mean it, and he swears he won't do it again."

It must be something in the air, because that night everybody was acting cuckoo for Cocoa Puffs. "Let me tell you something, Tasha. Any woman who takes a man back after he hits her, all she's doing is telling him it's okay to do it again."

"But he's going to counseling!"

"Good, he needs to. And what you need to do is find a man who respects you."

"He can't help it. His father used to abuse him."

"And that makes it right? Girlfriend, you have to respect yourself first before you can expect a man to show you respect."

"I know, but I've prayed on it and God wants me to take him back. I'm certain of it."

"Nooo, the Lord helps those who help themselves. If you go back to a man that hits you, that means you don't feel worthy of a man who won't."

"I believe everyone deserves a chance to change!"

What was up with these defensive women? "True, but are you willing to risk your life on it? What if he really hurts you next time?"

"That ain't gonna happen, I'm certain of this. He's been trying real hard to work on our relationship. In fact, last week he asked me to marry him and I accepted. So there's no way I'm letting my family or anyone else stand in the way. I just wanted to go on the air and say that, 'cause I know my cousins Alizé and Lingerie listen to yo show."

"If you're adamant about staying with him, then all I can do is wish you the best of luck. In the meantime, do me a favor . . . take some boxing classes." I ended the call, and the phone lines lit up with callers anxious to put in their two cents. "This is Nikki and you're on the air."

"*Tasha, you are pathetic. I would have taken a frying pan to his head!*"

I had to laugh at that one. "I know that's right, girl."

"*Trust and believe, I used to date a man who hit me. I used to think it was my fault. That maybe if I did things the way he asked me to instead of the way I wanted, maybe he would love me more and stop hitting me. But you can't change people like that. The more I tried to make him happy, the angrier he got and the beatings got worse until one day he hit me in front of my son.*"

"What!" I cried, adding dramatic effect. "Girlfriend, what did you do?"

"*Ms. Nikki, something in me snapped. I picked up my son's base-ball bat and I swung and knocked that fool hard in the arm, then I kept on swinging. I had him running out the door in his draws scream-ing murder!*"

"Good for you." I laughed, trying to lighten the mood. "I like to hear about a woman standing up for herself."

"*Humph! I might be a big girl, but I know I deserve better.*"

"Yes, you do. Next caller."

"*Ms. Nikki, this is Petra, and I'm calling in response to the call you got from Kimberly. Yep, that was me she was talking about. I'm the other woman, and as far as her husband is concerned, I'm the only woman in his life. Kimberly, get it in your head, Daddy ain't coming home!*" Click.

"Oops, there you have it! Kimberly, dear, if that don't give you a reality check, then I don't know what will." I noticed Tristan waving his arms in the air. As soon as he had my attention, he sig-naled for me to take line two. "Caller, you're on the air."

"*Hello, Ms. Nikki.*"

I groaned inwardly the second I recognized the voice. If it had belonged to anyone else, I would have considered the sound sexy and soothing. Instead, I was on the line with Mr. Loser.

I looked through the glass at Tristan, who was cracking up laughing, and stuck up my middle finger high enough for him to see it. "Caller, please introduce yourself," I said as if I didn't already know.

"Ms. Nikki, you hurt my feelings. I just knew you would never forget my voice."

I rolled my eyes. "Sorry, Charlie, but I hear hundreds of voices every week. I can't remember just one."

He chuckled. *"It's me . . . Junior."*

"Hellooo, Junior!" I said, trying to sound excited to hear from him. This man was like nails on a chalkboard—annoying as hell. "Long time no hear. What's it been, a month, maybe two?"

"It's been one month, two weeks, and three days, to be exact."

"Oh, boy! I take it your newest relationship didn't work out either."

He sighed. *"No, and I don't understand it because she was perfect. I really thought she was the one."*

"If my memory serves me right, as far as you're concerned, they're all 'the one.' " Junior had gone through so many relationships it was pathetic. Nothing ever worked and it was always the woman's fault. He was what the show *The Biggest Loser* should really be about. He would have no problem winning, because he was definitely a big, fat loser.

"No, this woman was crazy."

Listen to him tell it, they all were. "Come on, Junior. Tell me what happened, even if the truth hurts."

"What's there to say? I loved her, still do, and part of me wished she'd come back to me. I just don't understand why she ended it. I was there for her, giving her everything she needed and then some, but she had the nerve to say she needed some space."

I stuck my finger down my throat. Men like Junior were sickening. "Maybe you were smothering her."

"Nope. As soon as she said she needed room, I gave it to her. I guess I just loved her too much."

"Ugh! You're turning me off. Come on, Junior. A woman likes excitement and a little mystery."

"I gave her excitement! I bought her roses, surprised her with a massage. I cut her grass, washed her clothes."

I cut him off. "Like I said, all that catering is a turnoff. That seems to be a pattern of yours."

"What do you mean?"

"I mean you can't keep a woman! I know the truth hurts, but if anyone's gonna be honest with you, it's Ms. Nikki."

He laughed. It was a soft, eerie sound. *"That's what I love most about you."*

Just like everyone else. "Junior, you call every month to tell me how you've gotten dumped. At some point you have to realize they can't all be crazy. Maybe it's time you started looking at yourself."

"I'm a nice man."

"Didn't you get the memo? Nice guys finish last. As sad as it may sound, women don't want a man who wears his heart on his sleeve."

"I don't understand that. Women are always talking about how they want a good man, yet when they get a man who isn't trying to take their money or drive their car, they don't want him."

I sighed dramatically. "You're right, and it's a damn shame. However, we do know what we don't want, and that's a clingy man."

"I'm not smothering."

"Gotta be. You've been dumped five times in the last six months."

There was a noticeable pause. *"Wow! You've been keeping track. You obviously care more than I imagined."*

"Nah, don't get the shit twisted. I just got a good memory and you, my friend, are unforgettable."

"I'll take that as a compliment."

"Why? I wouldn't. True, there are some women out there who appreciate a good man who's also needy. Unfortunately, me and the hundred females I know don't. However, I'm gonna let the listeners be the judge. Let's see if there is one female listening tonight who'd go out with you. In fact, I'm gonna open up the phone lines and see if we can possibly make a love connection. This is Nikki Truth with *Truth Hurts,* and for any listeners who are just tuning in, I'm on the phone with Junior. Junior, say hello to the listeners."

"Hello."

I almost laughed at the way he tried to sound like Barry White somebody. "Junior is one of my faithful listeners. He is also a *good* man, who is unlucky with love. If there are any single women out there looking for a *special* kind of man, give me a call, because I'm about to hook you up." I couldn't help emphasizing *special,* because Junior was definitely a head case.

"I-I prefer picking my own women," he sputtered. I guess he was uncomfortable with me trying to help him out.

"Maybe that's the problem. You might be picking the wrong type, but I'm gonna hook you up."

"*Damn, Ms. Nikki,*" he began with a chuckle. It was obvious I was making him nervous. "*I respect your advice, but why you always have to be so hard? In fact, why you gotta put a brotha on the spot?*"

"Hey, I'm just telling it like I see it. In the meantime, keep your head up and take my advice for a change." I depressed the button, then took a few more calls and read several e-mails, but no one phoned in interested in going out with Mr. Loser. Not that I was the least bit surprised. By midnight my head was hurting and I was anxious to wrap up the show. "This is Nikki Truth at Hot 97 WJPC, ending another evening. When things get tough, remember the truth will set you free. Until next time." I leaned back in my chair as I took off the headset. By the time I placed it on the table, the sound of Jennifer Hudson was bellowing over the air. Tristan always knew what song to play at the end of each show. Sitting back in my chair, I had to smile. Tonight had been another fulfilling night. My producer came running over to my desk.

"You did it, girl! Another fabulous night." Tristan snapped his fingers. He's sweeter than a Krispy Kreme doughnut, but he is one hell of a producer and has been one of my closest friends for years.

"Thank you, sweetie."

He blew me a kiss, then pursed his cherry lip-gloss lips as he draped a hand at his narrow waist. "After Georgia comes on to take over the quiet storm, you wanna go grab an apple martini? I bought these shoes and I'm dying to be seen. Girlfriend is looking fierce!" He struck a pose, and I couldn't do anything but laugh. One thing Tristan knew was clothes. And even better, he knew how to get them cheap. Whenever I was in the mood for shopping, I took Tristan because he knew where to find every bargain from St. Louis to Chicago.

"Nah, I got an early day tomorrow at the bookstore. I was planning to go home and take a hot bubble bath and curl up under the covers."

He pursed his lips with disapproval, then sat his narrow ass on the end of my desk in front of me. "Miss Thang, I ain't even gonna try to beat around the bush about it. You need some dick in your life." I got ready to speak but he held up a heavily jeweled hand. "Hold on. Let me finish. Nikki, girlfriend, it's been six months, girl. Enough is enough. It's time for you to move on."

Tears burned at the backs of my eyes, and I let one roll down my cheek. Tristan was one of the few people I allowed to see me this vulnerable. He was right. I needed to start facing reality, but deep down, I wasn't ready yet to admit my marriage was over. "I know. You're right."

"Of course I'm right," he said with a toss of his fabulous weave. "Let's go get our drink on. I promise just one and we're out."

Tristan and I had been friends for almost five years, and that was long enough to know he wasn't going to give up until I agreed. I slipped into my winter coat, said good-bye to the rest of the night owls, then strolled out of the studio to my silver Lexus. Every time I saw my car it made me smile and gave me what I desperately needed—something to smile about. As I climbed behind the wheel and pulled out of the parking lot, I couldn't help but think about what Tristan had said. I needed to give up hoping and finally move on. Deep down, part of me knew my marriage was over, but a part of me still hoped and prayed we still had a chance. But I needed to do something because wondering what the future held was starting to drive me crazy. Luckily, I had my bookstore, Book Ends, and the best job in the world at WJPC radio. I still don't understand how I had been so lucky professionally.

I was already working for the station as an intern when the general manager agreed to let me liven up the first half of the quiet storm. I had this crazy idea to serve the needs of the hundreds of lonely listeners who tuned in at night by giving them the opportunity to call in and express their feelings. Hell, all the show required was common sense and my own style of bold, in-your-face advice. The crazy idea earned me thousands of loyal listeners. Even though it's part-time, I love the hell out of my job. Giving advice is something I'm good at. Instead of getting a degree in radio broadcasting, I should have majored in social work like my girl Trinette. Nevertheless, giving advice is what I do best. I don't hold punches. But no matter what I say or, better yet, *how* I say it, the listeners love me, and the calls and letters keep pouring in. That's why I was pulling out of the parking lot in a pretty-ass silver IS 350 convertible with butter soft leather interior. The proof is in the pudding. It's a damn shame. I could give other people advice about their lives while my own was a damn mess.

My husband and I are separated, or at least we have been since Donovan's unit, 138th Engineering Battalion, was activated and sent to Iraq. Lord, please forgive me. But his being sent to war was actually a blessing. We'd been having problems for some time, and the night before Donovan left, the two of us decided that maybe time and distance would give us a chance to decide if we wanted to either stay together or file for divorce. I guess he decided on the latter, because despite all my letters and care packages, I haven't received a single call or letter, nothing but a sorry postcard the first week he was there. I know his ass is all right, because my girl Tabitha's husband is in the same unit and she makes it her business to come to the bookstore just so she can rub it in my face how often she talks to her fat-ass husband.

After six months of nothing, I need to start facing the fact that my marriage is over and has been for quite some time. Yet a part of me still was not ready to let go. I don't know if I am just being stubborn or plain stupid like half the women who call in to my show.

Tristan made a right at the next corner, and I rolled my eyes when I realized where he was headed. I thought we were going to a bar close by and having one drink. Yeah, right. I should have known he was going to take me to his favorite hangout. Straight Shoot. A gay bar. Not that I mind. Hell, I sometimes have more fun with gay men than I do with straight muthafuckas, who are too busy trying to run game.

I climbed out just as Tristan came over switching his skinny ass toward me in knee-high, red leather boots. I'm hating, because he's got a walk that's out of this world, like he's related to Ms. J from *America's Next Top Model.* He's wearing black jeans, a white blouse and a red leather jacket with a wide belt cinched tight around his small waist. Tristan's five foot ten with mile-long legs. I'm barely five six, so he definitely makes a statement walking beside me.

I frowned with annoyance. "I thought you said one drink."

"We are!" Tristan batted his eyelashes, trying to look innocent. I know there is no way he's leaving early. Thank goodness I drove my own car. "I hope you ain't using me as an excuse to hook up with Brandon tonight."

Tristan pointed his long nail in the air. "Gurlfriend, puhleeze! He's yesterday's news."

"Since when?"

He snapped his fingers. "Since I found out he was messing around. Don't you know that sneaky bastard left a message for another bitch on my damn answering machine?"

"What!" I tried not to laugh but couldn't help myself.

I could tell he didn't see anything the least bit funny. "I guess he thought he was calling that bitch's house."

I shrugged. "At least you found out early."

"You right, because I was ready to rock his muthafuckin' world." He winked and signaled for me to follow him inside.

The club was real tasteful and clean with small intimate tables and chairs and low lighting. There was a big stage in the middle. Tristan moved to a long table in the back that was occupied by friends of his. Two of them I had met before. Coco and Mercedes. Both men were prettier than me.

Mercedes glanced down at the watch on his wrist. " 'Bout time you bitches got here."

"I know that's right." Coco gave Tristan a high five as he slid in the seat next to him.

"Sorry I'm late, but if y'all weren't listening, let me tell you, the show tonight was off the hook! Matter of fact, let me introduce the rest of y'all to the hostess with the mostess, Ms. Nikki Truth."

I waved and took the chair at the far end.

The other he/she I didn't know started squirming in his seat. "Oooh! Girlfriend, your show is the bomb! I never miss it."

Mercedes gave a rude snort. "She ain't lying. You've even answered her calls a few times."

I gave the one with the blond weave a long look. "Oh, yeah? When did you call?"

She looked uncomfortable. "Last month."

Mercedes filled in the details. "Girlfriend, here is Oasis. She called telling you her man insisted on the cat sleeping in the bed with them."

Laughing, I nodded my head. "Oh, yeah, I remember. I told you to tell him to get rid of the cat or you were leaving his ass."

"Yeah, and the next day he packed his shit and left," Oasis announced with disgust.

"Damn. I'm sorry."

"Wasn't your fault," she said, and made an exaggerated show of fanning herself. "I think that cat was licking a lot more than just his paws under those covers."

The table roared with laughter. Tristan signaled for a waiter and we both ordered a martini. The deejay was rocking some old school. I had gotten my drink and was having fun with the others when I felt someone tap me on the shoulder. I looked up, and it was a young slender woman with her head shaved bald and jeans hanging low on her hips.

"Yo, ma, you wanna dance?"

I looked up into the most amazing brown eyes I'd seen in a long time. Her lashes were naturally long and incredibly thick. Mascara had nothing to do with it. I would give anything to have eyes like that. I don't know how long I stared at her before I finally shook my head. "Nah, boo. I'm strictly dickly."

The look she gave me rang loud and clear. She could do

anything a man could do, only better. "Yo, don't knock it till you try it."

I smiled. "Not knocking it. I just prefer my dick to be attached, not strapped on."

"A'ight, ma. If you change your mind, you know where to find me." With a nod of her head, she turned on the soles of her Air Force Ones.

I watched her walk away and had to admit she had a hell of a swagger that made my nipples tighten. Damn, had it been that long since I had some?

I raised my hand and quickly ordered another drink. Yep, Tristan was right. I needed some dick—quick!

From *Heartbreaker*

Prologue

The summer heat ain't nothing to fuck with in Atlanta. All the hustlin' niggas on the street corners looked like tall sticks of meltin' chocolate, but we're all dedicated to the grind. Shit. We had bills, badass kids, and whining baby mamas ready to stick our asses in jail if we missed one damn child support check. Bitches don't be playin' about their fuckin' checks nowadays.

When I was fourteen, I fucked around and got my play cousin, Trina, knocked up. Now I had a beautiful eight-year-old daughter I hardly ever saw. Ain't my fault. Trina's parents shipped her ass out to her grandma's in Alabama pretty much after the baby was born. Some of my niggas said I got lucky not having her ass all in my face all the time. I just know it didn't stop her from being able to reach into a nigga's pocket. So my paranoid ass was out there hustlin' too. Shit. In this muthafuckin' economy a nigga ain't got no choice. Way things be lookin', Obama was the only nigga with a good job.

One thing about walking up and down Metropolitan Parkway in my fresh tee and black AKOO jeans was that I got to hear and watch how all the shawties be bangin' it. Every one of us niggas out there couldn't walk straight because our dicks were so hard, peepin' at big-ass titties and red-beans-and-rice booties squeezed into shorts that could double for panties. There was nothing but titties and asses shakin' as far as the eye could see.

I grew up in this godforsaken neighborhood back when the street was named Stewart Avenue and its reputation for drugs, prostitution, and murder were known statewide. The tall brick buildings were crack houses, and dodging bullets was how niggas got their daily exercise. Though I wasn't so lucky one time. Caught a bullet when I was fifteen, walking out of a Freddie's Hot Wings joint. It was bullshit because it was all over shit that didn't have nothing to do with me. Some miscellaneous nigga got hot over some other nigga for scuffing up his white Air Jordans. That non-aiming muthafucka just started shooting. The bullet that nailed my left shoulder felt like straight fire. I remember hitting the side-walk—hot sauce flying everywhere and my ass thinkin' I'm about to die.

My boy, Alonzo, claimed I was screaming like a bitch, and to this day his ass hadn't let me live that shit down. That's alright, though. What goes around comes around—and as big as my dawg's mouth is, it's just a matter of time before some nigga blazes his ass up. Now I wasn't wishin' that shit on him. I'm just sayin'. Muthafucka thinks he knows every fuckin' thang.

Alonzo and I were cool and everythang, but I'd be lyin' if I didn't say that every once in a while we got a friendly competition be-tween the two of us goin'. Nuthin' serious or anything. Though I might have crossed the line when I hooked with one of his baby mamas before I got locked down. But shit, what the nigga don't know won't hurt him. Besides, if he was so crazy about her, he would've given her his last name.

I survived that night outside Freddie's. 'Round here what doesn't kill ya makes ya stronger.

The crack houses were gone, but the buildings still felt like brick bars for people who were still strugglin' to make it out. That included my ass. Gettin' out wasn't as easy as it sounds. The street game ain't no joke. Most niggas I knew jumped into this shit 'cuz money didn't come no easier. The one true thing about drugs was that the product sold itself. But easy money knew how to hypnotize muthafuckas too. It convinced our weak asses that ballin' out of control was gonna last forever.

It never does.

And if you didn't wind up facedown on some hard concrete, then you're certainly gonna feel the cold pinch of the po-po's handcuffs when you least expected the shit.

"Delvon, yo ass ain't worth shit!" Tiffani, a dime piece I'd spent the last two nights fuckin', shouted from across the way.

I rolled my eyes at the sound of that bullhorn she called a voice. I kept it movin' though, hopin' I could outwalk her.

"I know you hear me, Delvon," she shouted, practically blowing my damn eardrums out when she rolled up on me.

I finally stopped. She mushed me on the back of my head. "I shoulda known that your ass hadn't changed a damn bit."

I laughed at her stupid ass. The only reason I was putting up with her shit was because she was ghetto fine and had pussy that tasted like candy. "Hey baby." I attempted to pull her into my arms, but she pulled back.

"Don't *baby* me, Delvon. You said you were gonna give me

twenty dollars so I can get some damn diapers for Kanye." She ran her hands through her tight weave and then crossed her arms, waiting for the next lie I was 'bout to tell.

"Look, I'm gonna get you your twenty."

"And what—my baby is supposed to just chill in pissy diapers 'til you feel like showing back up?"

"What the fuck? It ain't like that l'il nigga has my DNA."

Tiffani's face twisted so hard, it looked like it was about to pop off. Still, twenty dollars for two nights' worth of pussy was a bargain no matter how you sliced that shit up. "Look. I said I'ma gone get you your twenty. I just haven't swung by the ATM yet." I reached for her again, and *again* she stepped out of reach.

"Nigga, does it look like I have Boo Boo The Fool stamped on my muthafuckin' forehead? Yo ass ain't never *dreamed* of having no damn bank account."

I laughed because she was straight up tellin' the truth.

"The shit ain't funny, *Delvon*." She held out one hand while cradling a fist in the center of her hip. "Give me my shit."

I thought about fuckin' with her for a bit longer, but judging by her mean mug shot, she seriously wasn't in the mood for it. Fuck it. I was tired of dealing with her triflin' ass anyway. "Here. Take your muthafuckin' twenty." I pulled out a fat roll from my mornin' hustle and peeled off a bill, and to show just how generous my ass was, I peeled off an extra one. "Here. Consider it a tip."

Tiffani snatched the two bills out of my hand, but then eyed the roll I was stuffin' into my pocket like a Doberman drooling over a ham bone. Flippin' the script, her voice suddenly dripped with honey. "You comin' back over tonight?" She eased up on me, rubbin' her titties on my arms. But I ain't going out like that. I've gotten my nut. Now it was time for me to find a better grade of pussy to get me through this hot-ass summer. It wouldn't be hard. A pretty nigga like me ain't never had no trouble slidin' into home base.

"Nah. Nah. I'm cool. Thanks for the pussy, though. I'll recommend ya to a coupla my partnas." I stepped back and spotted a new dime piece sportin' some short shorts that had the bottom of her ass cheeks peekin' out and winkin' at me. "Goddamn!"

Li'l shawty hit me back with a wide smile. I bet I could bust that shit wide open behind one of these buildings. I reached down and readjusted my hard dick while lickin' my lips—a sign to let li'l shawty know I was down for whatever.

"Oh, hell naw." Tiffani jumped into my line of vision and got her cobra neck workin'. "How the fuck you gonna play me like that?"

"What?" I asked, blinking and playin' dumb.

"Fuck you, muthafucka. Yo ass will never change." Tiffani's nose twitched like I was somethin' nasty stuck to the bottom of her Payless shoes.

"Why? Because I keep shit real? Girl, you better go on with that." I laughed. "You know what I was about when you hooked up with my ass." From the corner of my eyes, I see Alonzo strollin' down the block, bouncin' a basketball and chattin' with that Crazy Larry. "A-yo! Alonzo! Wait up!"

"What the fuck? We're talkin'," Tiffani whined.

"Correction: you're talkin'. I'm walkin'. Later."

"Nigga, hold up," she shouted after me.

I tossed her a couple of deuces and kept it movin'.

"Alright," she yelled. "You're gone get yours one of these days. Watch!"

Alonzo and Larry seen me comin' and held up. As I rushed across the way I saw a couple of other niggas that had been hangin' on the block since my ass was in diapers. The original gangstas they called themselves—or O.G.'s. They used to be hard; now they look as if they were allergic to cocoa butter or Vaseline. Ashy from head to toe and lookin' as if they hit the glass dick on the regular.

Their surprise at seein' me back on the block was clearly etched into their faces. Truth be told, nobody was more surprised than my ass when my sentence was reduced because the state couldn't afford to hold so many niggas on bullshit charges.

Hell. What amount of weed they busted me for couldn't have gotten a cockroach high.

"Yo, nigga." Alonzo laughed, swappin' daps. "I thought you'd still be gettin' your dick wet or I would've hit you up sooner."

We did a one-arm hug and then pulled back like the shit never happened. "Just takin' a little break." A coupla more honeys squeezed past us standing on the sidewalk. I turned, my dick following the one with the jiggling booty like a homing device. "What—y'all can't say excuse me?" I asked with my slick, on-the-prowl smile already in place.

The one chick that was so high yella she practically belonged in a Crayola box smiled. As her hazel green eyes performed a slow drag down my six foot two, muscular frame, I knew my pretty caramel complexion and my honey-colored eyes was making her think how pretty a baby between us would be.

Alonzo stepped out front. "What's your name, li'l mama?"

I bit back my annoyance at the nigga interruptin' my flow.

"Jelissa," she purred.

"Jelissa, nice." Alonzo reached up and lightly brushed a curl away from her cheek, making sure to caress the side of her face. When she smiled, it was over his shoulder at me and I knew my ass was in. For the first time, I noticed the orange Creamsicle in her hand. She put it up to her mouth and unfurled this incredibly long pink tongue and started lapping up the melting icicle like a porn star practicing for her close-up. My shit was hard as fuck.

"You got a man, Jelissa?" Alonzo asked.

"Yeah," she admitted to my surprise. "But he ain't here right now." She cut a look toward me. The kind of look that promised nothing but freaky, butt-nasty sex, and you know a nigga was always down for that shit.

Impatient, Crazy Larry started bouncing his basketball. "We playing or what?"

"Y'all go on ahead. I'ma holla at Jelissa for a minute," I said, easing in between my man and what I hoped to be some sweet pussy.

Alonzo looked pissed, but I've always scored more bitches than he did. You'd think by now he would accept the shit.

"Sheeeit," Crazy Lazy grumbled.

I looked over in time to see Crazy Larry rollin' his eyes. Then Larry just put it to me straight. "Look, nigga, we ain't got all day to wait for you to play with some more busted-ass ghetto pussy."

Jelissa snapped out of her sex trance. "Hey!"

He ignored her. "When you get through busting a nut with her, why don't you just meet up with us tonight up at The White Room?"

"The White Room? Where the fuck is that?" I asked.

Alonzo smirked. "Aww man, it's this sweet spot out in Alpharetta."

I laughed. "Y'all niggas hangin' out in suburbs now?"

Crazy Larry wrapped one of his big, meaty arms around my neck and damn near put my ass in a headlock. "Yo ass gonna be hangin' out there too once you see the bitches that joint rakes in. Bitches with money." His eyes shifted back over to Jelissa. "Not these used-up hos we got still hangin' out here. You'll probably need a shot or something after fuckin' with this one. Didn't I hear yo ass got chlamydia or something?" he asked Jelissa.

My dick just shriveled up.

"You know what—FUCK YOU, muthafucka." Jelissa's sex kitten act was long gone and she was clearly in full bitch mode. "I ain't gotta take this shit."

"Then take yo skank ass on then." Larry laughed as if he got a high from pissing her off. "Ain't nobody stoppin' your ho patrol out here. But I bet Lamon ain't gonna like hearing you giving his shit away to every Tom, Dick, and Delvon."

Jelissa's yella ass turned white.

I couldn't help but laugh.

"Yeah, that's right," Crazy Larry kept on, smirking. "I know your boy. Nigga locked down and *this* is how you roll?"

Jelissa's friend, a thick big girl in clothes two sizes too small, moved back into the scene and tugged on her girl's arm. "C'mon, Jelissa. These niggas are whack."

"Y'all bitches are whack," Crazy Larry corrected, cupping his dick as he looked Jelissa's friend up and down. "Why don't you go home and dust that dandruff off in that whack-ass weave. Maybe then I'll let you ride some of this good dick. I love big girls."

"Kiss my ass," the girl shouted, smacking her round rump.

"Wash it and maybe I will." He flicked his tongue out as if to show her what she was missing.

I was cracking up. If these bitches didn't know that this crazy nigga would say just anything by now then their asses deserved exactly what the fuck he was shovelin' out.

Jelissa gave me a nasty look and I couldn't do anything but shrug my shoulders. Hell, I didn't do nothing to their stupid asses.

"What the fuck ever." She cut her eyes and I was left to watch her strut away.

Crazy Larry's heavy hand slammed across my back. "I ain't never seen a nigga get more strung out over pussy in my life."

I rolled my eyes. "And I ain't never seen a nigga do so much cock blockin' in all my life. What's up with you, nigga?"

"Shit. I just did your ass a favor and this is how you act?" He tossed up his hands as if saying I was on my own.

"Alright, y'all. Squash that bullshit," Alonzo said, sounding as if he was tired of the fake drama. "D, why don't you just come out to The White Room, check it out, and see if you like the vibe? Hell, it ain't like you got shit to do anyway. I'm sure by now you done pissed off whatever bitch you've been fuckin' with anyways."

"You know me so well." I laughed.

"Then it's settled," Crazy Larry declared. "You're hangin' with your boys tonight. Now let's go play some damn ball before I fuck around and lose my muthafuckin' high."

I gave in. Why not? Maybe it was time for me to leave these ghetto hood rats alone and find myself a real classy woman with *no drama*.

"9-1-1, what's your emergency?"

"Hello? We need help! There's been an explosion. Please send the fire department!"

"What's the address?"

"2355 Abbott's Way. It's the Walkers' estate. Please hurry. There were people inside!"

"We're on our way. Do you know what caused the explosion?"

Silence.

"Sir?"

"Yes. I did it."